DAWN OF THE DRAGON QUEEN

Asvoria smiled. "We will return to the manor and bring the children to us. Then, we will take back my amulet and return to the original plan."

"So many dragons to pick from," Ophion said, glancing in the direction of the ancient black, his head now resting in slumber. "Whomever will you choose?"

"I think," Asvoria said, drawing out the words until her thoughts mingled with Nearra's own, "that I know the perfect host."

Nearra screamed, No!

"Oh, yes," Asvoria whispered. "Now hush."

The Daystar amulet would soon be theirs and, with its return, Asvoria would finally set into motion the plans she had devised over two thousand years ago.

"It is almost time, my dear familiar," she whispered to Ophion as they flew. "Tomorrow, our new life begins."

THE NEW ADVENTURES

THE NEW ADVENTURES

VOLUME
8

DRAGON
SPELL

JEFF SAMPSON

COVER & INTERIOR ART
Vinod Rams

MIRROR
STONE

DRAGON SPELL

©2005 Wizards of the Coast, Inc.

Distributed in the United States by Holtzbrinck Publishing. Distributed in Canada by Fenn Ltd.

Distributed to the hobby, toy, and comic trade in the United States and Canada by regional distributors.

Distributed worldwide by Wizards of the Coast, Inc. and regional distributors.

Art by Vinod Rams
Cartography by Dennis Kauth
First Printing: July 2005
Library of Congress Catalog Card Number: 2004116934

9 8 7 6 5 4 3 2 1

US ISBN: 0-7869-3744-0
ISBN-13: 978-0-7869-3744-8

605-96712000-001-EN

U.S., CANADA,
ASIA, PACIFIC, & LATIN AMERICA
Wizards of the Coast, Inc.
P.O. Box 707
Renton, WA 98057-0707
+1-800-324-6496

EUROPEAN HEADQUARTERS
Hasbro UK Ltd
Caswell Way
Newport, Gwent NP9 0YH
GREAT BRITAIN
Please keep this address for your records

Visit our web site at **www.mirrorstonebooks.com**

FOR RACHEL MORGAN-WALL,
THE FAIRY QUEEN

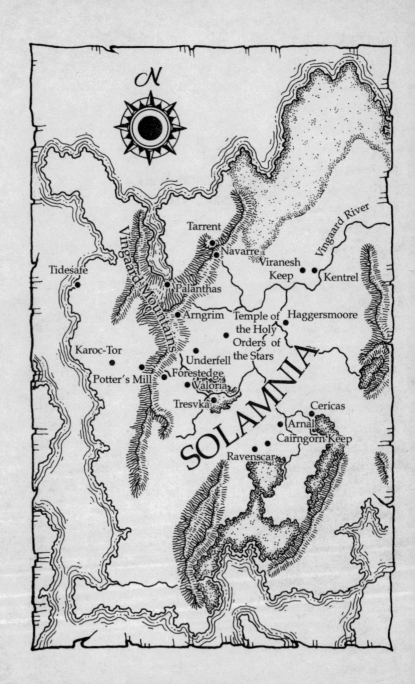

Contents

CHAPTER 1

THE FIRST STEP

"Curse them all!"

The words rounded the corner before their speaker did, echoing harsh and angry between the cracked walls. Davyn watched as a girl followed, her eyes narrowed into slits of cold fury.

He wondered if today would be the day that he would have to kill her.

She could hardly be called a girl now, of course. At one point that was who she was—a lovely, spirited young peasant girl with silky blond hair and a disarming smile. Her name had been Nearra and Davyn had loved her.

Now all that was left of Nearra was her body, a shell of youth and beauty that housed the dark soul of a long-dead sorceress, Asvoria.

Asvoria stormed past Davyn where he sat on the bottom step of a spiraling staircase. Stopping to stand among tangled vines in the decaying hall, she tilted her head to regard a partially moss-covered painting on the wall. Dusk's molten light streamed through cracks in the broken ceiling and glinted off the golden detail of her flowing green gown.

The painting depicted a fierce red dragon soaring over one

of Solamnia's many forests. Asvoria studied the painting for a long time. Davyn forced himself to breathe quietly so as not to disturb her.

Then, with a flick of her wrist, the painting shredded as though mauled by some vicious beast. Remnants of the brittle parchment drifted to the ground.

"I can't imagine the painting did anything to deserve such treatment," Davyn said.

Asvoria glanced sidelong at him, her eyes cold. "Not the painting, my dear. Red dragons. Felaren, Magmus, all of them. They seemed like good candidates. I underestimated the difficulty of this task without the Daystar and my sword."

"Ah, well," Davyn said. Daring to meet her gaze, he brushed a strand of unruly, sandy brown hair from his eyes. "Perhaps that means it's time to give it up."

Snorting, Asvoria shook her head. "I keep you here to serve me," she said. "I do not keep you here to offer your opinions. There are other dragons." She stepped away from the painting, with a sigh. "A red one would have been nice, though. For old times' sake."

Davyn closed his eyes. Images from old dreams flashed through his mind, dreams he'd had of Asvoria transforming into a great dragon and devouring them all. He couldn't help but shudder.

Asvoria started strolling regally down the corridor. Her steady footsteps echoed around him. "Either way. I can't wait much longer. The first step must happen tonight, whether I have a host or not." She stopped suddenly. "Davyn?"

"Yes?" Davyn bounded to his feet and started to follow.

She kept her back to him. "Yes *what?*"

Feeling disgusted with himself, Davyn clenched his fists. "Yes . . . Dragon Queen."

Asvoria nodded in approval. "Come with me. I want my newest follower to bear witness."

Davyn took several slow, deep breaths to keep his muscles from tensing. He had only come to Asvoria because Shemnara, the seeress of Potter's Mill, had predicted that to rescue Nearra's soul he would have to serve Asvoria and bide his time. He had been biding his time for weeks, watching the sorceress come and go as the manor grew from three walls shrouded with vines to what it was today. But no chance of rescue had arisen.

Upon his arrival, Asvoria had taken his bow and quiver, and the sword of the Dragon Knight, the sword that he had planned to use to sever Asvoria's soul from Nearra's.

The weapons and the rest of his belongings were locked away in a tower to which he had no hope of gaining access. Davyn hadn't put up a fight, to keep up the illusion of his servitude, and had instead followed Asvoria's every order to the last detail. The majority of his tasks had involved little more than scrubbing floors or hanging the dragon paintings that now lined the walls. On occasion the sorceress would request his company in some abandoned alcove where she would boast about her past accomplishments and future plans. She seemed to expect him to congratulate her as she spoke of massacring his friends.

Most of the time, though, he was left to roam the halls of the manor, more of which were added every day. It was almost as though she was attempting to torture him with the tedium of it all. He'd tried to go outside one day, to escape the dank hallways, and found some sort of invisible barrier blocking his way. Although Asvoria seemed more than willing to allow Davyn freedom within the overgrown manor that acted as her new stronghold, she apparently wasn't willing to trust him.

As well she shouldn't, Davyn thought. She had killed Elidor, Davyn's blood brother and friend, and she planned to kill others. There was no way he was going to let that happen. And having watched Davyn for a year from the back of Nearra's mind, Asvoria was surely aware of his intentions. Everything they said to each other, every action they made in each other's presence, was a calculated farce. He knew it. She knew it.

What he didn't know was why Asvoria still kept him around.

"I don't believe I've ever allowed you in here." Asvoria's voice startled Davyn from his thoughts and he found that they had reached a dark wooden door laced with vines. An ornate letter A was carved into the wood, a stylized dragon arching between its lines.

Turning her head, the sorceress gave Davyn a sly grin. "I've spent most of my energy creating this room as of late. I think tonight will be the perfect night for you to see it."

"I'm sure it's great," Davyn muttered.

Without bothering to respond, Asvoria pushed the door open and stepped inside. It was the most complete of any room in the constantly growing manor. More paintings of dragons lined wood-paneled walls decorated with intricate molding. Plush armchairs covered in silk cloth were arranged atop red and gold rugs in the corners. In the center of the room was an intricately carved table. On top of the table sat many strange artifacts and bottles, an open spellbook, and a pair of half-melted candles.

Davyn looked up. A large, craggy hole in the ceiling revealed the lavender sky. He could barely make out a familiar constellation in the shape of a five-headed dragon. He knew the stars would shine brighter once night was fully upon them.

On the eastern wall, a pair of sheer curtains fluttered in front of two tall glass doors. One of the doors was slightly ajar.

"Impressive," Davyn admitted.

"Well, Valoria's remains don't come close to the brilliance of the city before it was destroyed, but it'll serve for now." The sorceress walked to stand before the table. "Still, the ruins aren't without beauty. Why don't you take in the view? The balcony door is open."

Not knowing what Asvoria was up to, but knowing he didn't want to risk disobeying, Davyn did as he was told.

Chilly evening air met him as he moved between the flowing curtains and stepped out onto the stone balcony. Bumps bristled on his bare forearms.

Asvoria was right. Below, the devastated town of Valoria seemed almost beautiful by the last of the sun's rays. It had long ago been a grand city of Asvoria's followers, but little was left now beyond crumbling walls huddled in groups between the broken streets, where neighborhoods had once been. Flowering vines twined up through cracks, moss hung in cascades from jagged stones. Endless and dark, a forest had reclaimed the city's remains, seeming to spread out forever in every direction.

The main street led from the foot of Asvoria's new manor, between ruined buildings, to a tower and protective wall on the opposite end of the town. Davyn furrowed his brow as he saw the tower. It was half the size it had been when he first arrived, now barely reaching the canopy of the trees. Bit by bit, Asvoria had stolen stone from the tower's outer wall and used it to rebuild the manor.

Davyn's stomach tightened and what little hope he'd had left fell away.

He had been very specific in his directions to Jirah, Rina, and Mudd. He had told them to use the tower as a landmark to find him once they'd located Catriona, Sindri, and Maddoc.

After weeks of living with the sorceress, he knew that he needed the help of his friends to defeat her. But it seemed the sorceress's hiding spot was even more hidden now than it had been before. Would his friends ever find him?

"Lovely view, isn't it?"

Startled, Davyn turned to find Ophion crouched on the balcony's wall like a living gargoyle. The shapeshifter was in a human form, but its entire body was colored to match the gray stone behind him. Only its wide eyes—so blue that they seemed to glow with an inner light—let Davyn know where it sat.

Ophion killed Elidor, Davyn thought. Ophion killed him at Asvoria's command and here I am, doing nothing.

Clenching his hands, Davyn tried to repress his rage. It wasn't time yet. Ophion would die at his hands, he was sure of it. But not now.

From the room behind him, Davyn heard Asvoria whispering complicated words. He started to turn to see what the sorceress was doing, but a movement from below caught his eye.

A single ogre wandered aimlessly out from the forest and stopped between a cluster of bushes and a mansion's remains. Broken beams jutted from the rubble as though they were spears that had felled the once great home.

The ogre, tall and overly muscled, scratched a boil atop its head and looked around as though confused. Moments later, another ogre lumbered out from the trees.

"What's happening?" Davyn asked. Ophion didn't answer, and Asvoria's chanting grew louder.

Davyn felt a distant rumbling and saw the two ogres stumble as the ground shook beneath them. Seconds later, dirt and the stones of one of the long-destroyed roads burst up in a jagged line as something large coursed beneath the ground. The trail came to a stop a yard from where the ogres stood. The rumbling stopped along with it.

For a moment, all was silent. The ogres looked at one another, and both shrugged.

Then, a massive pinkish brown head burst through broken stone and grass and thrust toward the sky. The head had no features at all save for a tiny slit at its end that could possibly be a mouth. The head rose higher into the oncoming night's sky, its segmented body following behind like a long, fleshy, pulsating neck.

The giant worm stopped and jerked its nub of a head from side to side before aiming it down at the two ogres. The ogres and the worm stared at each other for a moment, completely baffled.

"An Urkhan worm," Davyn whispered, remembering lessons on Krynn's creatures from Maddoc. "But none live in Solamnia." He shouted through the open doorway, "What are you doing!"

Asvoria ignored him, her chants growing louder. As her cold voice overtook Davyn's ears, more creatures burst from between the buildings and from behind the trees. Clusters of red-faced, scowling goblins clung to the broken walls as they eyed the worm and the two ogres with caution. Farther away Davyn saw a pride of orange-furred beasts that resembled cats with narrow heads. As the cats neared the goblins, they let out warning hisses and pulled back flaps of skin on their heads. Davyn's stomach churned at the sight of the bloody muscle clinging to their skulls.

Slithering through the underbrush came large serpents, their scales patterned to look like red and black diamonds. Behind them, swarms of multi-legged, giant insects took in the scene with beady black eyes. Man-sized, wingless birds with deadly-sharp talons scraped at the ground in their fear. Every last creature seemed in a state of dazed confusion.

Asvoria's chanting stopped and almost immediately she appeared at Davyn's side. She turned to him and tilted her head. "An impressive turnout, don't you think?"

"What—" Davyn started to ask, but Asvoria brushed him aside and went to the balcony's edge. Her dress and hair billowed behind her as she held her head high, raised her hands, and once again began to chant.

Davyn was leaping forward, his hand outstretched to grab the sorceress's arm, when he felt a strong hand clutch his shoulder and pull him backward. He fell to the cold stone floor of the balcony and gritted his teeth.

Ophion peered down at him, its eyes flashing with amusement as a smirk creased its face. "You should know better than to stand close to a sorceress when she casts a spell," it said, voice devoid of inflection, yet somehow still mocking.

Asvoria lowered her hands and stopped chanting. Without turning, she tilted her head back. "Get up," she demanded.

His heart pounding, Davyn forced himself to his feet. Only then did he hear the terrible wailing of dozens of monsters gone berserk. He stumbled to the balcony's edge and gasped.

Though they had once stood side by side in shared confusion, all the creatures now screeched in primal rage and pounced on each other, using their own natural weapons or whatever they could find around them to kill one another.

Davyn saw one of the ogres who had first wandered into the town slamming the other ogre's head repeatedly against the ground. The first ogre didn't notice the worm until it was too late. It had already lunged forward to bite off its arm.

"What is this?" Davyn asked, quickly turning his head to avoid seeing any more death. "What are you doing?"

"You'll see, dear boy." Turning to him, Asvoria reached out a slender hand and caressed Davyn's cheek, sending a cold chill down his spine. "Oh, how you'll see." With a last, delighted look at the ongoing battle, she pulled her hand away and walked back inside.

Thrusting aside the wispy curtains, Davyn followed her. As he stepped all the way through, the glass door slammed shut. "You didn't answer my question. Tell me what you're doing!"

Asvoria closed the book on the table. "The only followers I have left are you and Ophion," she said without looking at him. "Ophion is my familiar and I trust him more than any being on this planet trusts anyone else. You, on the other hand, are only here to kill me. Not exactly the army I need, now is it? I had to find another way."

Vast wings rustled from the sky above the room, interrupting Davyn's protests. Ever so carefully, a furry flying beast descended through the hole in the ceiling. Stretching out leathery, veined wings to catch the air, it lowered its mangy, wolf-like body to land on the floor beside Asvoria. As the sorceress climbed upon its back, the creature studied Davyn with its intense blue eyes.

"Have a good night," Asvoria said. "Don't wait up." She laughed and the winged beast that was Ophion bunched its powerful back legs and leaped up into the sky.

With a frustrated yell, Davyn picked up one of the bottles from the table and threw it after her. The bottle shattered as it reached the hole, as if it had hit a wall. Viscous red liquid splattered throughout the room.

Davyn threw himself into one of the armchairs and put his head in his hands. His whole body shook with frustration. If ever there had been a time he needed to strike with the Dragon Knight's sword and free Nearra, it must have long passed.

He had failed, and now he was trapped and helpless. His only hope lay with his friends and—he hated to admit it—with Maddoc.

As the distant wailing of the dying monsters slowly faded away, Davyn looked back up through the magically sealed hole. The constellation of the five-headed dragon glowed startlingly bright and Davyn knew with sudden clarity that it wasn't the gods of good that were watching over Krynn that night.

CHAPTER

2

SOUNDS IN THE NIGHT

Twigs cracked.

The sound echoed through the trees, jolting Catriona from her light sleep.

Adrenaline raced through her body. Her hands instinctively flew to the dragon claws—two curved, serrated swords—at her side.

Bunching the muscles in her back, she flung her upper body forward, then rolled into a crouch, ready for the impending attack.

All was still and silent, save for the crackling of the fire behind her.

It took her a few moments to remember where she was. The clearing was black in the night, the tall grass and weeds brushing against her boots and thighs. A wall of trees surrounded the little clearing, so dense that it was impossible to see through.

Catriona scanned the trees. She tried to calm her breathing.

"Did we wake you?" Sindri asked from behind her. "I tried not to be loud, but—"

Pointing one of the dragon claws at him, she let out a shushing sound. Ever so slowly, she pushed herself up to stand her full six feet.

There was nothing.

Letting out a long, slow breath, Cat put the two swords back into place on her belt.

"I'd say our fair knight is a bit jumpy." Maddoc studied Catriona with concerned eyes.

"I heard something." She turned away from the firelight so as not to ruin her night vision.

"Maybe it was a deer?" Sindri suggested. The little kender sat cross-legged next to Maddoc near the fire, fidgeting with his hoopak staff. His purple cape and blue shirt, so garish in daylight, seemed almost noble by the dim silver and red light of the partial moons.

"I hope so, Sindri." Kneeling in the matted grass where she had been sleeping, she found her armor next to her pack and began to put it on. "But I haven't seen any animals since entering these woods."

"Ooh! Do you think it was those things we heard earlier?" Sindri bobbed his head eagerly.

The great chorus of roars and bellows that had risen through the trees to the north had been a collection of sounds more terrifying than any Catriona had ever heard. The monstrous din ended only moments later, just as swiftly as it had begun, and it had been eerily silent ever since.

"I hope not," she said. "But we have to be ready for anything." Cat finished fastening her breastplate and checked to make sure her helmet was firmly on her head. Like any kender, the noises didn't concern Sindri at all, and Maddoc showed no fear.

But Cat was worried. Those awful sounds must have come from exactly where they were heading: Asvoria's hiding place deep within these endless woods.

Catriona walked to the fire and crouched near Sindri. Splayed between them was one of Maddoc's ancient spellbooks, its pages yellow in the flickering firelight. One of the pages depicted a woodcarved image of black-robed mages engaged in bloody destruction of a foe—dark sorcery. Cat looked at Maddoc in surprise.

Maddoc stared back, eyebrows raised. Cat hardened her features. She wasn't in the mood for the wizard's mind games. She gestured toward the book. "Well, continue. Don't let me keep you from your lesson."

"You heard her, Sindri," Maddoc said, pointing at the spellbook. Sindri scooted closer to the fire.

As Maddoc resumed his instruction, Cat studied his face, all sharp features and carefully tended, close-cropped facial hair. With his slight wrinkles and long gray hair he seemed almost like some fabled, regal king. He was handsome, at least for a man his age.

No, not just a man. A wizard. Or, at least, a former wizard. Cat never knew quite how she felt about him. It seemed such a short time ago that he was their sworn foe. He had sent Catriona and her friends into all sorts of dangerous situations without their knowledge, all to release the soul of the long-dead sorceress that he had placed inside the body of their friend, Nearra.

But now Maddoc was powerless. His plans to study Asvoria ruined, he offered them his help to contain her before she could destroy the world and, most importantly, him.

Catriona had to admit that Maddoc had been beyond helpful. His knowledge of Asvoria had been invaluable in keeping the sorceress from regaining the Aegis, the sword that would have made her powerful beyond measure. After Catriona and Sindri failed in their quest to return Elidor's effects to his family, the wizard located them in Palanthas. He vowed to help them find Davyn and had secured directions to Asvoria's new stronghold (though he never revealed how he had gained this information).

Now, perhaps most importantly of all, he was teaching Sindri the spells that could potentially free Nearra from the sorceress that possessed her body.

The wizard and kender were engrossed in the text now. Sindri bounced with excitement, full of far more energy than he should have had, considering the late hour. Maddoc nodded in encouragement.

Cat started to worry about Sindri. She couldn't help it—what reason could Maddoc have for showing the kender dark magic spells? What sort of effect would that have on someone like Sindri, so eager to learn any magic he could?

"Maddoc," Cat said as she stood. "May I have a word?"

Maddoc looked up from the book. "Of course." He stood, his black robes billowing around him.

Cat led him away from the fire, toward a knot of trees.

"I need to talk to you," Catriona said as they walked out of Sindri's earshot, "about what you're teaching Sindri."

Maddoc raised one of his black eyebrows as he leaned back against the trunk of an aging oak. "I am teaching him exactly what you asked me to teach him. Or did you forget the terms of your oath?"

"I haven't forgotten," Catriona said. Before Elidor's death, Maddoc had vowed to do everything in his power to free Nearra, if Catriona would promise herself to his service.

Maddoc brushed a stray strand of crimson hair from Catriona's face, letting his wrinkled hand rest on her cheek. "What is the problem, my dear?" He smiled warmly.

An uneasy feeling fluttered in Catriona's gut. She jerked her head, and Maddoc pulled away. "I want to make sure that you aren't teaching Sindri anything he shouldn't be taught."

Maddoc smiled again and lowered his head. "I'm afraid Sindri is so eager that I couldn't keep him from reading every spell in my book even if I had the magic to do so. He likes to know things, as any true wizard does. We're discussing dark magic, but our little kender wizard is clear in his view of right and wrong. He is not as impressionable as you think."

Cat studied Maddoc's eyes. She could read nothing of his

intentions. Above them, the leaves rustled in the night breeze.

"All right," she said after a moment. "But I'm going to be watching you all the same."

Maddoc nodded. "I understand. But I have faith in your strength, Catriona. Have faith in Sindri and myself, and we'll get through this."

The former wizard pushed himself away from his tree and started to walk back toward the fire, but Catriona reached out to grab his arm. "Don't tell Sindri I questioned his resolve," she said. "I don't want him to think I don't believe he can take care of himself."

Maddoc nodded, then resumed his path back to Sindri. Cat watched from the edge of the trees as he sat next to the kender and flipped through the pages of the spellbook.

There was another crack, sounding from deep within the woods. The dragon claws were in Catriona's hands in an instant and she whirled around to face the trees.

"Someone's coming," Maddoc called out.

Cat said nothing. Proudly brandishing his hoopak staff, Sindri ran to her side.

"Shall we check it out?" he asked, strolling toward the dark woods without waiting for a response.

Cat grabbed him by his shoulder, careful to keep her blade aimed away from him. "Stay here, Sindri. I'll go alone."

Eyes narrowed, Sindri looked up. "Come on, Cat. I don't need to stay behind and be protected. Do we need to have this discussion again?"

"No, it's not that," she said. "It's just that you can't get hurt, not now."

Sindri narrowed his eyes further. "And what makes you think I'd get hurt? I know how to take care of myself, you know. I don't always need you protecting me."

"Sindri, no, it's—"

Maddoc stepped forward. "What I believe Catriona is trying

to say is that you need to save your strength for the confrontation with Asvoria. We'll help if needed, but then and only then."

Sindri looked back and forth between the old man and the warrior. Then, with a glance at the woods and a sigh, he stepped back toward the fire. "All right. But if it's anything interesting, tell me about it in complete detail, got it?"

Catriona nodded, then stalked into the trees.

The dense canopy above blocked out almost all of the moonlight, casting the forest floor in shadow. Snuffed by the branches above, the pale red and silver light faded away.

Wind whispered between the wide trees and the smell of decaying leaves and fresh soil filled her nose. Ahead of Catriona lay a rotting log covered in toadstools.

The mossy forest floor kept her footsteps silent as she neared the log. Anyone who wanted to be quiet here certainly could. So what was it that they had heard?

There was a crunch as yet more twigs were crushed beneath someone's feet. Catriona crouched down and leaned against the squishy fungus covering the log. She twirled one of the dragon claws back and forth as she waited.

Something was moving through the trees to the west, something dark and big. Its scent was overpowering, a wild odor so noxious that it made Catriona want to gag. Trying not to make any noise at all, she waited for it to pass.

But, then, there came more crunches. Other dark figures moved through the woods on the other side of the log from where she crouched, though she couldn't tell how many by the sounds alone. Heart pounding, Catriona took a chance and peered up over the log.

Crashing through the underbrush were four goblins, some sort of large lizard, and a big insect with multi-jointed legs. Some were missing limbs and all were bloodied and bruised. They moved slowly but surely eastward, toward the clearing where Maddoc and Sindri were waiting for her to return.

There came a rustling of leathery wings and the large, shadowy form of a flying beast tore through the canopy to hover above the monsters. It turned its furry head side to side, seeming to study the creatures and make sure they were going the right way.

Then, the flying creature landed. Wings receded and became arms. Fur disappeared and its head shrank into the shriveled, red-skinned face of a goblin. Fully transformed, it walked to stand in front of the only goblin that seemed even semi-conscious. It barked out commands in the harsh Goblin tongue.

Mind racing, Catriona crouched back down to hide behind the crumbling log. The winged beast who was now a goblin could only be one creature: Ophion. And if Ophion were leading a small cluster of monsters to their clearing, that could only mean that Asvoria knew they were on their way to her stronghold. Somehow she knew exactly where to find them.

After the creatures had passed, Cat leaped to her feet and ran south through the woods. She had to get back and warn Sindri and Maddoc.

So concerned with what she had just seen, Catriona noticed too late that the monstrous odor had grown stronger.

As she rounded a tree, she found herself face-to-face with an ogre.

Cat skidded to a stop and braced for the ogre's attack. But instead, it stood watching her with a dim expression on its face.

One of its arms was missing and dark blood seeped from the wound. With its pale skin and sunken eyes, the creature appeared to be on the verge of death.

Ever so slightly, its mouth moved. In a wheezing gasp, so low that Catriona almost didn't hear, it said, "Help me. . . ."

Catriona started to run past the creature, and suddenly, its eyes came alive and its lips curled into a snarl.

It lifted its only remaining massive fist and punched forward, straight at Catriona's head.

CHAPTER 3

UNEXPECTED Aid

The ogre's fist met Catriona's helmet with a loud clang. Her mind reeled and her ears rang. She fumbled with the dragon claws, desperately trying to get them into attack position.

The ogre clenched its one bulbous fist tighter and leaped forward, spit flying from its snarling lips. Catriona could do nothing but scramble backward. Bellowing, the ogre closed in.

Cat backed into a tree with a heavy thud. She took a deep breath, inhaling the ogre's rancid stench. She clenched the dragon claws tighter, holding them perpendicular, one high and one low.

The creature was four steps away . . . three steps . . . two . . .

With a yell, Cat lashed out with the dragon claws. They raked through the ogre's bare neck and belly, shredding through the flesh like a real dragon's claws. What little was left of the ogre's blood seeped through the two new wounds and it stumbled over its own legs. Its face still stuck in a mask of fury, the ogre fell at Catriona's feet with a heavy thump, dying as it hit the ground.

Catriona's head was pounding. She could only stare at the ogre lying facedown in the soggy leaves beneath her. Blood dripped from the edges of the dragon claws, hitting the creature's lifeless back with heavy plops.

And then, with a start, Cat remembered the others. Leaping over the ogre's body, she raced ahead.

The monsters walked on through the trees as though they had heard nothing. Like the ogre, the gleam of awareness in their eyes was so faded that it seemed likely they could see or hear nothing at all. They continued to head straight toward the clearing. If they were like the ogre, as soon as they saw Sindri or Maddoc they'd go into some sort of rage and attack them.

What has Asvoria done? Catriona thought.

"Hello."

Cat whirled around at the sudden voice and blinked in surprise. Leaning against a tree, regarding her with crossed arms and a smirk, was . . . herself.

"The redheaded warrior," the other Catriona said in a voice that seemed at once familiar and terribly foreign. Her *own* voice, the real Catriona realized.

"Whatever are you doing in these woods?" The not-Catriona's deep blue eyes, the only feature that showed they were not one and the same, twinkled with amusement.

"Ophion," Cat said. She clenched her dragon claws tight, ready.

"So, you remember me? It's been so long, I wasn't sure you'd—"

Cat lashed out with a dragon claw. Ophion jumped back. But the jagged edge of the sword sliced through the shapeshifter's cheek. Before Ophion could react, Catriona turned and ran.

Jumping over fallen branches and racing around trees, Catriona forced her limbs to pump under the weight of the armor. Sweat coursed down her back and still her head pounded. The disgusting noises of shifting flesh and sloshing innards sounded from behind her.

Cat dared a look over her shoulder to see that Ophion had transformed back into the giant winged creature. Its furry muzzle was opened wide to bare sharp, shredding teeth. Claws at the ends of its leathery wings clutched at branches and gripped into the dirt, pulling Ophion forward far faster than Catriona could ever hope to run. Looking straight ahead, Cat focused all her energy on reaching the clearing.

Veering right, Catriona bounded through a tight cluster of trees. Moments later she heard Ophion grunt before taking wing and flying up through the canopy. Leaves and branches showered down.

Ophion could easily have transformed into something smaller to chase her and Catriona didn't know why it hadn't. Shaking off the uneasy thoughts, she focused on running.

Catriona burst into the dimly lit clearing. She stopped only when she came to stand right in front of Sindri and Maddoc.

She gulped for breath. "Monsters . . . six of them . . . Ophion is leading them here."

Maddoc stood up and gestured toward her bloodstained swords. "What happened?"

"There used to be seven," she said.

Sindri scrambled to his feet. "What kind of monsters? Any I've never seen? Should I use a spell? Oh!" Sindri's eyes fell into a look of concern as he noticed the dented helmet. "Cat, you're bleeding."

Catriona reached up with one of her gloved hands and felt the side of her face. When she pulled her hand away, her fingers were stained with sticky red blood. Catriona's head throbbed harder, as though someone was beating a war drum between her ears. She closed her eyes and tried to will the pain away.

I need to focus, Catriona thought. I need to keep them safe.

"Get ready," she said between clenched teeth.

"Cat—" Sindri started to say.

Before he could finish, wings flapped above their heads.

Catriona opened her eyes and looked up. Ophion's large, furry form hovered above the clearing, watching the three of them with its glowing blue eyes. She could almost have sworn that a smile crossed its beastly face at the sight of the three of them together. Gracefully arcing its wings, it descended, landing lightly on the northern edge of the clearing.

The moment Ophion's claws touched the grass, the monsters stumbled over one another into the clearing. One of the goblins had already lost one leg, and it hopped forward in a way that would have made Catriona laugh if she hadn't felt so frightened. The creatures stopped. Blinking in the firelight, they stared at Sindri, Catriona, and Maddoc.

"What's wrong with them?" Sindri asked. "They look like they've been in a fight."

Cat shook her head, her heart beating faster.

Behind the monsters, Ophion continued to watch the trio. The strange smile still on its face, it flattened its wings and walked backward into the shadows of the trees.

"Sindri," Maddoc whispered. "The spell we were discussing last night. Use it."

The kender looked up at him curiously. "Now?"

The change in the monsters came in an instant. Their eyes flashed with rage and their mouths curled into snarls. The lizard's tail whipped back and forth. The goblins let out war cries and raised their fists to the sky.

The one-legged goblin charged forward. The motion caught the eyes of the crazed goblins and the lizard. In their madness, they could not discern friend from foe. They leaped for the lame creature and began tearing its remaining limbs from its body.

The giant insect dodged the fray and charged toward Catriona.

"Now!" Maddoc yelled.

Pulling a small vial of black liquid from a pouch on his belt,

Sindri raised his hands and began mumbling in the spidery language of magic.

The giant insect's stride was awkward because of its missing legs, but that didn't slow it down. Its two razor sharp mandibles—surrounded by hundreds upon hundreds of beady black eyes—opened and closed.

Raising her dragon claws, Cat turned her head to the kender, trying not to let the fear show in her eyes. She had never much liked insects. Especially not giant ones.

Sindri, however, didn't seem the least bit worried. His eyes were narrowed in complete concentration as the strange words seeped from his lips. Ink from the vial dripped down his forearm and red and blue mist began to flow from his fingers, but still the monster charged.

"Sindri!" Catriona yelled. Sweat beading at his temples, he ignored her.

The insect tripped over its legs. Its beady black eyes clouded with a purple mist and it screamed.

"Ha!" Sindri pumped his fist in triumph, then turned to Catriona with a broad grin. "And you were worried."

At the sound of Sindri's voice, the insect stopped screaming and instead cocked its head to listen.

"Behind the fire!" Maddoc shouted. "Now!"

Grabbing Sindri's arm, Catriona raced around the fire. At the sound of their footsteps, the giant insect once again made chase, ignoring its sudden blindness.

"Would you look at that," Sindri said, craning his neck backward so as to see the monster chasing them. "What do you suppose it needs all those eyes for?"

Ignoring him, Catriona dived behind the ring of stones surrounding their fire. Maddoc was already there and had picked up a rock. He smashed it repeatedly against the other stones and shouted, making as much noise as possible.

"What are you doing?" Catriona yelled.

Hearing the noises, the insect leaped. For a terrifying moment, Catriona thought it would land directly on top of them. Covering Sindri's small body with her own, she raised her weapons in preparation, not daring to blink.

Instead, the monster landed in the fire. The flames blazed as though they had been doused with grease. As the creature squealed in pain, an acrid scent filled the air. The insect leaped away from the fire and ran back into the woods, leaving only a trail of flaming underbrush in its wake.

As the insect's screams faded into the night, the three remaining goblins and the lizard turned their attention to the trio as though noticing them for the first time. Once again the goblins raised their fists and let out shouts of war.

There was no time to plan a defense with Sindri or Maddoc. The creatures were on them in seconds.

Raising her dragon claws high, Cat jumped toward the nearest goblin. The red-faced creature ducked the blows and leaped backward, snarling. It picked up a clump of dirt and flung it at her face. Cat spun away, just in time.

As she turned she saw Sindri out of the corner of her eye, valiantly trying to fight off the two other goblins with his hoopak staff. He swung it around as they had been taught by Set-ai, so long ago. Knocking one of the goblins onto its back, he whipped the staff around to smack the other across the head.

Unfortunately, in his exhilaration, he didn't notice that the first goblin had kicked itself back onto its feet. It snatched the hoopak staff from Sindri's fingers and swung it at the kender's skull.

"Sindri!" Catriona cried, but she couldn't see what happened next. Her own goblin barreled into her armored chest with a loud clang. She fell backward, using the momentum to kick up her legs and fling the creature off of her. It landed next to the fire, rolled, and was back on its feet in an instant.

Letting out a cry that made her head ache even more,

Catriona pushed herself to her feet and swung the dragon claws forward. They met the goblin's exposed red neck with a sick squelch as metal cut through flesh and then bone. The creature's head rolled through the dark grass. Its body stood for a moment before collapsing backward.

Catriona spun around, her face a mask of resolve. Sindri had pulled the dagger she had given him from his boot and was trying to get his staff back from the goblins, but he was no match for two of them. Meanwhile, over near the trees, Maddoc had picked up a handful of jagged rocks and was tossing them at the lizard. Its fang-filled snout snapped open and shut in response. Fear filled Maddoc's eyes.

I have to help them! Catriona's thoughts screamed. She began to race forward and a wave of dizziness washed over her. She fell to her knees, her head still throbbing from the ogre's blow. Tears of frustration welled at the corners of her eyes.

Maddoc let out a shout. The lizard's thick tail whipped around and hit the old man in his middle, tossing him backward. He crashed against a tree and crumpled to the ground.

Catriona heard Sindri yell too, and she turned away from Maddoc. One of the goblins had taken his dagger and was swinging its arm back and forth so fast it was a blur. The dagger sliced through Sindri's wrist and, cradling it, he stumbled backward.

Get up! Cat commanded herself. Without her they were lost. Without her they'd—

There was a soft twang and something flew through the air past her face. The lizard creature roared, and Cat turned to see that it had just been about to take Maddoc's head in its jaws. Fortunately for Maddoc, a white-shafted arrow had plunged into the lizard's back. Rearing its head, the lizard turned to find its attacker.

Another arrow flew almost silently through the air, landing hard in the chest of the goblin with the knife. Its face froze, and it fell backward.

Running out of the trees were three people: two girls and a boy. The girl with the bow was slender with almond-shaped eyes and curly hair the color of untarnished gold. Cat didn't have to see her ears to know she was an elf.

The other girl's pale face seemed somehow familiar, though Cat wasn't sure where she'd seen her before. Looking to be no more than thirteen or fourteen, she too was slender, though her body was gangly rather than graceful. Her black hair was pulled back into a short, tight braid and she brandished a short sword.

The boy, also wielding a sword, had unruly black hair and lips that seemed unable to do anything but grin. "Mudd," Catriona whispered, recognizing the boy as he grew closer. He was a little taller and his once-skinny arms more defined, but it was definitely the boy she'd met back in Potter's Mill.

Mudd raced toward the wounded lizard. The black-haired girl barreled toward the goblin that was still attacking Sindri. The elf nocked an arrow on her bow and aimed it at the goblin at the exact moment the black-haired girl stepped between the archer and her target. Already on the verge of releasing, all the elf could do was move her bow to the side so as not to hit her companion.

The arrow flew through the air, whizzing past the human girl's face. It sunk into the goblin's shoulder, far from its mark. The goblin ignored the arrow and kept swinging the staff at Sindri's head.

"Hey!" the black-haired girl cried. Scowling, she turned and shot the elf a dirty look.

Mudd reached the lizard, leaped over its snapping jaws, and raised his sword high. Fumbling with the weapon, he managed to aim it down before slicing it in a swift arc toward the creature's spine. The blade plunged through the rough hide of the beast's back and into its heart.

The black-haired girl swung wildly at the goblin. The flat of her sword knocked the staff out of its hands. The goblin hurled itself at the girl.

She held her sword straight, and the goblin impaled itself, its own momentum stabbing the sword deep into its chest. With a look of disgust, the girl shoved the now dead goblin off the point of her sword with one of her booted feet.

Silence settled over the clearing. At the edge of the forest, Maddoc rose with his head in his hands and his face contorted in agony. The black-haired girl and the elf looked around, breathing hard. Catriona still was unable to climb to her feet.

"Mudd!" Sindri cried. Cradling his injured arm, he picked up his hoopak staff from where it had fallen and ran forward to meet their old friend.

"Well met, Sindri," Mudd said. "Looks like we got here just in time."

"Wait," Catriona whispered. "Wait!" she said again, forcing herself to yell. "There's still—"

Again there came the sound of leathery wings flapping to catch the wind. Everyone turned to see the winged beast that was Ophion burst from the shadows between the trees and leap high into the sky. The black-haired girl and Mudd raised their swords. The elf lifted her bow. Catriona forced herself to her feet and brandished her dragon claws, waiting for the impending attack.

Instead, Ophion considered them all with a cocked head, then turned and flew off into the dark horizon.

The others breathed sighs of relief at its retreat. But Catriona's concern had only grown. This time she was certain.

Ophion was smiling.

CHAPTER

4   MUDD AND THE SISTERS

I never thought I'd get a chance to see the inside of my arm," Sindri said, studying his wound. "I just wish there was a way to do it without it hurting so much!"

Rina frowned, but Sindri didn't notice. He continued to twist his arm back and forth, watching as the slick blood glinted in the firelight.

Rina had of course heard about the insatiable curiosity and unique lack of personal fear inherent in all kender, but she had never seen it up close. It was more than a little disconcerting.

"Well, yes, fascinating as this gory wound is," Rina said, "you must hold still. I need to bandage this up." She reached into her pack and pulled out a long strip of cloth.

The kender obliged, though his small body shook with eagerness. His eyes never left the cut.

It was a bit awkward for her to be bandaging a person she had only met a few moments before, but there had been no time for introductions. Rina had immediately crouched to tend to the kender's wound as the others dragged the bodies of the goblins away from the campfire. The old human man in the black robes sat near the fire, head resting in his palms.

Rina glanced up from her work and saw the three young humans carrying the body of the headless goblin to lay it near the trees where the lizard had been killed.

Rina noticed Jirah glance at her as the trio finished their grisly task, and for a moment their eyes met. Rina could read no emotion on her face, and the human girl spun around as though surprised to have been caught staring.

With a shake of her head, Rina turned her attention back to the kender. "All right," she said, giving the bandage one final tug. "All done. A white bandage is hardly as interesting to look at as your bones, but it's probably preferable to infection."

"Amazing!" The kender raised his arm in front of his face. "It doesn't even hurt anymore."

"My mother used to be a healer," Rina said. "She taught me a few secrets, though I'm hardly an expert."

"*Used* to be?" The kender tilted his head and looked up at her inquisitively.

"She's in politics now. Not quite the same woman she was back when . . . Well, anyway, you should be fine now." Turning from the kender, Rina looked back at the humans. They were done, it seemed, and were heading back to the fire.

Dark clouds swirled across the sky, blocking the moons and thrusting the woods deep into shadow. It didn't bother Rina much, since elf vision was made for the night, but even she could tell that the clearing seemed smaller somehow.

"I'm glad that's over with," Mudd said as he grew closer. "Perhaps someone should make a point of introducing goblins to the concept of bathing. Get Sindri all fixed up?"

Rina nodded, unconsciously brushing a lock of curly hair behind her pointed ear. "Good as new. He should be healed up and handling weapons with the best of them in no time."

"Are you sure he'll be all right?" Jirah asked as she sidled up beside Mudd. "Last time Rina 'healed' someone's arm, it had to be removed."

"He'll be *fine*, Jirah," Rina said.

"That's good to hear," Catriona said. She was tall, her jaw line hard, her neck sinewy with muscle. Her face revealed pain, though whether that was from the wound to her head or from something far deeper Rina couldn't tell.

"Thanks for your help," Catriona went on. "I'd taken a pretty hard blow and couldn't fight my best."

Mudd grinned and slapped the warrior on her armored back. "No worries, Cat. It was our pleasure to help."

Catriona winced.

"Maybe we should introduce ourselves," Jirah said. She glanced quickly between the group huddled around the fire. "It wasn't an accident that we ran into you."

"I was just wondering why Mudd and two girls were wandering about these woods," Sindri said. He had walked over to the old man by the fire and now sat cross-legged next to him. "I couldn't imagine any good reason you'd be out here all alone. Well, maybe one, but it didn't seem likely."

Mudd laughed, and Rina couldn't help but grind her teeth at the sound of his endlessly loud voice. Of the humans she'd met since leaving Southern Ergoth, only Davyn hadn't seemed so terribly vulgar. Even Jirah, who had at first seemed so quiet, had proven to grow more *human* the longer they knew each other. She wondered if she'd ever get used to them before firmly reminding herself, yet again, that it would be worth the effort in the end. It had to be.

Mudd jumped forward and put his hands on his hips in a proud pose. As always, the human boy was full of so much pent-up energy that it made Rina feel a bit unsettled. "Sindri, my friend, we are here on a mission. A mission to find you three, no less, a mission it seems we have succeeded in completing. I'd say that makes us quite the little team, wouldn't you, Rina?"

Rina looked up and nodded. "Yes, somehow we managed, although you three certainly threw us for a loop coming here before we could find you and bring you here ourselves."

"Hold on," Catriona said, raising a hand. "Who sent you to find us?"

"Davyn," Jirah said.

As soon as the name was mentioned, Sindri's eyes came alive with excitement while Catriona looked down. The old man's look was much harder to read, but something about the way his dark eyes looked up into her own made Rina shiver.

"He sent us to find you," Jirah continued. "Shemnara told him that she had a vision about him serving Asvoria and biding his time. So he's there now."

"Where?" the kender asked.

"Asvoria's manor," Jirah said. "Doing exactly as he was told. Serving the sorceress and waiting."

The old man by the fire let out a short, bitter laugh and everyone turned to stare. He glanced up and raised an eyebrow, but said nothing.

"That doesn't sound like much of a plan," Sindri said. "You would think serving Asvoria would only help her, wouldn't you? But, oh, Davyn is so lucky! I wish I could have pretended to serve her instead. I wonder if she would have taught me some of her secrets?"

"I don't like it," Catriona said, shaking her head. "Although I'm glad to hear Davyn finally came to his senses and wants to help save Nearra again, something about all this isn't right."

Mudd shrugged. "He's there with Asvoria, and now we've found you. We're supposed to all head back there as soon as possible, before Asvoria can do whatever it is she's planning to do."

"How did you three get involved in this?" Catriona said, glancing at Rina. "Why are you helping us?"

"We were called on to help Davyn," Mudd revealed, "after Jirah here attacked him in a tavern. Got on his case about Nearra, so he decided he needed to help her."

"You know Nearra?" Sindri asked Jirah.

Startled, the black-haired girl stammered for a moment before composing herself. "I'm, well, her sister."

"I knew you looked familiar!" Sindri cried and jumped to his feet. His purple cape fluttered to the back of his knees, his shaggy black hair to his shoulders. He looked a bit like a stage magician. Certainly not how Rina had heard kender tended to look. "How wonderful to meet you!" he said.

Jirah gave the kender a distasteful look. "Thank you, I suppose."

"So, Nearra's sister attacked Davyn," Catriona pressed. "What then?"

"They came back to Potter's Mill," Mudd said, "and Shemnara told us about this Dragon Knight who had the key to freeing Nearra."

"How is Shemnara?" the kender asked. "I wish I could see her. Wow, we all have so much catching up to do!"

Catriona gently put her hand on the kender's shoulder and stepped forward, eyes focused. "The Dragon Knight," she said. "Did you find him? Will he help us?"

Mudd shook his head. "No Dragon Knight. Well, not exactly. Shemnara sent us out to find others to help us, which is how we met Rina here. But the Dragon Knight we found was dead, and his heir was fat and crazy."

"Shemnara thinks Davyn's the Dragon Knight now," Rina added. "And I think she's right. He has one of the Dragon Knight's swords and he received his blessing."

"What's your story?" Catriona said, turning to study the elf. "Why were you chosen to help Davyn?"

"I'm . . ." Rina began, finding she didn't quite know what to say. This human girl was so big, her demeanor so brutish and forceful. But there was an air of sadness and determination about her that somehow spoke to the elf.

Rina held her head high. "I am Rinalasha Lelaynar," she

said. "And I am Elidor's sister."

The kender gasped. Catriona closed her eyes, then bowed her head. "It was my deepest honor to have known Elidor. He died saving our lives, and I will not let that go unavenged." She looked up, deep into Rina's eyes. "You have my word."

Rina bowed her head in return. "Thank you."

"What an interesting coincidence," the old man said, speaking for the first time. His gaze met Rina's, and she narrowed her eyes. "The sisters of the two fallen companions coming to the rescue."

Mudd turned, his smile gone as he regarded the old man. "So, this is Maddoc. Davyn wasn't sure if you caught up with Sindri and Cat, but he said you might be here. You're shorter than I thought you'd be."

Maddoc snorted and shot Mudd a condescending look. "I'm sitting. And you shouldn't believe everything you hear."

Rina's limbs trembled in anger. "Maddoc. Elidor is dead because of you."

"And my sister is possessed," Jirah added.

Maddoc looked directly into Rina's eyes, and she did not look away. "You have no chance of success without me. Only I can teach Sindri how to free Nearra. I suppose you'll just have to put up with me for the time being."

"Davyn told me about everything," Mudd said. Crossing his arms, he went to stand above the old man. "He told me you're powerless now, or so you say, and he told me that you're the only person who knows Asvoria inside and out, so we need you. But he also told me if you were here to keep my eye on you."

Maddoc shook his head, an amused look on his face. "That's my son for you."

"Excuse me," Jirah said. She stepped forward, head slightly bowed. "You said you're teaching *Sindri* the spells?"

"I am indeed," Maddoc said, his thin lips pursed into a tight smile. "Did Davyn neglect to mention that Sindri is a wizard?"

Sindri beamed proudly.

Rina stared. "A *kender* wizard? Davyn mentioned something about magic, but I thought perhaps Sindri had an artifact or something. A kender *wizard*? Really?"

Jirah glared at Sindri. "Surely you're joking. Kender cannot be wizards."

Sindri's eyes narrowed. "I'll have you know that I am descended from a great kender wizard and that my mother foresaw me becoming a wizard just as great while she was gardening. Raistlin himself admitted me to the very famous Greeves Academy of Thaumaturgical Studies in Palanthas, and tonight I cast a really powerful blinding spell on a giant bug. So how is it that kender cannot be wizards?"

"They just can't!" Jirah shouted, clenching her fists at her side. "Especially not if—" She stopped herself and shook her head. "Never mind."

Rina looked at Jirah sideways. Red flushed her face, almost as though she was angry at the kender. Certainly someone who would be so daring as to attack Davyn wasn't exactly demure, but this was strange, even for a human.

"Well, whether or not kender can be wizards hardly matters now," Maddoc said. "The fact is that our friend Sindri has access to some sort of magic, and I am helping him to use it. As it stands, Sindri may well be our only chance to free Nearra."

Jirah let out a slight snort. "And when exactly do we plan to do this freeing?"

"As soon as we reach Asvoria's stronghold," Catriona said. "Whatever plans she's made, it's obvious she's started."

Rina nodded. "The sooner the better."

Jirah turned to Rina and tilted her head. "Maybe we should wait for Davyn to come find us and let us know what he's found out. Someone certainly needs to give you a few archery lessons before we go storming anywhere, at the very least. You almost killed me earlier with that wild shot."

"Excuse me?" Rina demanded. She scrunched her eyebrows and looked into the human girl's darkly smiling eyes.

"Oh, I'm sorry," Jirah said. "I'm sure you *meant* to graze my cheek and miss that goblin's heart, right?"

"Well, if you hadn't—"

"No need to apologize." Jirah brushed past Catriona to stand closer to the fire. "But now that we've found Davyn's companions, perhaps it's time you went on your own way."

"What on Krynn are you going on about?" Rina raised her chin. "Did you get hit in the head? Did I do something to offend you?"

Jirah waved her hand dismissively. "I just meant there's no reason for you to continue to risk your life. It's not like you have any real stake in freeing Nearra, not like the rest of us. My sister still has a chance to live, but your brother—well, he's *dead*. Fighting Asvoria won't bring him back."

Rina clenched her jaw. "But Davyn—"

"Davyn would understand. We have a tough battle ahead, and I'm sure he wouldn't want another mistake like that to cost one of us our lives. He told me himself, back in Viranesh Keep, that he doesn't really need your help."

"I don't believe you." Rina narrowed her eyes. "If anything, he doesn't need—"

Mudd stepped forward and placed a hand on Rina's shoulder. "Now, now, ladies, let's not get feisty." He shot Jirah a meaningful look.

Catriona shook her head and started to gather her things from around the fire. "We need to move," she said. "Ophion is probably reporting to Asvoria as we speak and could be on the way back with more monsters. We can decide later about waiting for Davyn or—"

Wincing, she stopped talking and kneeled in the grass, pressing her hand against her head. Eyes closed tight, she hissed through clenched teeth.

Bounding to the warrior's side, Sindri rest a hand on her shoulder. "Cat? Are you all right? Are you still hurt?"

She waved a hand to reassure him, but her expression did not change.

"Hey, Cat, we can rest here." Mudd knelt beside her and Sindri. "We'll take turns with watch."

She shook her head. "It isn't safe."

"You need sleep, Catriona," Maddoc said. Rina was surprised to hear what seemed to be genuine concern in his tone. "Dawn is coming. With all Asvoria has done this night, it's unlikely she's going to bother with us right now."

The warrior let out a disgruntled sigh. "Fine. Let's rest then. But I'm taking first watch."

Jirah plopped her pack on the ground with a heavy thud. "Before we sleep," she said, rustling through the pack's contents, "I think there's something all of you need to know."

Finding what she was searching for, Jirah pulled her hand free from the pack and showed everyone a plain wooden box. Opening it, she revealed a small black statue worn smooth with age. It was intricately carved in the shape of a dragon. Rina recognized it as the artifact Shemnara had given back to Jirah before they left Potter's Mill.

"This is the Trinistyr," the black-haired girl explained. "It's the reason I sought out Davyn. There's a curse placed on it, one that Nearra has been foretold to break."

"And that's bad?" Sindri asked.

"Oh yes," Jirah said. She glanced down at Sindri. "You see, no one knows exactly how the curse will be broken. All we know is that when it is, the power of the gods will have to flow through Nearra's body and back into the Trinistyr."

Catriona nodded in grim understanding. "And that means . . ."

"That means," Jirah finished, "that if the curse is somehow broken while Asvoria is connected to Nearra, she'll have access to the power of the very gods themselves."

Mudd let out a low whistle. "With that kind of power, no one on Krynn will be able to stop her."

Everyone fell silent, staring at the small black statue Jirah held in the box. She caught their eyes one by one before snapping the box shut, the sound overwhelmingly loud in the quiet night.

5   VICTANT

The toad croaked.

Asvoria glanced sidelong at the little brown creature. It sat in the mud beside her, staring at absolutely nothing, not the least bit afraid of the giant human standing so near it.

It croaked. Again.

Asvoria had been standing in the swamp for hours, ever since Ophion dropped her off. The shapeshifter had headed back to the woods to take care of the boy's traveling companions, while she stood here waiting for the dragon to return.

Asvoria didn't like waiting. She'd already spent two thousand years waiting. She didn't want to waste any more time.

She'd expected the dragon to return by now. And yet, here she stood, ankle deep in thick mud, her only companion a dirty toad.

The toad prepared to croak again. The thin membrane under its fleshy neck bulged out as it slowly filled with the humid air. Asvoria lifted her hand and mumbled a few choice words.

No air was released. No croak sounded. Instead, the skin continued to grow and stretch. The small creature's body shook with agony.

Then, with a tiny, insignificant pop, the toad exploded.

Asvoria considered the creature's remains, then looked away. "Where is he?" she muttered, absentmindedly wiping amphibian gore off the side of her dress.

It would serve you right if he never came. The voice was tinny and soft, as though hearing someone from far away. The girl in the back of her mind could be such a bother sometimes. Usually she left Asvoria alone, choosing instead, Asvoria imagined, to wallow in self-pity. There had been times early on when the girl had built up enough pure will to manage to keep Asvoria from killing her friends. But those acts seemed to have sapped the girl of any further strength.

"Why such hostility, Nearra?" Asvoria said aloud. "Do you realize that if all goes well, soon I'll be free of your frail little body? What you do with it then is of no concern to me. If I were you, I'd want things to go well."

Never.

It was such a waste to speak to her. Nearra was helping her to fulfill plans that would change Krynn forever, and yet she could not appreciate it!

Asvoria shook her head. She knew she shouldn't care what opinions the girl held. Still, she thought, it never hurts to be on good terms with the voices in your head.

She chuckled at the joke despite herself. "Nearra, your little girl mind has rubbed off on me more than I thought."

No part of me will—

Asvoria pushed back Nearra's personality, shoving it into the far corners of her mind. Nearra's soul was now bound to Asvoria's own, thanks to the magic of a dragon well—the same magic that gave Asvoria the power she needed to resist Maddoc's spells of paralysis and fully emerge in Nearra's body.

She had tried to make the best of a bad situation by allowing the girl to speak up. After all, her pitiful mewling often proved amusing. But, true to form, Nearra had quickly grown tiresome.

To Asvoria's annoyance, it took a little effort to submerge the girl. She still felt tired from the spells she'd performed earlier that evening. But her exhaustion only strengthened her resolve to be free of her humanity once and for all.

The swamp's murky scent overwhelmed her delicate nose and mud gushed around her ankles. In the distance a bird called and another responded. Flies buzzed around her head, and Asvoria dimly thought that perhaps she should have let the toad live until it had devoured the pests.

Then, she felt it, tingling at the back of her mind. To Nearra, the feeling translated as dragonfear, the sense of complete terror that paralyzed most beings. Asvoria, however, felt only dragon-awe, since she shared the dragon's alignment with darkness. Adoration flooded her mind.

Finally, Victant had come home.

He descended from the sky, his vast, powerful wings raising up such a wind that the muddy water rippled fiercely. Asvoria's hair and dress whipped around her body and the flies gave themselves over to the gusts and were blown away.

The dragon could only be seen against the dark, murky scenery by what little silver and red moonlight seeped through the clouds and glinted off the edges of his perfectly black scales. An immense shadow, he landed in the mud beneath two spiny trees that jutted toward the sky.

Asvoria couldn't help but stare in longing. He was hardly as big as the other dragons she had tried—and failed—to coax into being her host, but he was beautiful all the same. She trembled as she watched him, wondering what it would be like to see through those shrewd eyes, to fly with those vast wings, to rip a creature apart with those razor-sharp claws.

This was her last chance. Without the artifacts the children had stolen from her, she had no other options. Tomorrow night the black moon, Nuitari, would be at its highest point, and the possession needed to happen then. Already she'd started to raise her army. After so long, she was so close . . .

The dragon snorted, the sound echoing over the quiet waters. Asvoria noted that the birds that had been calling to each other only moments before had fallen silent.

"I know you are there," the dragon growled.

"As I knew you would," Asvoria said, willing her emotions to hide, for her voice to remain steady. She was a queen, after all.

Once again the dragon snorted. "I sense magic on you. And I suppose that means you believe yourself capable of facing me and living to tell the tale."

Leaving the shelter of the shadows, Asvoria trudged as regally as she could through the mud. She could see the dragon clearer now. His eyes watched her with malice.

"Victant," Asvoria said, "hear me out and you may find your destiny to be far greater than you had ever imagined."

The dragon's eyes narrowed and his wings shuddered slightly. "My name to mortals is Nimbus," he snarled. "And yet you dare use my true name."

Asvoria couldn't help but smirk. "You knew as soon as you sensed me that I was no mere mortal."

Cocking his great head, Victant considered Asvoria. Then, baring teeth stained with fresh blood, his head shot forward, stopping just in front of Asvoria's own. The young body Asvoria possessed was dwarfed by the dragon's snout alone; his nostril was as big as her entire head.

Again he snorted. The smell of musty decay overwhelmed Asvoria, clinging to the back of her throat.

For a moment, the dragon did not move. His eyes, even blacker than his shimmering scales, scanned Asvoria from head to toe.

He pulled away. "Speak. Quickly."

"I am Asvoria. Long ago, I ruled as queen, and long ago I made great plans that would forever change the face of this world. I was defeated by my betrayers and before I could reemerge, the dragons left Krynn."

"And now that we're back, you've come back as well?"

Asvoria nodded. "You are intelligent, Victant. I have heard great things about you. Which is why you were chosen."

The dragon dug his sharp talons deep into the mud. "Chosen for what?"

"To be my next form. With your body and mind as the host of my soul, together we shall—"

A deep rumbling rose from Victant's chest, bursting forth from the dragon's jaws as booming laughter. Asvoria frowned.

"My body? Your soul?" Again the dragon laughed. "I suppose you searched far and wide for one of the reds or blues, and now you're settling for one of us small blacks? How amusing. Tell me, Asvoria, how many dragons have you approached in your little quest before coming to me?"

Asvoria stayed silent. He had guessed right, of course, but he didn't need to know that. Long ago her plans of ascension had involved transforming her own body into that of a dragon, but it involved years of spell casting timed to complete on the Night of the Eye. Now, possession was her only option.

Without the sun-shaped amulet known as the Daystar and the emerald-flecked sword called the Aegis, she was woefully unprepared to possess a dragon by force. Unfortunately, as she had rapidly found out, not many dragons were willing to hand over their bodies for someone else to control.

So it was that she had heard of Nimbus, whose true name was Victant. He had apparently been a faithful servant during the War of the Lance, which was unusual for a black dragon. He was a follower in need of a leader now that his had long since met his bitter end. A perfect candidate.

"What sort of dragon you are now does not matter," Asvoria said after a moment. "Not with what we will become. The two of us will meld as one, and no more powerful a being will exist on Krynn. Nothing could stop us."

"So, you plan to take over Krynn, then?" Victant's scaly lips curled into a condescending smile. "How . . . unique. Tell me, sorceress, what about you is so special that you believe you will succeed where the Dark Queen herself has failed so recently? And with only one dragon, no less."

"I don't plan to take over Krynn," Asvoria said, lifting her chin in haughty pride. "Dragons are the most exquisite creatures ever to have resided on this world of ours, Victant. They deserve to be worshipped, and yet all the species live apart, fending for themselves. With my ascension, dragonkind will be exalted and every being on Krynn will serve us. Willingly or otherwise."

"Serve *us*?" Victant said, his lips now rising into a sneer. "You are not a dragon, sorceress, and may you never be. To think, being forced to intermingle with other dragons . . ." He shook his head.

Asvoria clenched her fists, almost unable to keep herself from screaming in frustration. She was so close! "But think of the power our kind would have!"

"I have more than enough power." Victant sneered. He tilted his head. "You are a pest. Would you like to see my special way of dealing with pests?"

Letting out a devastated, rage-filled cry, Asvoria raised her fingers and began speaking the spells that would tear this insolent creature's flesh from his bones. But as she did, Victant lifted his long, sinewy neck and reared back his head. Black, acrid liquid seeped from the edges of his lips.

Quickly Asvoria shifted her spell casting. She raised a wall of mystical energy only seconds before the thick black acid spewed from Victant's mouth to engulf her.

The acid slid down Asvoria's mystical shield, burning into the mud. As it did, she looked up to find that Victant had disappeared. Frantically she looked up and to the sides. Nothing.

Too late she noticed the water rippling beside her.

Victant's head burst from beneath the murky pond. An immense wave slammed into Asvoria. She fell to her back, sputtering as slimy water filled her nostrils and coated her throat. The swamp water pushed her through the muck and grass until she thudded heavily against one of the spiny trees.

Finally, the wave pulled back. Hacking, Asvoria climbed to her knees and glared at the dragon. Victant stood at his full height in the water, wings slowly flapping. His teeth were bared, his eyes narrowed.

"You are lucky, sorceress," he said. "If you had approached me only a year ago, I'd have fought you until you were so weak you couldn't even move your lips, let alone cast a spell. Then I would have eaten you, starting with the least necessary bits so that you'd be alive for every last bite. But I know you would be a powerful opponent and I am too old and tired to waste the energy it would take to defeat you. Besides, I have a full stomach. I suggest you leave before I change my mind."

Asvoria rose. Her blond hair hung in clumpy tendrils over her shoulders. Drops of mud clung to her back like leeches. She stared at the creature, rage coursing throughout her entire body.

"You will regret this," she said. Then she turned and walked away.

Behind her, Victant chuckled to himself before settling down to sleep. In the distant corner of her mind where the girl hid, Nearra joined in his laughter.

"Shut up!" Asvoria screamed, stamping her foot in the mud. "Ophion! If you're not here, I'll—"

There was a rustling in the reeds to her right and Ophion appeared. Its body was the ambiguous, featureless form of a human, the color of its skin shifting to match the water and sky behind him. Only its blue eyes stood out among the dim scenery.

"Things didn't go well?" Ophion asked, bowing.

"What do you think?" she snapped. "Tell me that the boy's companions are dead."

"They are not."

Digging her fingernails into her palms, Asvoria couldn't help but scream. First her artifacts were stolen, then she was forced to waste energy raising an army of the dead because she couldn't find any willing followers that she trusted, let alone a dragon willing to be her host. Now this. Dark thoughts of Ophion writhing in agony at her feet flitted through her mind. "And why not?"

"I never had a chance to find the elf and the two humans," Ophion said, daring to lift its head. "I ran into the boy's original companions. The fool wizard, the redheaded warrior, and—"

"The kender," Asvoria finished. "The one who stole my Daystar amulet."

Ophion nodded. "I let them live so that they could bring the kender to us. No doubt he'd try and use the amulet, and then . . ."

Asvoria smiled. "We will return to the manor and bring the children to us. Then, we will take back my amulet and return to the original plan."

"So many dragons to pick from," Ophion said, glancing in the direction of the ancient black, his head now resting in slumber. "Whomever will you choose?"

"I think," Asvoria said, drawing out the words until her thoughts mingled with Nearra's own, "that I know the perfect host."

Nearra screamed, *No!*

"Oh, yes," Asvoria whispered. "Now hush."

She pushed away Nearra's personality. As Ophion changed into a flying beast, Asvoria turned to watch Victant. "We will meet again, dragon. And then you will know true pain."

With Ophion changed, Asvoria climbed upon its hairy back. She patted the nape of its neck, and Ophion took wing.

The Daystar amulet would soon be theirs and, with its return, Asvoria would finally set into motion the plans she had devised over two thousand years ago.

"It is almost time, my dear familiar," she whispered to Ophion as they flew. "Tomorrow, our new life begins."

6 PLANS AND REUNIONS

An icy cold droplet of water plopped against the back of Sindri's head. Then another on his shoulder, and still another on the roll of parchment in his lap.

Sindri looked up. Gray clouds swirled like fire smoke, hiding the sun's bright orb and filtering its light into a soft haze. More droplets fell, hitting Sindri's cheeks and smearing the charcoal on the paper.

"I've been in need of a good wash," Sindri said to no one in particular. "But now's probably not the best time."

Rolling up the parchment, Sindri put it and his piece of charcoal into a pocket on the inside of his cloak and looked around the clearing. He hadn't been able to sleep well and had taken over watch from Catriona after a few hours of restlessness.

His bandaged right arm still throbbed with a strange numb pulse, and on top of that he'd been unable to keep from reliving the night's events over and over again in his mind. As soon as it was light enough to see, he set about writing down all the details of the attack and the unexpected visitors, so as not to forget anything when he told the tales of their adventure in the future.

Sindri scanned the clearing to see if anyone else was awake. Mudd and the elf girl Rina were still fast asleep, and Maddoc lay with his eyes closed near the smoldering, ashy remains of last night's fire. Whether Maddoc was actually asleep or not, Sindri didn't know. Never could tell with him.

Catriona was leaning against a tree across the clearing, where she had insisted she sit all night while keeping watch, even after Sindri had officially taken over. He grinned when he saw that her eyes were closed. He hoped she was having good dreams. Noticing the streaks of blood on her face, Sindri made a note to himself to ask her what it was like to be punched in the head by an ogre.

Only Nearra's sister, Jirah, was awake. She was on the opposite side of the clearing from where Cat lay, sitting cross-legged and facing toward the trees. Her pack lay open beside her as she looked at something in her hands and mumbled to herself. Strands of untamed black hair stuck out at odd angles from her untangling braid.

Sindri was walking toward Jirah before he even realized he had begun to move. As he came closer, he saw that what the girl held was a small oval mirror in a silver frame. Her blue eyes, so like Nearra's, were furrowed in concern, and still she muttered to herself as she studied her reflection. The only time she looked away was to cast quick glances in the direction of where Mudd and Rina lay sleeping.

Whatever was she doing? Perhaps she was practicing for a speech? Sindri had heard of people talking in mirrors to prepare. In fact, his aunt Moonbeam knew a king who would practice his speeches in front of a magical mirror that would constantly interrupt to tell him how awful he was doing. But why would Jirah be giving a speech? Curiosity taking over, Sindri started to walk forward to ask the girl himself.

"Sindri."

Sindri turned at the sound of Maddoc's voice and saw the

former wizard was now sitting up next to the fire. The hood of his black cloak covered his face and hid it in shadow.

"Come here a moment." Maddoc lifted a wrinkled hand and beckoned Sindri closer.

Anxiously, Sindri looked back and forth between Maddoc and Nearra's sister. Jirah was oblivious to him and Maddoc, as she appeared to be in heated discussion with her reflection. Raindrops beaded on the mirror's glassy surface, but she didn't seem to notice.

"Sindri," Maddoc said again, and with a sigh Sindri forced himself to turn away from Jirah. He'd just have to ask her about it later.

Wet grass squelched beneath his boots as he walked to Maddoc. Sindri plopped cross-legged on the ground beside him. Maddoc's gray eyes studied the kender from beneath his hood.

"You did well last night," Maddoc said after a moment. "A little slow, but well nonetheless."

Sindri nodded eagerly. "I think at first I mixed up a few of the words, but I got it in the end. It worked, although I can't seem to remember what it was exactly that I said."

Maddoc glanced at the sleeping companions lying beyond the makeshift fire pit. "Nuitari will be at its peak tonight," he said, still turned away.

Sindri tilted his head and regarded Maddoc with a curious look. Nuitari was the black moon that no one but the black-robed mages could see. In fact, few people on Krynn even knew the moon existed. Sindri himself had never managed to make it out in the night sky, though he'd tried. He'd always wondered what exactly a black moon would look like.

"Nuitari?" Sindri whispered, glancing over at Catriona's sleeping form. "That moon only grants power to dark wizards."

Turning back to face him, Maddoc sighed. "I'm well aware."

"Then what does it matter if it's full?"

"Because," Maddoc said, gently resting his hand on Sindri's shoulder, "Lunitari and Solinari are both waning. Tonight, dark magic will be more powerful. Asvoria will have the upper hand, which is no doubt why she has set her plans into motion. You must know this."

Sindri nodded. "I didn't know. I never really paid attention to the moons."

"You should start," Maddoc said. "Their cycles are very important. In fact, I've been thinking about it. I'd say that you would have better luck tonight were you to use black magic spells."

Sindri lifted his head with a start and frowned.

"No," Sindri said, his voice hard. Then, softening his tone, he shook his head. "We already talked about this. Just because I wanted to see what kind of spells there were, that doesn't mean I want to be a black-robed wizard. I'm not evil."

"I know, Sindri," Maddoc said. "And I can tell you're convinced you're right. But know this: dark magic does not have to mean bad magic. As a white-robed wizard you are limited by your own morality. With dark magic morality holds no sway and, unlike neutral magic, the power can be limitless. You would certainly never use it for evil, would you?"

Sindri shrugged, then shook his head. "No."

"Then perhaps it is something you should consider. If you only use the spells to stop someone like Asvoria, then what is the harm? Does that make sense to you?"

Fingering his hoopak staff, Sindri shrugged again. "I suppose."

Maddoc sighed and closed his eyes. "Just my own point of view. I didn't expect you to understand." Opening his eyes, Maddoc glanced back toward the other companions. "Looks like the others are waking. Shall we join them?"

Sindri nodded, then jammed his hoopak into the muddy ground to help him stand.

Lending Maddoc a hand up, Sindri found his mind racing.

Black magic was evil. That's what everyone said. But what if Maddoc were right? He'd always dismissed the thought before. What if it was only in how Sindri used the power, not what the power represented? Could he maybe be a good, dark mage?

And what would it be like? Did dark magic feel different, somehow? Maybe if he tried just one spell, just to know how it felt, then stopped if he couldn't control it . . .

Shaking his head, Sindri tried to push the thoughts away. It was silly to think such things. They had their plans to stop Asvoria, he knew the light magic spells, and they would work. They just had to.

"Good morning," Mudd said as they grew close. Rain dripped from the tip of his nose, and he glanced up. "Or, well, good noon, I suppose. This rain wasn't the wake-up call I'd hoped for, but it'll do in a pinch."

Catriona scrunched her eyes, then arched her back and stretched her arms. "Is everyone else up?" she asked.

"I am," Rina said from behind Sindri. Startled, he turned to find the elf girl standing only a few feet away. He hadn't heard her approach.

Arms behind her back, Rina held her chin high in appraisal, her delicate features unreadable. Golden hair, once curly, hung in thick wet tendrils to her waist. At Sindri's surprised look, her lips curled into an amused smile.

Scrambling to put the mirror back in her pack, Jirah rushed over from across the clearing, almost slipping on the slick grass. She stopped there under the trees and offered a quick shrug.

Wincing slightly as she stood, Catriona regarded the small group with serious eyes. "Now that we're all rested, we have to decide what we are going to do next. Apparently, some of us want to wait for Davyn to tell us what to do."

The elf girl raised her eyebrows at this, though she didn't comment.

"But some of us want to run right in and find him instead," Catriona went on. "Either way, this isn't going to be simple. We can't just walk up to Asvoria's door and politely ask her to hand back Nearra's body."

"Then perhaps we shouldn't stand here and discuss things," Maddoc said, looking darkly at the others from beneath his hood. "Now is not the time to take votes and argue points."

Crossing her arms, Rina looked at Maddoc down her nose. "I certainly don't think you should have any say in what we do."

"I agree," Jirah said. "And I still think we need Davyn. No one here knows what to do like he will. And some of us definitely need his guidance." At this she gave the elf girl a pointed stare.

Rina's mouth dropped and her hands shot to her side. Her fingers tensed as they neared the long daggers strapped to her waist. "What are you implying?" Rina demanded.

"Nothing!" Jirah said, holding her hands up as though to appease the other girl. "Just, you know, he knows the entire situation, and—"

Catriona held up a hand to stop her. "Come on, enough," she said, her voice firm. Turning to Mudd, she crossed her arms. "Davyn couldn't have expected he would simply find us in the woods. Was there a meeting place?"

Mudd nodded. "The town. The directions said there was a big watchtower which we could see over the trees while traveling north. We were to meet him there."

"Fine," Rina said, nodding her head. "Let's go then. Perhaps Davyn will already be waiting for us. If not, then we can take action and get this over with."

"I think you should go first, then," Jirah muttered.

Snorting, Rina put her hands on her hips. "What is your problem with me?"

"We really don't have time for this," Maddoc growled, and both girls scowled at him.

Sindri tilted his head back as far as he could and looked north over the trees. All he saw were leaves and gray sky.

"Maybe the clouds are covering it," he said, "but I don't see any tower."

"What?" Mudd said, brow furrowed. "But it was definitely there before, I saw it just the other day when we were getting closer and—" He stopped speaking as he scanned the horizon himself. "It can't be."

"What?" Catriona asked, turning her head to look as well. "What is it?"

"It's gone," Mudd said, his shoulders slumping. "There's no way we can find Asvoria's manor in these woods without a landmark."

"Of course there's a way," Catriona said. "The creatures that attacked us last night must have left a trail. We can follow it."

"Ooh, do you suppose we might run into the monsters again?" Sindri asked.

"Typical kender," Jirah muttered. Sindri frowned. Sometimes the girl was somewhat friendly, though a little on the nervous side. These bursts of hostility seemed downright incomprehensible. He'd have to ask her about that, too, when he asked about her magical mirror.

Not caring that his clothes had soaked through and now clung to his small body, Sindri raced back to the fire and stuffed his gear into his pack. This was it. In only half a day's time they'd finally face Asvoria. Sindri would win the battle, and no one would ever tell him that he couldn't be a wizard, ever again.

"Are we ready?" Catriona asked, standing near the trees. Everyone else, packs slung over their shoulders and weapons at their sides, nodded their heads.

"Then let's go." Head high, Catriona regarded the group with a stern look. "It's time to go free Nearra."

The companions walked single file through the underbrush, Catriona in the lead and Mudd taking up the rear. The woods were dark under the foliage. Rain dripped from the leaves and landed with tiny plops in puddles between the logs and weeds.

A small orange frog croaked from the center of a leaf where water had pooled, and Sindri couldn't help but watch it in wonder. So engrossed by this sight, he didn't notice that Catriona had stopped until it was too late. He bumped into her legs and fell backward into the mud.

"Why did we—" He looked up and saw that Catriona had one hand held high to signal the others to stop. Her other hand reached for one of the dragon claws.

Everyone halted. Slowly reaching for the sword strapped to his back, Mudd looked at Cat out of the corner of his eye. "What is it?" he asked.

"There's something out there," she said. In a flash, the other dragon claw was unleashed. Brandishing both fiercely, she stepped forward to peer through the bushes and vines that surrounded them.

No longer distracted, Sindri could hear the movement clearly. Puddles splashed. Tree branches snapped.

Catriona was right. Something large and clumsy was coming closer.

"Cat!" Sindri cried out in excitement. "It's coming from over here, and fast, too!"

Before anyone could react, a figure burst between the trees. It was a human male, that much Sindri could tell. Rain dripped from his straggly brown hair and into his eyes. Bright red scratches covered his arms, and his whole body shook as he gasped for air.

The figure collapsed in the mud at their feet. Catriona

stepped forward warily as Sindri reached out a hand to touch the boy's shoulder.

The boy looked up at Sindri's touch. Deep lacerations covered his face, and Sindri heard Jirah gasp. It took a moment for the kender to realize that this mangled face was one that he knew.

Davyn had returned.

7 REMAINS

Catriona watched Davyn as he tilted his head back and gulped greedily from the waterskin Mudd had given him. Water dribbled from between his injured lips and ran down his chin.

A mix of emotion—relief, anger, concern, and lingering hurt—washed over Catriona. They had been hoping for months to find Davyn, but now that the moment had finally arrived, Cat wasn't quite sure what to say.

After one last gulp, Davyn lowered the skin. He looked at the small group with eyes so swollen Catriona could barely make out the blacks of his pupils between his slitted eyelids. A sick feeling lurched in her gut.

"Thank you," Davyn said, his voice strained. Mudd's usual grin was gone and he nodded gravely as he took back his skin.

"What happened?" Rina asked. Gracefully, she slipped between Catriona and Mudd and came to kneel at Davyn's side. Gingerly she touched one of the open wounds on his face, then pulled back as Davyn winced.

"Rina, be careful!" Jirah yelled. "You're hurting him!"

"Sorry," the elf girl said to Davyn, ignoring Jirah. "We need to do something with these wounds. Wrap them up or—"

Davyn shook his head sharply and tried to look at her through his damaged eyes. "There's no time," he wheezed. "We have to move, now. I barely managed to get away alive this morning, but I had to find you all and make sure you were on your way. It's begun."

Catriona closed her eyes and clenched her jaw. Of course they had heard the eerie howling and had faced Ophion. But now it was definite—Davyn was there and had seen for certain.

Groaning, Davyn rose to his feet. He tried to take a step, then stumbled. Both Catriona and Mudd jumped forward to catch him.

"Careful now," Mudd said. "You're hurt, my friend. Letting you rest a few moments longer won't make us late to stop Asvoria."

Davyn gripped Catriona's arms and tried to look at her. "No. We have to go now, we have to stop her."

"Yes," Maddoc said from where he had stopped to lean against a tree. He was the only one who hadn't rushed forward to greet Davyn. "We've done nothing as of late except plan a way to stop Asvoria. Sounds like you tried the same. And failed."

Catriona turned her head and looked back. The former wizard's face was hidden in shadow. Of course this was probably an awkward reunion for both the old man and his adopted son, but they had to work together now.

"Yes, I failed," Davyn said sadly. "I hope your plans have gone better."

Maddoc tilted his head back and regarded Davyn through narrowed eyes. "They have. I have been teaching Sindri the spells needed to free Nearra."

Nodding thoughtfully, a small smile appeared at the edges of the boy's damaged lips. "Good," he said. "Very good." Then, gently pulling free from Mudd and Catriona's grip, he started moving down the path made by last night's procession of monsters. "We can talk more as we go."

Immediately, Jirah ran to his side. "Let me help you,

Davyn," she said. "I've really missed you. I knew you'd come find us, even though *they* didn't want to wait." Nodding absentmindedly, Davyn let the small girl put an arm around his waist and help him forward. Catriona saw Rina swallow and raise an eyebrow, but she said nothing as she adjusted the pack over her shoulder.

"I suppose we should follow," Rina said with a glance at Catriona. "He might bleed himself into unconsciousness and maybe then he'll let me tend to him."

Cat nodded. With a glance at Sindri, Catriona quickened her pace to walk at Davyn's side.

"I know this is urgent," she said in a low voice as she strode to match his speed, "but we can't rush in."

"Davyn's a leader," Jirah said from his other side. "He knows what he's doing." Catriona didn't respond, and instead glared at the black-haired girl. Jirah quickly turned her head to look at the trees.

"It is good to see you, Davyn," Sindri said. Catriona looked down to see that the little kender had run forward to join them. His tiny legs were a blur as he rushed to keep up, and he looked up at the ranger with his hand above his eyes to block the rain.

"We've missed you," he continued. "We didn't know where you went."

"I wish you'd talked to us," Catriona said. "Told us where you were going. I know we were fighting, that we were all angry. It was a bad time. But I think we would have understood, and we wouldn't have had to run into you like this."

Davyn shook his head and glanced behind his shoulder at Maddoc, Mudd, and Rina. He seemed not to be listening to a word they were saying, and all the concern and relief Catriona felt at his arrival started to drift away. Anger and hurt rushed to fill the void they left behind.

"We don't have time to discuss this now," Davyn said. His

tone was cold, and he glared at them through his swollen eyes before turning to look back at the path ahead. "Later. We need to move."

Stunned at his harsh tone, neither Catriona nor Sindri could say anything. They slowed their pace as one, leaving Davyn and Jirah to walk ahead.

"He left us," Sindri said, glaring at the ranger's back, "and when we meet again, he acts like he isn't even sorry. What sort of friend is he?"

Cat shook her head. "Not any kind of friend, Sindri." She looked at Jirah. "Maybe he has new friends now. But he's right, we need to move."

Sindri sighed and looked away, but Catriona grabbed his shoulder. He turned his head and caught her eye.

"You ready to do this, Sindri?" she asked.

"Of course!" he said. "Why don't any of you have any faith in me?"

"Sindri, no, I believe in you. But you've seen what Asvoria has done before."

Scowling, Sindri shrugged her hand off his shoulder. "I know what I'm doing, Cat. And I'm going to win, you just wait."

"Sindri—" Cat reached out a hand to grab his arm, but Sindri quickened his pace and ran ahead. With a sigh, Catriona let him go, hoping that somehow, some way, everyone would be able to pull together before the battle began.

Hours passed and Catriona hiked forward, eyes on the two in front of her. Davyn marched through the trees and the underbrush. He was focused only on the journey forward. Catriona noticed Jirah try to start a conversation, as she had done many times already, but Davyn only replied in grunts.

"See?" Mudd said from where he walked beside Catriona. "When I push this button, the blade retracts."

Mudd held up his right hand and demonstrated the device. On his index finger was a ring with a small blade jutting out. Pressing an invisible button on the side of the ring, the blade retracted in a blur. There was no sign that it had ever existed.

"That's a wonderful invention," Catriona said, unable to help smiling at Mudd's eager expression. She hadn't gotten to know him very well during their first encounter, which had unfortunately involved the deaths of some people close to him. But now they had more time to talk. It turned out Mudd had spent the last several months being trained in the ways of fighting from Set-ai, just as she had been so long ago. It seems he'd also spent his time acquiring some unusual devices.

"I suppose," Cat said, glancing at the ring, "that you only use this with the best intentions?"

Mudd tried to look serious, glancing back and forth as though expecting to see someone spying. He couldn't keep it up for long, and he laughed. "I only ever use things like this for good. Any purse I ever cut open deserved to be cut open."

Cat shook her head in amusement, then looked over her shoulder. Sindri and Maddoc followed behind, now deep in discussion. The elf girl, Rina, walked alone.

"Mudd," Cat said, not taking her eyes off of Rina. "How about you walk with Davyn and Jirah for a while? I'm going to join Rina."

Mudd nodded and picked up his pace, and Catriona began walking at Rina's side.

"We never got to speak much," Catriona said. "And I thought it rude to leave you walking alone."

"Thank you," Rina said. Her eyes shifted to Davyn and Jirah.

"He ignored you back there," Catriona said. "He didn't seem pleased to see any of us, actually."

Rina nodded. "I don't know why. Before he was so—" She

stopped, shaking her head. "Never mind. If he'd rather talk to Jirah, that's his business."

"What was Jirah talking about, that he didn't need you?" Catriona asked. "That doesn't seem very much like Davyn."

"I don't believe anything she says for a second." Rina said. "She has a crush on him, and she's jealous of any girl who even mentions his name. Still . . ." Rina frowned. "I don't understand why he didn't want to stop and make plans with me—with us, I mean."

Catriona nodded and fell silent, unwilling to enter in the middle of a feud she knew nothing about. Jirah had been rude to Rina, but Silvanesti elves were also notoriously prejudiced toward humans. Maybe that was clouding Rina's judgment. Still, surely if she was journeying with them, she couldn't have that low an opinion of humans, could she?

The woods grew darker and the patter of rain against leaves lessened. Night was approaching and they'd yet to reach the manor. Catriona took a breath and noted the wind shift. It had been coming at them from the east, but now it blew at them from the north.

Death. That was the first word that popped into Catriona's mind when the scent reached her nose, carried toward her on the new wind. The stench was rancid and sour, acrid and bitter. Catriona's eyes began to water. Beside her, Rina crinkled her nose.

"What is that wonderfully awful smell?" Sindri asked. The little kender ran toward them with his eyes wide. Catriona only shook her head, trying her best to hold her breath.

"We're here!" Davyn called. He, Jirah, and Mudd had reached the edge of the trees. Only Davyn was looking back. Jirah and Mudd seemed unable to look away from whatever it was they were seeing.

Catriona ran as fast as she could to join the others. The smell grew worse as she came closer, so horrendous that it brought back echoes of the pounding headache that had only recently faded away.

Davyn stood aside to let Catriona through. That was when she saw the aftermath of Asvoria's spell.

They had exited the forest near the base of a broken tower. It rose several stories above them, its wall ending just below the canopy of the trees. Twin bronze doors at the base of the tower, stood tall—guarding whatever lay inside. The once-cobblestone streets were now broken and overgrown. Clusters of crumbling buildings choked beneath wild undergrowth. Only one building stood completely intact: a large manor at the far end of the ruins. Several stories high, it seemed an unusual mismatch of arches and stone patterns. Moss and vines clung to its side, and its windows were completely black.

Littering the streets between the trees and overgrown walls were the bodies of the creatures Asvoria had called to her manor. Limbs and torsos were piled in bloody heaps. Heads looked up at the sky with blank eyes. The immense body of what had once been a giant worm lay through the mess like an ancient, felled tree.

The massacre was far more than Catriona had imagined. She tightened her lips in a hard line.

"Why did she do this?" she asked of no one in particular. "What possible reason could she have had for doing this?"

Davyn, his back turned to them, stepped into the town, carefully making his way through the random body parts.

"Remember Arngrim?" he asked, his voice quiet.

Catriona furrowed her eyes in confusion. "Of course I do. But what does that have to do with this?"

Davyn turned around. His startling blue eyes were no longer swollen. "The curse of undeath Asvoria placed on Arngrim wasn't just random vengeance," he said. "It was an experiment."

"An experiment for what?" Sindri asked, not noticing the change in Davyn's appearance.

"You'll see." He laughed, a dangerous, deadly laugh. His features grew soft, his body became taller and sinewy, and his hair began to flow long and red. The tone of the laughter rose in pitch as the creature who wasn't Davyn at all now changed into a female form.

"Ophion!" Catriona yelled. "It was a trick!"

Before they could make a move, Ophion was fully transformed. As in the woods, the shapeshifter had become Catriona herself.

"Come and get me, warrior." The familiar yet foreign voice sent a chill down Catriona's spine.

Ophion turned and ran through the field of bodies, leaping over arms and legs and bounding past severed wings. The shapeshifter was heading straight for the manor.

Catriona clenched her fists and began to follow. That was when she saw her.

The sorceress stood on a balcony on the highest story, her hands outstretched.

Despite herself, Catriona couldn't help but think it was Nearra. She had the same long blond hair, the same lovely face. Even the way she held herself was the same. No one would have been able to tell it wasn't the same slender girl Catriona once knew, were it not for the wicked, dangerous expression on her face. No, such an expression could only belong to someone like Asvoria.

"What is she doing?" Jirah yelled, pulling her sword free and coming to stand by Cat. "What did Davyn—Ophion—what did he mean about Arngrim?"

Cat didn't answer. She didn't have to. In front of them a single clawed hand had started to twitch.

Cat's body tensed as a tingle raced down her spine. "By the gods," she whispered. "She can't be doing this."

In the center of the town, the giant worm shuddered. Near it, tendrils of red flesh coursed from a goblin's arm, connecting at random to an ogre's massive shoulder. What had once been a giant bird, its eyes gouged out, started climbing to its feet.

"What do we do?" Mudd asked, his voice trembling.

Cat took a breath and closed her aching, exhausted eyes. "Get ready," she said, hands going for the dragon claws. "Just get ready."

DEAD AND ALIVE

The creatures rose in twos and threes until not a torso or a limb or a head was without the rest of its parts.

As they stood, the mismatched creatures formed an impenetrable wall. They stared at the humans, the elf, and the kender with glassy, empty eyes.

With a shudder, the worm lifted from where it lay among the bodies. It rose high into the sky. Attached to its body were goblin arms and ogre feet and bird talons and spindly insect legs. The talons and claws grasped at the air spastically, though the rest of the creature did not move.

Catriona watched the scene with detached horror. It was so surreal and so unexpected that it felt as though she were living in a nightmare. The stench of death was stronger now. A dull pounding throbbed at her temples.

Above the creatures on the balcony, Asvoria watched them with a look of triumph. Her violet eyes met Catriona's own as if to say, *your move.*

"Would you look at that!" Sindri cried. He watched the scene with his mouth wide open.

When Catriona and the others made no move, Asvoria

twitched her hand. As one, the monsters crouched and reared back into attack positions. Some leaped to the tops of the broken walls, others reached for pieces of the broken street to use as clubs.

Then they froze, like terrifying exhibits in some museum of the macabre.

"It's an army," Mudd said, coming beside Catriona. "Asvoria made herself an army."

"A nice, obedient army," Maddoc said. He watched the scene before them with an expression very much like awe.

Still the nightmarish creatures did not move. Cat clenched the dragon claws tighter, waiting. She would not rush into death, nor would she rush her friends into death.

"What do we do?" Mudd asked.

"I don't know," Catriona said. "We can't rush in. We can't fight our way through them. We need to think this through."

Jirah clutched at Cat's arm. "Maybe Davyn, the real Davyn, maybe we can call for him and—"

"Davyn isn't coming to save us, Jirah," Rina said. "We have to attack our way through. Either way, Asvoria will kill us. At least we should go down fighting instead of cowering or running away."

With one swift move, the elf nocked an arrow and let it fly straight toward the nearest, motionless beast. It plunged into its flesh with a soft thunk. The creature didn't react.

Sindri crept forward. "They aren't even alive. It's just a trick to scare us."

Catriona clenched her jaw firm and straightened her shoulders. "Sindri, I know you're eager, but Asvoria wants us dead. This isn't a trick."

Puffing his chest out, Sindri spun away from Catriona. "I'll prove it!"

Before she could make a move, Sindri bounded forward, his tiny legs carrying him between the broken walls. He reached a goblin with three spider's legs arcing from its back and swiftly knocked it on the head with his hoopak.

"See!" Sindri yelled. He turned his back to the monsters and faced his friends with a big smile. "They're just giant dummies!"

The goblin creature twitched and clenched its claws.

"Sindri, look out!" Catriona raced forward.

She shoved Sindri aside, let out a cry, and impaled the spider-leg goblin with her dragon claws. The creature did nothing. Slowly, it tilted back its head to look up at her. Its eyes were milky and dry.

Confused, Catriona pulled her sword free and stepped back.

"Cat!" Sindri yelled, as he scrambled to his feet. "Was that really necessary?"

Shaking her head, Catriona said, "I saw it move. I didn't want you to get hurt."

He only shrugged and looked back at the motionless creatures.

The others crowded by the two of them, weapons drawn. "By the gods," Jirah said as she reached Catriona's side. "Why aren't they fighting us?"

There was another great rustling as the hundreds of creatures moved to the side, coming out of their attack positions. They clung to the walls and climbed up the few trees that had sprouted in the broken homes, revealing a narrow path between their ranks. The grass that had long ago broken through the ancient road was now crushed and stained with dark blood.

"She's not trying to stop us, that's why." Catriona looked up at Asvoria, smirking as she waited. "She wants us to reach the manor. This isn't right. She sent Ophion to set this whole thing up and take us here. Now she has a whole army ready and waiting to kill us as soon as we do whatever it is she wants us to do."

"Maybe," Jirah said, glancing nervously at the creatures still staring at them, some with empty eye sockets. "Or maybe she just wants to trap us in the middle of her zombies and then attack. We'd have no escape."

"We wouldn't have an escape either way." Mudd's usual shameless grin was gone and his hands shook.

Cat glanced back at Rina, who still stood ready with her bow. "We have to go back," she said to the elf. "Letting us through like this, it has to be a trap."

"Well, then that's her mistake, isn't it?" Sindri said, sticking his hoopak staff firmly in the ground and glaring up at Asvoria. "She may think she's trapping us, but it's us who will be trapping her." Defiant, Sindri pushed past Catriona and Mudd and strode between the crowd of monsters.

Catriona wanted to have faith in Sindri. She wanted to believe he could free Nearra. But amid all the mismatched monsters, he seemed as tiny and helpless as a toddler.

"Well?" Rina asked, taking a few steps before turning to face them. "Are you coming or not?" Looking pointedly at Jirah, she thumbed over her shoulder. "Davyn's in that manor. If you want him so bad, you're going to have to walk through them to get to him."

Trembling—with fear or anger Catriona couldn't tell—Jirah shoved past Rina and ran down the path after Sindri.

"What are you trying to prove?" Cat said in a low voice as she gripped Rina's arm.

Rina shrugged. "Nothing. I just want to avenge my brother." Turning, she too ran after Sindri.

Trying to contain her unease, Catriona made a choice. They had to stick together no matter what. Dragon claws held ready and with a quick glance at Maddoc and Mudd, she followed. She heard Mudd muttering to himself and the rustling of Maddoc's robes as they took the rear.

The walk to the manor door seemed achingly long. With every step, Catriona expected the monsters to come alive and try to rip out her throat.

But with each step, still there was no movement. Though the creatures stood, they were as dead as they had been when they were lying on the ground.

Their smell surrounded her like a thick cloud, and her eyes watered. Cat was afraid if she breathed in the stench, it would fill her lungs and poison her body.

After climbing carefully over the tail of the frozen worm, Sindri ran straight to the manor door. Confidently, he reached up and tried to push it open.

"Locked!" he cried. He turned and looked back at his friends with a scowl on his face. "I knew Asvoria was evil, but so evil that she locks her doors? How can they be used for their true purpose?" He shook his head in disgust.

Catriona quickened her pace and burst free from the path. She gulped at the fresh air blowing from behind the manor, air that was free of the smell of death. The others were quick to join her.

"Why don't you—" Mudd started to say.

Once again, Catriona heard the sound of hundreds of bodies moving. She spun around, dragon claws raised, certain now that Asvoria had launched her attack.

But the creatures still stared at her and her friends, their eyes frozen. The monsters had merely shifted to fill in the gap that had been their path.

Cat's anger rose. Asvoria was toying with them!

Mudd let out a slow, shaky breath. "All right, then. All right."

Rina, who faced the monsters with her bow held taut, dared a glance back at Sindri. "Why don't you use your lockpick?" she asked. "Don't all kender keep one with them?"

"I'm afraid I don't have one," Sindri said with a shrug. "I used to have one, but I seemed to have misplaced it at my cousin Dorny's house. I did have Elidor's for a while, but I thought it only fitting to send it back with his belongings. Of course, with my powers, I have no use for one anyway. I'll just cast a quick spell."

"No," Maddoc said, shooting out his hand to grab Sindri before he could turn around and use his magic. "Don't fatigue yourself unnecessarily."

"Lucky for you, Sindri," Mudd said as he rustled through his pack, "I happen to be an expert locksmith. Or, well," he said with a grin, "in theory." He produced a set of lockpicks. Tools in hand, Mudd set down his sword and crouched in front of the door.

"Why would Asvoria lock the door?" Jirah said. "She seems to be leading us here. What? Does she just want to play with us some more?"

"Maybe it's not us she's trying to keep out," Cat said, remembered Davyn. "Maybe she wants to keep someone in."

There was a loud click, and Mudd groaned in frustration. "Blast it! I can't seem to get it open."

Maddoc brushed past Catriona and Jirah and went to the door. "Move aside, boy. Asvoria no doubt locked this with mystical—"

Before he could finish speaking, the door opened, hinges creaking.

Mudd looked up at Maddoc. "Looks like Asvoria wants you inside first."

"So it does," Maddoc said. He turned to Sindri and tilted his head. "Shall we be the first to use the door for its true purpose?"

Sindri grinned and bowed with a flourish. "It would be my pleasure." With his head held high, he walked forward to stand beside Maddoc. As one, they entered the dark interior of the manor.

Catriona gave one last glance at the eerie army, then turned to follow. "Sindri, wait! We need to stick together and think this through before you face Asvoria." She reached the doorway just as Mudd got back to his feet.

The wooden door slammed shut in her face.

Mudd shouted, "What in the Abyss—"

Jirah screamed.

Catriona whipped around. The zombie army had come to life. Fangs and claws bared, the creatures surged forward.

Catriona held her swords high, let out a Solamnic war cry, and raced forward to protect her friends.

CHASING THE DARK

The door slammed behind Sindri.

"Cat!" Sindri tugged on the rusted iron door handle. It didn't budge. He heard a scream followed by Catriona's familiar war cry, then a chorus of snarls and yowls.

Sindri's stomach dropped. He longed to see Asvoria's spell in all its glory now that the zombie creatures had come to life. But he couldn't bear to think of his friends getting hurt.

"Maddoc!" Sindri yelled as he pulled at the door with all his strength. "Help me!"

Maddoc placed a gentle hand on Sindri's shoulder, and Sindri looked up. The former wizard was but a shadow in the darkness.

"Asvoria has trapped us inside," Maddoc whispered. "I can sense the spell and it is powerful. She wants us in here. You were right before. That will be her mistake."

"But our friends!" Sindri cried.

Shaking his head, Maddoc pulled Sindri from the door. "There's no going back. We must head up."

Sindri took a breath and tried to block out the sounds of the battle raging outside. Maddoc was right. Cat would be fine. She had to be. And he had a mission to complete.

71

Raising his hoopak high, Sindri whispered one of the first spells Maddoc had taught him. "*Shirak.*"

As though it had been set aflame, the woven sling at the top of his staff flared with light. Its soft yellow glow filled the manor's foyer.

Sindri gasped in wonder at the sight of an ancient, wilting willow tree taking up the corner of the room. Its roots jutted up in bumps through the broken stone slabs that made up the floor. Some sort of well-worn cloth was arranged between the roots like a makeshift throne. The tree's long branches seemed withered, its leaves tinged with gray.

Beyond the tree, tangled vines and moss clung to the walls in thick curtains. The stone patterns Sindri could make out on the walls were oddly arranged, as though the walls were made up of many different pieces of wall, stacked atop one another like some giant puzzle.

Aside from plain square pillars that supported the upper stories and the dying willow tree, the first floor of the manor was completely bare. In the corner was the beginning of a spiral staircase.

With a nod at Maddoc, Sindri and the former wizard headed toward the stairs.

Claws gripped at Mudd's arms, bared teeth lunged toward his neck, and powerful legs tried to kick his own out from beneath him.

He almost wanted to laugh. None of this could possibly be real.

Instead, he mimicked one of Catriona's war cries and sliced his sword through a serpent's torso, cutting it in half. Innards sloshed to the ground and he made a face.

"Keep moving!" Catriona yelled over the din of the monsters' screams. "Head for the tower!"

The undead creatures came at them from all sides and Mudd lashed at them with his sword as he shoved his way through. He could barely make out the giant metal doors of the broken tower, glinting in the soft glow of the partial moons.

A sharp pain lanced through Mudd's forehead. Blood dripped into his eyes. He blinked it away as he desperately pushed through the crowd of zombies.

When he was young, before his little sister Hiera was born, Mudd's parents had taken him north through the mountains to visit Palanthas. The city was nothing like his home in Potter's Mill. The glimmering white buildings were giants that spiraled high into the sky. The long streets were clogged with hundreds and hundreds of humans, elves, dwarves, and every other race imaginable.

It must have been a festival of some kind, because Mudd remembered a vendor giving away free sweets. There had been a mad rush. He tried to make his way through alone, but the crowd felt like a wall, closing in, crushing him. His father had to wade through the excited mass to save him.

He never did get his sweet.

As Mudd forced his way through the monsters, all he could remember was fighting through that crowd as a child. This was exactly like that, except these creatures were trying harder to kill him, and there was no one to come to his rescue.

Grunting, he pulled his sword free from the gut of a goblin and found himself finally free of the monsters.

In front of him was a wall at least three stories high, though broken around its top edge.

He'd made it. He reached the tower's outer wall.

"Help!" He turned to see that his escape had come at the expense of Jirah. The monsters that had attacked him were now circling her.

Jirah stumbled backward. A massive, bear-like beast reared back on its hind legs. It raised a single paw. Jirah screamed and covered her face with dirty hands.

Mudd leaped forward and brought his short sword down in a quick arc. The bear-creature's paw flew threw the air. Unperturbed, it continued its attack. The bloody stump at the end of its arm swung past Jirah's face.

"Come on!" Mudd cried. He pulled the girl to her feet and they turned and ran.

Up ahead, they could see Catriona and Rina standing near the tower's wall, both with hair tangled and wild. The two girls shoved against the bronze doors, which still stood sturdy despite the lack of support for the top hinges.

Mudd and Jirah reached the door and joined the push. The door inched open.

"Harder!" Catriona yelled. "Put all your strength into it!"

Back muscles aching, Mudd did as he was told. Daring a glance to his side, he saw the monsters stumbling over themselves as they tried to find their prey. They were so packed together in the tight streets that they were unable to move quickly.

"Asvoria must be distracted with another spell," Rina said, between grunts. "If she were overseeing this attack, we'd be dead by now. These undead monsters are hardly capable of organizing themselves."

"Thank Paladine, she's got other things on her mind," Mudd said.

"Stop talking and push!" Jirah screamed.

Finally the door inched open far enough for them to fit through. Jirah was the first to slip through the crack, followed by Rina and Catriona.

Looking back, Mudd saw some of the zombie monsters free themselves from the surging army and race toward the wall. He sucked in his stomach and forced his way through the crack.

"Hold it shut!" he yelled as he came through. Catriona and Rina pushed their full weight against the door just as several bodies slammed into it from the other side.

"We need a barricade," Catriona said. "Jirah! Start pushing some of those stone blocks over here!"

The door pushed farther inward as something even larger hit it from the other side.

Come on, Mudd thought as he strained to hold the door closed. Davyn. . . Sindri . . . Someone . . . Do something. We can't hold out much longer.

Sindri and Maddoc made it up a single flight of stairs before a buzzing sounded in the back of the kender's mind.

He gasped in wonder and reached out his hand.

"What is it?" Maddoc asked.

Sindri didn't answer. He hadn't given it much thought before, but the darkness beyond the radius of his staff's light seemed suddenly captivating. Sindri just knew there were untold secrets to be found in its depths.

He had to discover what the darkness concealed. Mind still buzzing, he held his staff forward and ran.

"Sindri!" Maddoc gasped from behind him. "Wait!"

As Sindri raced forward, the buzzing became a tingling sensation in his head. All thought of Asvoria and of the monsters, of Catriona and of his friends disappeared, as he followed the darkness. Doorways flew past him, as the darkness led him down an empty, decaying corridor and up more spiraling stairs.

At last, the staircase spit him out into another corridor, this one just as decrepit as the last. Parchment lay in tatters on the ground, and vines snaked through moss on the dark stone walls. Every few feet, a painting hung from the wall, all depicting dragons. Some had what appeared to be claw marks through them.

Almost as swiftly as the desire had come upon him, Sindri realized that the darkness could be chased no farther.

He found himself in front of a door at the end of the corridor. Carved into the wood was a symbol he recognized from the ruins of Navarre—an ornate letter A with a dragon twining about it.

He shook his head and blinked, as though coming out of a deep sleep. "Maddoc?" he said, then spun around to see if his mentor had managed to follow. The corridor behind him was empty.

His legs ached as though he'd just climbed a mountain.

That's interesting, he thought. I can't seem to remember the trip.

"Sindri?"

Sindri gasped in surprise at the familiar voice. He followed the sound down the corridor, and into a new staircase, one that seemed to wind up into a tower.

There, lounging on one of the steps, was Davyn.

"Davyn!" Sindri cried. Before his excitement could get the better of him, he peered into the ranger's startled eyes. They were dark and brown.

"Just checking," Sindri said with a satisfied nod.

"Sindri," Davyn said, brushing his unruly bangs up from his forehead. "How did you get here? Where's Catriona?"

"Cat . . ." Sindri let his voice trail off as he remembered the battle raging outside. Shaking his head, he turned to look back at the door at the end of the hall. It felt as though there had been something inside his head, needling through the nooks in his brain, hiding something from him. He didn't much like the feeling.

"I need to find Asvoria," Sindri said. "She's starting her plans. Catriona and everyone are fighting outside."

"Mudd, Rina, and Jirah—they found you?"

Sindri nodded.

"Listen, I'm sorry about abandoning you and Cat."

Sindri shook his head. "We already had this conversation. Well, not us exactly, but someone who we thought was you, and the other you was sort of right. We'll have time to talk about this later, after I beat Asvoria."

"You're certainly confident," Davyn said. "You must have learned some things since we were last together."

"Lots!"

Davyn nodded thoughtfully. "Sindri, Asvoria is in the main room beyond that door at the end of the hall. I have a sword that can save Nearra but it's locked up in the tower." Davyn pointed to the staircase rising above him. "Maybe if you have a spell . . ."

Sindri dimly remembered Maddoc's warning about saving his magic, but he shook away the thought. One little spell couldn't hurt. "Of course!" he said with a bow. "Opening doors is easy for someone with my mystical knowledge."

Davyn let out a small laugh. "Sindri, it's been too long without you. Well, go ahead, then."

Brushing past Davyn, Sindri raced up the tower stairs. At the top was a hatch in the ceiling. Just as Davyn had said, it was locked.

Recalling the spell, Sindri pointed his fingers at the door and recited the words. He expected it to open immediately, but still the door remained locked. He concentrated harder, willing the spell to work. Sweat dripped into his eye and colored smoke began to wisp from his fingertips.

Finally, he heard a soft click. The trapdoor sprung open.

"There," he said, then gasped for air despite himself.

"You all right?" Davyn asked. He had climbed up the stairs after him, and now he put his hand on the kender's shoulder.

"I'm fine," Sindri said. "Just hurry, I'm not sure how long the door will stay open."

Davyn studied Sindri's eyes for a moment, then nodded. "All right. Wait here, we'll go to Asvoria together. No more splitting up."

Taking a breath, Davyn crouched low and jumped. He grabbed the opening's edges with ease and hefted himself up into the darkness beyond.

Sindri intended to wait. He really did. He had already lost Maddoc somewhere in the bowels of the manor, and certainly a trained ranger like Davyn would come in handy with Asvoria.

But, when Sindri looked down the steps after Davyn disappeared up into the tower room, he saw the darkness yet again. And once again, he felt the tingling in his brain forcing him to follow.

He barreled down the stairs.

This time when he reached the door with the A symbol, it was open. Sindri peered into the room and saw no one.

He took a breath to calm his excitement and stepped forward.

The first thing Sindri noticed was the large hole in the ceiling. Lamps, shining with a white-blue glow, lined the walls. In the center of the room, a table stood, covered with melted candles and spell books and all sorts of interesting artifacts.

Sindri walked to the table and ran his hand along its top, taking in the cold metal objects and glass bottles. To Sindri, it seemed some of the objects disappeared from the table as he passed. His cloak grew heavier.

"Sindri Suncatcher," a cool female voice said. Sindri looked up from the table and saw Asvoria standing on the balcony beyond the tall glass doors. She turned to him and smiled a dangerous smile.

"I've been waiting for you."

10   SINDRI'S SPELL

H ello Asvoria," Sindri said. "I've come to stop you."

"Did you?" she said. "And here I thought it was I who brought you here, to stop *you*." Turning to look back over her balcony, she gestured toward the fighting below. "Why don't you come out here and see how my spell worked out. I know you're curious."

Crossing his arms, Sindri forced himself to scowl. He really did want to see, but he wouldn't let her know that.

"No," he said, his voice steady. "You are evil and I won't let you hurt any more people."

With a snort, Asvoria turned her head and regarded Sindri with a smile. It was Nearra's face Sindri saw, but that was definitely not Nearra's smile.

"Such big words for such a small creature," she said, then tilted her head. "You interest me, kender. Despite all logic, you seem to actually possess some sort of magic. I watched as you were granted your power from the dragon spirit, and I watched as you used that power to shatter my sword. There are people who would kill for what you were given."

"I don't know what you mean," Sindri said with a frown. "I've always been a wizard." Reaching his hand down his shirt, he began to pull free the golden, sun-shaped Daystar amulet.

"Oh, not always," Asvoria turned back to the balcony. Wretched howls drifted up from the battle below.

"You were just another delusional fool," she went on. "I suppose it's lucky for me that you don't understand how your magic works and instead try to conform yourself to what Maddoc and the orders have been teaching you. Perhaps then I'd actually be worried that you'd keep me from possessing a dragon."

Confused, Sindri shook his head. "A dragon? You can't do that! And you're wrong about my magic. It's—" He stopped and shook his head again. "You're trying to trick me. Which means you are afraid of me, after all."

No more talking, he thought. Thinking fast, he tried to recall the spell of protection Maddoc had told him to raise, only to find that he couldn't quite remember the words. He knew them before. He'd studied them on the way here, just hours ago. But fatigue clouded his mind and sapped him of the energy needed to call forth the spell. No words would come.

Sindri's mind raced. Then pain flooded his body. His insides ached as though he were being crushed from within.

Asvoria laughed and stepped in the room from the balcony. Hand raised, her eyes were focused directly on the kender. "Idiot creature. No one actually believed you would be able to stop me. Not me and especially not your friends. And we were right."

With a twitch of her hand, more pain shot through Sindri's body and he let out an agonized yell. With a crazed look on her face, Asvoria strode closer to Sindri, sending another jab of magic into his body as she did.

Trying to focus through his pain, Sindri forced his hand to reach up and grab the Daystar. With a shout, he shot his hand forward. Focusing the mystical amulet at the sorceress, he countered her spell and sent it firing back at her.

Screeching, Asvoria flew backward onto the balcony and

landed on her back. Sindri collapsed to the ground and gulped for air, his body still aching.

Get up, he told himself. Finish her. Free Nearra!

Sindri bounded to his feet and ran forward, purple cape fluttering behind him. He brushed aside the white curtains and skidded to a stop on the stone balcony. At his feet, Asvoria clenched her eyes closed and groaned.

Not daring to speak, Sindri pulled the amulet free from his neck. He would not hesitate and let her get the upper hand again. Trying to work past his fatigue, he brought to mind the spell that would free Nearra: he was going to imbue Asvoria with so much anti-magic energy that she would be unable to keep her hold on Nearra's body. She would cease to exist.

Feet planted firm and the Daystar aimed directly at Asvoria's heart, Sindri cast his spell.

With what little light seeped through the hatch, Davyn carefully made his way through the rubble in the tower room. A feeling of grim anticipation overcame him as he found what he was looking for.

Tossed unceremoniously in a corner were his belongings—his pack, a quiver of arrows, his bow, and, most importantly, the sword of the Dragon Knight.

Davyn gathered his things, picking up the sword last. He felt a rush of adrenaline as he gripped the hilt. This was the sword he would use to sever Asvoria's soul from Nearra and free her. This was the weapon that would save the girl he loved.

Behind him, he heard hinges creaking. Startled, Davyn turned to see the hatch beginning to close. Leaping over stone blocks, he dived through the narrowing gap.

Davyn landed on the stairs in a heap, and the trapdoor closed above him with a heavy thud. Brushing himself off, he stood.

"Sindri?" The kender wizard was gone. Not even Asvoria's

impending ascension could stop the insatiable curiosity of a kender.

It couldn't have been more than ten minutes, however. What trouble could Sindri have possibly gotten into?

Steeling his nerves, Davyn started down the stairs. At the bottom step he set down his pack and rifled through it until he found Elidor's old flute. He rubbed it gently between his fingers, then tucked it behind his belt.

Leaving the pack, his bow, and his arrows behind, Davyn went to face Asvoria.

As the words of the spell left Sindri's mouth, they were erased from his mind, taking on their new life as magic. A warmth filled his body, starting in his heart and spreading throughout his limbs.

The power coursed from within him and took hold, and the words came faster and faster until they were a blur of noise even to him. The Daystar glowed bright and white.

I'm doing it! he dared to think. I'm going to win!

With a terrifying roar, something grabbed the kender from behind, pinning his arms to his sides and breaking his concentration.

"You will not destroy the Dragon Queen," a voice hissed in his ear. Though two strong arms already held Sindri tight, another appeared from behind him and yanked the Daystar free from his grasp.

"No!" Sindri screamed. "Put me down!" He kicked his legs and struggled to free himself, but the arms holding him seemed unbreakable.

"You are a faithful servant, Ophion." Asvoria rose from where she had fallen, one hand on her forehead. She glared at Sindri. "My amulet."

The arm holding the amulet stretched out from behind Sindri

and deposited the Daystar into Asvoria's hand. Sindri felt a rush of anger as her slender fingers encircled the medallion.

Hanging the Daystar from around her neck, Asvoria let it fall into place in front of her chest. "Back where it was meant to be," she said, then let out an exhilarated laugh. "It worked! My ascension shall come!"

"Never!" Sindri screamed. Baring his teeth, he turned his head and bit hard into the arms surrounding him. It was like biting into rubber, but he wrenched his head back and forth like a rabid dog until he tore through the flesh. Dark red blood flowed past his lips.

With a hollow cry, Ophion dropped Sindri. The kender landed on his feet. Without thinking, he ran to whip Asvoria across the head with his hoopak.

Her face cold, Asvoria raised her hands and spoke. Immediately Sindri stopped in his tracks, closed his eyes, and began to shiver.

Vaguely he felt himself lifting up from the balcony and rising into the sky. He opened his eyes and looked down. His friends huddled inside the broken tower. The zombie army still came at the doors unrelentingly, trying to break through.

"Cat," Sindri tried to say, but no words would come. Then a sharp pain coursed through his body. It accumulated in his head, where it felt as though someone had jammed an icicle into his skull.

Images of death and destruction forced their way into his mind. He saw his friends slaughtered. He saw his family hanging by their necks from trees. He saw villages burning. Darkness filled his body.

Sindri's lips opened wide in cackling laughter. Die, he thought. All of you, die! Glee overwhelmed his emotions.

Then, just when Sindri thought he could handle no more of the deadly ecstasy, the dark spell drifted away. He gasped for breath as he realized what he'd just felt. Tears welled at the corner of his eyes, but Sindri felt incapable of crying.

"What did you do?" he asked in a small voice. He looked down at Asvoria from where he floated in the cold night air.

She watched him, her expression malicious. With a flick of her wrist, she released the spell holding Sindri aloft and he started to fall.

Sindri could do nothing but stare as air rushed around him.

Asvoria watched him over the edge of the balcony, her cold eyes boring into him. Above her, Sindri saw it for the first time. Nuitari, the black moon.

"It's like a hole in the sky," he whispered.

Near it, a glittering winged form flew over the trees. A sleek, beautiful creature with copper scales.

"Raedon," Sindri whispered, then remembered what Asvoria had said about possessing a dragon. "No, anyone but Raedon."

With the endless, awful sounds of the battling monsters filling his ears, Sindri finally hit the ground.

The world went black.

11 Possession

Raedon tilted his wings and circled above the dark forest. It had been a long flight, but finally he could see the image that had appeared in his head early that morning—a great manor rising up from the overgrown remnants of a pre-Cataclysm city.

"Aha." He smiled, baring great glimmering fangs.

It had been months and months since Raedon had felt a summons. He'd spent many of those months in the care of the young centaur Ayanti. She tended to the shattered bones of his wing and helped rid him of the deadly venom that had coursed throughout his body. Now the pain of those injuries and the agony of his defeat at Asvoria's hand were only memories.

He'd often wondered what happened to his young friends after they set off in search of Asvoria, but neither he nor Ayanti had heard any word. He'd gone back to the tunnels of his mountain home and tried to continue his life.

But now, lately especially, every trick he played on a gully dwarf and every new item he added to his horde did nothing but momentarily distract him from his worry. It seemed he had grown attached to the young mortals during their short time together.

85

When more months passed and still no word came, his worry slowly turned to dread. Then, as he lay half-asleep in the early morning, a single word had bubbled up into his thoughts.

Tarkemelhion.

His True Name. A name found in the mind of someone he thought was lost—Nearra. His heart had leaped with joy in knowing that at least one of his young companions was still alive.

Images had followed the summons in rapid flashes. He saw Nearra, as Asvoria, fighting a hideous monster. He saw Asvoria scream out in pain as magic came at her from a shadowy figure in a corner. And he saw Nearra, free of Asvoria's soul, running for her life through the corridors of the manor he was now growing near.

Raedon knew better than to fully trust these images. It had been by blindly following a summons that he had almost been killed before. But he had to see if Nearra was all right and to help her in any way he could. Without regard to the safety of the mystical items he usually guarded so closely, he burst out of his lair and sped as fast as he could in the direction that had been implanted in his mind.

Raedon grew closer to the manor, and only then did he see the mass of monsters surging within the city's destroyed streets. His shrewd eyes saw the battlefield as clearly as if he were in the thick of it. He made out flaming red hair that could only belong to the girl warrior, Catriona. There were others cowering behind crumbling walls along with Catriona, but no one he knew. Where were Davyn, Sindri, and Elidor?

Raedon adjusted his wings to match a shift in the wind and began to circle down. The copper dragon intended to find the answer these questions. But first, he had to save Nearra.

"Don't worry, little one," he said to himself. "I'm coming."

The door to Asvoria's chamber was already open as Davyn approached. As he neared it, he could hear the distant sounds of a monstrous battle, but he couldn't worry about that now. If he knew anything about his friends, it was that they could take care of themselves.

Stepping into the room, Davyn dared to allow himself brief hope that Sindri had succeeded with his spells. Maybe he would find the kender sifting through Asvoria's belongings while Nearra, the real Nearra, sat by and watched with an amused smile.

Instead, Davyn found no sign of Sindri. From the balcony, he heard muffled voices, and then Asvoria strode through the curtains and back into the room.

"Ah, Davyn!" she said. "So you decided you wanted to see the show after all. I thought you might mope on the stairs all evening. I found that upsetting."

Sword held ready, he said nothing.

"The idiot kender was just here," Asvoria went on. "But I had to send him on his way." Head held high in regal pride, she strode past Davyn to stand next to the table and glance up through the hole in the ceiling. "He did bring me a lovely gift, though."

Only then did Davyn notice the amulet swaying in front of Asvoria's chest. The golden Daystar glinted bright in the lamplight.

Sindri. She'd done something to Sindri!

"No!" Davyn reared back his sword and raced toward the sorceress. He leaped onto the wooden table, sending bottles and candles clattering to the floor. Letting out another yell, he prepared to thrust the sword down and pierce Asvoria's vile heart.

Asvoria's eyes grew wide and her lip trembled. In a soft voice she said, "Please don't hurt me, Davyn. I love you."

With a scream of frustration, Davyn plunged the sword forward, but stopped short of Asvoria's chest. She stood there, impassive, still looking at him with confused eyes.

He tried to force himself to impale the sorceress, but his arms would not move. He'd had dreams of this. He saw himself sticking his sword into Asvoria and nothing happening. Later, he saw himself using the sword, but only after it gave him the sign to do so. Looking at the sword now, he saw no sign, and he wondered, as he always did, if this was even the right sword, if using it would only kill Nearra and leave Asvoria unaffected.

Asvoria's gentle expression melted away. She let out a bark of harsh laughter. "You still can't hurt me," she said, her voice slick with hatred. "Because I look like *her*." Raising her hand, she mumbled words Davyn couldn't hear. Bright red light shot from her fingers and Davyn flew back through the room. He slammed against the wall and slumped to the ground.

Rounding the table, Asvoria approached Davyn, her hand still outstretched. Her eyes were cold now, her features tight. Her lips moved and, as they did, purple energy coursed over her hands.

"I wouldn't do that if I were you."

Groaning through the pain in his back, Davyn turned his head to look at the doorway. Standing there, staring at Asvoria with intense eyes, was Maddoc.

Ignoring the former wizard, Asvoria continued casting the spell that Davyn knew would kill him.

"I studied you for decades," Maddoc went on, not moving from the doorway. "I know your power is vast and I longed to study it. But even you have limits. Your plans have yet to be completed, and already you've used much energy this night."

Stopping mid-word, Asvoria glanced at Maddoc. The crackling purple energy dissipated and she lowered her hand.

"Stop while I'm ahead, then," Asvoria said. "Such good advice from someone who never bothered to follow it himself."

Before Maddoc could respond, a face devoid of features save for bright blue eyes peered down through the hole. "He comes, mistress," Ophion said. "The dragon is here."

Asvoria tilted her head back, smiling. "It is time!" she declared, her voice breaking with emotion. "Finally, it is time!"

Leaving Davyn on the floor and turning away from Maddoc, the sorceress went to stand beneath the hole. "Take me up," she commanded. "And bring those two as well. I want both of them to bear witness."

Ophion's skin blackened and puckered as twisty tentacles sprouted from its bulging body. Two of the tentacles wrapped around Asvoria's middle and pulled her up through the ceiling. Others gripped Davyn's feet and latched onto Maddoc's wrists.

Davyn lost his grip on his sword as he was wrenched up. The world went upside down, and blood rushed to his head. Ophion lifted him through the hole, then tossed him unceremoniously on the roof. The wind was knocked out of him as he landed, and for a moment he couldn't breathe. Maddoc landed heavily beside him.

Gasping for air, Davyn tried to catch his bearings. The hole in the ceiling was in a lower corner of the flat roof of the manor. The rest of the roof was wide and open, ringed by a low wall. What looked like white sand had been poured out in massive, intricate patterns and in the center of it all were shards of crystals and gems laid out to resemble a sword. In front of that was a plain glass ball.

The night air was cold as frost, and wind whipped Davyn's unruly hair into his eyes.

Asvoria looked up at the sky with a broad smile on her face, strands of her blond hair wisping about her face in the night breeze. Davyn followed her gaze and only then saw the dragon approaching. Its scales glinted copper in the dim reddish-silver moonlight, and a sinking feeling opened in Davyn's gut.

"Raedon," he whispered. Fighting the pain in his back and arms, Davyn tried to climb to his feet. There was still time. He had to stop her.

Before he could move, a dark form tackled him and threw him back against the low wall. As rubbery flesh covered his mouth and his body, Maddoc thrashed beside him, caught under the creature's grip as well.

"Quiet now," Ophion whispered, the voice seeming to come directly next to Davyn's ear. "Just watch." The shapeshifter had colored its skin to match the stone wall, keeping itself, Maddoc, and Davyn hidden from view.

Raedon circled closer, coming to land on the roof. Desperate rage flooded Davyn's mind. He struggled to free himself, but it was no use. Ophion's grip was too strong.

He was going to have to watch, helpless, as yet another friend was destroyed at Asvoria's hand.

Raising his wings to catch the air, Raedon slowed his speed to land lightly on the roof of the vast manor. Nearra, or at least someone who looked like Nearra, sat cross-legged among strange symbols that had been made atop the dark stone. Her shoulders were slumped, and blond hair covered her face.

Repressing his dragonawe so as not to startle her, Raedon made his way toward the girl. As he came closer, he saw that she sat before a glass ball and precious stones piled in the shape of a sword.

A deep unease settled over the copper dragon, but he fought it down. Gently, he nudged the girl with his immense head. "Nearra," he whispered. "I am here."

The girl looked up at him with startled eyes. Tears had stained her cheeks. "Raedon?"

Her eyes were violet, he noticed immediately. Opening up his mind, he tried to sense the girl's thoughts, but there was nothing. Surely if Asvoria still resided in her body he'd feel it.

Calming down, Raedon lifted his lips in a dragon version of a human smile. "It's me, little one. I heard your call."

"Oh, Raedon!" the girl cried. Broad smile on her face, she leaped to her feet and raced forward to hug the dragon about his great neck. He bristled at her touch, but then felt waves of pleasure as he remembered the first time she'd hugged him—the first time he'd ever been touched by any human.

Closing his eyes, Raedon nudged her gently with his head. "You have been through a lot, Nearra," he said. "But it's over now. We can help your friends and—"

Something cold touched his chest, right above his heart, and Raedon's mind seized up. Opening his eyes, he saw the girl still hugging him, but now she had some sort of amulet pressed against his scales.

"Nearra?" he whispered.

The girl chanted words of magic, faster than he could understand them, and Raedon realized too late that he had been tricked. The amulet was the Daystar, an item used by Asvoria to reverse enchantments—an item that could even be used to reverse Raedon's own extra-sensory perception.

Before Raedon could react, a bright white light flashed from the amulet, blinding him. As it did, pain ripped through his body. His muscles seemed to be shredding beneath his skin. Phantom fingers dug into his mind and tore it to pieces.

For the last time, Raedon opened his mouth. He let out a roar so full of anguish that even the creatures embroiled in the battle below momentarily stopped as its sound reached their ears.

Then the white light faded away, and the girl clutching at Raedon's chest fell into a heap at his feet.

CHAPTER 12

THE DAYSTAR DRAGON

Davyn held his breath as he watched Asvoria fall. At the same moment, Raedon's screams ended, and he too collapsed to the stone roof.

For a long moment, nothing seemed to happen.

Then Raedon opened his eyes.

Davyn let out his breath with a quick, hopeful laugh. The spell hadn't worked. Raedon was alive!

The dragon stood, limbs trembling. But something about its coloring was wrong. The tips of the copper scales seemed to be stained black.

As the dragon stood to its full height, Davyn saw that a great scar had seared itself across the dragon's chest. It looked as though Raedon's scales had melted and bubbled up before hardening into the shape of a stylized sun—the symbol of the Daystar.

Blinking eyes that were now violet, the dragon's lips pulled back into a smile. It reared back its head and let out a laugh.

It was at the sound of this cold laughter that Davyn knew for certain.

Raedon was gone.

Asvoria had completed her ascension.

Ecstasy.

The word was all Asvoria knew as she opened her new eyes for the first time. It was overwhelming power, the likes of which she thought she'd never know.

Nothing was greater than this. *Nothing.*

She gripped her claws into the dark stone of the roof. She flexed her wings and shook her great head. With each beat of her new heart, she felt intense magical power coursing throughout her body.

She was no longer trapped in a fragile human form, forced to live under the archaic rules of humanity that were created on a whim by unseen gods. Her power had been limited and always would have been.

Now, she was the greatest being Krynn would ever know. She was the Daystar Dragon, and all the races of the world would bow before her.

Asvoria stepped over Nearra's fallen body and walked to the corner of the roof. Her muscles trembled with each step, and she almost stumbled. There was so much strength in these limbs that she was unsure how to move.

A piece of the wall seemed to melt away as she neared the corner, revealing the haggard forms of Davyn and Maddoc. With her new dragon sight, Asvoria could see Davyn's nostrils flare in anger.

"I have succeeded," she said. The words burst from her jaws like deep, booming thunder.

"You have," Maddoc said from where he leaned against the roof's low wall. He looked up at her with awe-filled eyes.

Asvoria let out a snort. "I suppose, Maddoc, that I should thank you for all your hard work. Without your help, I might never have achieved my destiny. I knew the moment I saw you from my tapestry that you were the one. It was simple enough planting ideas into your mind, but I never imagined the depths your obsession would take. You would have done anything to know my secrets."

The old man's eyes looked away, and Asvoria saw confusion cross his face. "My thoughts . . ." He began, then looked back up at her, anger creasing his features. "I was under my own control. Everything I did, every experiment I created to mimic your own, they were of my own design!"

Asvoria snorted once again. "Believe what you like," she said, then shot her head forward. The stench of Maddoc's fear filled her nostrils. "You were only a tool to me, Maddoc. You were nothing but a pawn, and that is how it will be written in the history I have created."

Opening her mouth, she breathed the acid that would kill the man and his adopted son. Jaw clenched, Maddoc waited for death with defiant eyes.

Nothing happened.

Confused, Asvoria pulled back. There was so much about the dragon's body she needed to discover, and apparently one of those things was how to use its breath weapons. Not wanting to show weakness, she turned to Ophion. The shapeshifter was still in the form of a human, its torso colored black and shining with stars.

"Kill them," she commanded. "I will take care of the others."

With that command, Asvoria unfurled her wings, leaped, and found herself flapping into the sky.

She let out a triumphant roar that echoed throughout the dark forest. She was flying!

She circled above her monster army, then descended to kill the children that had been plaguing her, once and for all.

Soaring low over the monster army that had fallen still at the lack of her magic control, she found Davyn's companions, hiding in the remains of the tower that once stood tall at the eastern edge of the town. Some of her undead creations looked to have scaled the wall, but their limbs were severed, their bodies stuck to the earth with dozens of white-shafted arrows.

The red-headed warrior, Catriona, stood atop the tower's broken outer wall, blood-stained swords held ready at her side. A look of hope flitted across her face. She had spotted the flying dragon and no doubt mistook her for an old friend.

Asvoria smiled. At that moment, the warrior's face dropped. She'd seen the dragon's eyes, seen its sun-shaped scar.

Catriona dropped the dragon claws. They clattered to the stone wall and fell the ground below. Though tears now streamed down her face, Catriona held her head high and waited.

Now you die, Asvoria thought. And you die as a failure.

Outstretching claws as sharp as swords, Asvoria swooped down for her first kill as a dragon. The girl warrior closed her eyes and waited for death.

Then, pain. Sharp, searing pain at each of Asvoria's joints, as though something large and unseen had gripped her limbs and was trying to wrench them free of her body. Claws clutched at her back, trying to pull out her spine.

Letting out an anguished roar, Asvoria closed her eyes. Thrashing her head back and forth, she snapped her jaws, trying to grab at the creature she was sure was attacking her.

There was nothing.

Trembling from the pain, Asvoria spun herself around to flee the unseen force. It was only when she flew a few feet back toward the manor that she heard it. Screams echoed inside her head, but they weren't her own. They were the screams of a young girl.

The pain lessened the closer Asvoria grew to the manor, and that was when she knew. Though she was free from Nearra's body, the two were still connected. The same power from the dragon well that allowed Asvoria enough strength to overcome Maddoc's spells had forged a connection between Asvoria and the girl that was still unbroken. There was no creature attacking her. It was this unbroken bond trying to pull her back to her former body.

She'd been so close!

Shrieking in rage, Asvoria flew back to the manor. None too gently, she landed on the roof and stalked toward Nearra's body. Though the girl's screams had died away, the closer she came, the more apparent the girl's presence became.

In the corner of the roof the former wizard lay unconscious. The boy Davyn was trying his best to fight Ophion, who had turned into a wolf and was biting his heels. Embroiled in battle, they paid no attention to Asvoria.

Leave him alone!

The voice blared in Asvoria's head and she turned with a start. It was Nearra, but the girl still lay in an unmoving heap. Her limp hand had fallen among the crystals that acted as a stand in for the Aegis.

You have what you want, her voice continued. *You don't need us anymore. Go away, Asvoria. Go begin your reign and leave us alone.*

"Shut up," Asvoria whispered, her deep voice rumbling from within her chest.

Go away! Leave us alone! GO AWAY! LEAVE US ALONE!

With an angry cry, Asvoria shot her head forward and wrapped her jaws around the comatose girl's middle. But as the first of her teeth pierced the girl's weak flesh, Asvoria felt a sharp jab of pain in her side.

Curse the gods! she thought, and pulled back her head. Exhaustion at all she'd done that night finally caught up with her, and it was only made worse by the girl's endless screaming. Asvoria clenched her eyes closed.

"Ophion!" she bellowed.

GO! LEAVE! GO! LEAVE! GO! LEAVE!

With one last snarl at the boy, Ophion turned and bounded to Asvoria. Still in wolf form, it bowed at her feet.

"Transform into something that can fly," she commanded. "And carry this girl. We must leave."

Looking up at her with piercing blue eyes, Ophion tilted its head.

GO! LEAVE! GO! LEAVE! GO! LEAVE!

Asvoria stamped one of her clawed feet. "Just do it! And make sure she stays close to me."

Davyn crouched beside Maddoc, panting. Sweat streamed down his forehead.

Asvoria had lifted up from the roof and now hovered over the unmoving army. Her scaly lips moved as she spoke low words that Davyn couldn't hear.

Near Nearra's body, Ophion's snout hardened into a beak and its front legs shifted into vast, feathered wings. With an eagle's call, it flew to Nearra's fallen body. Gripping her shoulders with its talons, it lifted up from the manor.

"No!" Davyn got to his feet and started to run toward them, but his legs were so weak. He stumbled and fell.

With the eagle-Ophion at her side, Asvoria turned from the manor and flew west. Davyn lay on his back and watched the two of them and Nearra soar above the manor before disappearing into the dark night.

As they flew away, there came the sound of hundreds of creatures moving in unison and then the crunching of branches as the monster army entered the forest and followed Asvoria's retreating form.

Davyn closed his eyes.

Asvoria had won.

13 RAMPAGE

For a long time, Davyn lay on his back and watched the sky. The red and silver moons were but slivers. The stars seemed to shine brighter in the absence of moonlight.

Tilting his head, Davyn saw a glowing green orb sitting in front of the crystals that had been laid out like a sword. Crawling over the roof, Davyn picked up the glass ball and cradled it in his arms.

"I'm sorry, Raedon," he whispered.

Hacking coughs sounded from the low wall. Davyn looked over to see Maddoc trying to rise.

Davyn swallowed the bile that had filled his throat and walked to the wizard. Maddoc had saved Davyn's life, but had it been to help him or to help Asvoria complete her plans? And was what Asvoria said true? Had all of Maddoc's plotting and scheming sprung from commands she had planted in his mind?

With the glowing orb in the crook of one arm, he offered his other hand and helped Maddoc stand. In silence, the two lowered themselves through the hole in the roof and landed in Asvoria's study. Davyn collected the Dragon Knight's sword from where it had fallen. In the corridor, he gathered the rest of his belongings.

Carefully placing the glass orb inside his pack, Davyn and Maddoc went down the flights of stairs, making their way deep into the bowels of the dark manor. Eventually they reached the first floor. Red and silver moonlight streamed through the now-open door, highlighting the willow tree throne in deep pink.

It was strangely silent as Davyn stepped outside. The night air was cold, and remnants of the hideous scent still wafted on the breeze.

"Davyn!" a voice cried. Peering across the open, crumbling streets, he saw a haggard group of people walking toward them.

At the sight of him, the four quickened their pace. Leaping over stone blocks and running through bloodstained grass, they ran to meet him.

"You're all right," Davyn said. He opened his arms as they neared and found himself enveloped in their embrace.

"We were worried," Jirah said. Her features seemed even paler than usual, but she still seemed happy to see him.

"It's good to see the real you, boss," Rina said. She was as beautiful as ever, and Davyn couldn't help but return her smile before nodding and looking past her.

Skin ashen and eyes shaded with dark circles, Catriona stood behind Mudd, Rina, and Jirah, the only one who hadn't rushed to embrace him. Tears had stained her cheeks and her arms lay slack by her side. To Davyn, it seemed that her raging spirit had finally broken.

With a nod of understanding, Mudd moved aside and patted Davyn on the back. Setting his pack and his sword down, Davyn walked to stand before the redheaded warrior. He noticed that he was now almost as tall as she was.

"Davyn," she said, her voice hoarse.

"Cat," he said. "I'm sorry. About everything."

Cat nodded, then lowered her head. "I failed, Davyn. We didn't save Nearra and now Raedon is lost. I couldn't get everyone to work together, we didn't have a plan. Everything is my fault, I . . ."

Unable to go on, her voice trailed off, and Davyn pulled her forward into an embrace. He knew how she felt, for he felt the same guilt.

"You did the best you could, Cat," he whispered in her ear. "Nothing that happened this night is your fault. Your job was to keep your friends alive, and you succeeded. Never forget that."

Hiding her face deep in his shoulder, she let out a gasping sob. "It's just so hard, Davyn," she said. "I don't know if I can do this anymore. I'm so tired."

The memory of their last battle with Asvoria echoed in Davyn's mind. He closed his eyes. Though it was Elidor who died that night, each of his friends had been changed in their own way. Catriona had wanted to fight her rage. Davyn wanted to flee from his. He didn't know about Catriona, but he knew now that he would never run away again.

"Hey," Davyn said, gripping her shoulder in reassurance. "You're starting to sound like me. Remember our last conversations before I left?"

She took a deep breath and pulled away. "Of course I do. I was so angry that you wanted to run away."

Davyn nodded. "You told me that I would live in shadow the rest of my days for not trying. And you were right. I tried to run, but I couldn't escape my destiny. So now I've embraced it. We may have failed tonight, but we haven't lost. Not yet. The Cat I knew would never give up."

"You sound positively grown up," she said, a hint of pride in her voice. "What exactly happened while you were away?"

Davyn shrugged and said nothing, then pulled her close for one last hug. Her body seemed to lose the tension he felt when he first embraced her and he knew that, at least to her, his words had meant something.

"Where is Sindri?" Maddoc asked.

The old man had been quiet and withdrawn ever since the battle had ended. Now he looked frantically among the ruins, eyes wide and manic.

"Blast it, you children," Maddoc shouted. "Help me find Sindri!"

"What happened?" Mudd asked. "Why are you looking down here?"

"Sindri faced Asvoria by himself," Davyn said, trying desperately to see the kender's form in the dark night. "They were on the balcony, and he . . ."

"She didn't." Catriona scowled. "If he's dead, I'll . . ." She didn't have to finish.

Rina grabbed Davyn's arm and pointed at a cluster of bushes beneath one of the manor's dark windows. "He's there," she said. "I can see him."

Davyn raced to the bushes. There, Sindri lay on his back and gazed up at the night sky.

Davyn shook the kender gently. "Sindri. Are you all right?"

Sindri turned to Davyn, his eyes shining. "There's a hole in the sky."

Davyn nodded. "Can you move, Sindri? Did she hurt you?"

The kender shook his head slowly. As the others came to surround him, his face lit up. "Hello," he said. "It was quite interesting, falling. I saw Raedon. Where is he?"

"Gone," Davyn said. "Asvoria possessed him, then took her army and left."

At this, Sindri's cheerful expression faded and his eyes fell into sadness.

"I saw things," he said softly. Gripping Davyn's shoulders, Sindri looked into his eyes. "She's going to kill people, Davyn. Lots of them. We have to stop her."

"We will," Davyn said. Anger bubbled up to displace all of his doubt and sorrow.

Davyn turned to face the small group with his jaw clenched and hands balled into fists. "Asvoria may have Raedon and her army," he said, "but we are all still alive, and that's all that matters. She should have killed me when she had the chance, because I'm not going to rest until she's dead. I'm done running and I'm done waiting. Asvoria will not win."

Mudd nodded, and Rina smiled. Jirah bit her lip, but did not disagree, and behind her Maddoc watched the group, eyes still distant.

Catriona stepped forward, a sparkle of the spirit he knew flashing in her eyes. "I won't rest either," she vowed, then bowed her head. "Lead and I will follow, Davyn."

"Me too," Sindri said.

"We all need sleep," Davyn said. "But tomorrow we will set out."

Everyone nodded, and Davyn turned back to help Sindri.

Asvoria flew west. Her plan had succeeded. But becoming a dragon was only the beginning.

The sun had risen, casting gold over the forest beneath her. The tips of her wings brushed against the tops of the trees and scattered dew. Cool, early spring wind met her face. It would prove to be a lovely day.

They'll never expect a thing, Asvoria thought.

Beside her, still in the form of a giant eagle, Ophion flew with Nearra clutched in its talons. The shapeshifter gripped the girl gently, but Asvoria could feel pressure against her shoulders all the same. Again she cursed the dragon well, cursed this bond. At least the girl had fallen silent after Asvoria had left her friends alone.

Beneath her, the trees rustled. The monster army traveled

JEFF SAMPSON

unseen beneath the foliage, following faithfully and silently. She could sense each and every one of them, feel them as though she shared their legs. With all the magic energy it took to control an undead army this size, she would have collapsed to exhaustion long ago were she still a sorceress, even one as powerful as she had once been.

But not now. Not as the Daystar Dragon.

In the distance, a town came into view. She'd researched it in the past months and knew it was the perfect location for her first strike.

Forestedge was one of many villages located along the base of the Vingaard Mountains, though it was by far the most prosperous. To the north was a great river that flowed east, where it circled around the vast forest that gave the village its name. To the south was the hilly land, and to the west, of course, lay the mountains.

This put Forestedge at a prime location. People came by river to trade and to use the great mills that had been built upon its banks, and hunters trying their luck in the forest often stayed at one of the village's many inns. There was also no shortage of travelers looking to rest after journeying over the hills or to gain strength before tackling the mountains.

Most importantly, high upon the cliff face were caves that had belonged to a long dead dragon.

Her new home.

With her thoughts, Asvoria commanded her zombie creatures to stop in the trees as they reached the edge of the forest. She flew on.

Beneath her was a small farm. Pens held cattle and pigs. The first small shoots of the crops stood out as dots of green on deep black soil.

She hovered above the silent village beyond the farm, planning the most effective means of attack. Smoke wafted from chimneys, farm animals called out, and awnings rustled as vendors set up stalls in the market in the center of town.

The market. That would be where most of the villagers would be. She would send her army through the streets, tearing people from their homes and destroying them. Then, they would converge on the market.

Asvoria bared her teeth in the mimic of a smile, a habit of human expression she would never be rid of. It would be wonderful.

"By the gods," a small voice whispered beneath her. "A dragon."

Tilting her head down, Asvoria saw a girl, kneeling in the soil. Her long black hair was pulled back against the nape of her neck, splaying out in a mass of braids against her back. Her jaw hung open and dirt streaked otherwise lovely features.

The girl looked very much like Asvoria had when she herself was young. The sorceress snorted at the thought. The person Asvoria was at this girl's age had disappeared long before she died at Captain Viranesh's hand.

"Tatelyn, it's time to come in." A lanky boy with brown hair ran from the village into the field, a large grin on his face. He didn't seem to notice Asvoria and Ophion, hovering in the sky.

"Brigg, look," the girl called out, tearing her eyes away from Asvoria. "There's—"

The boy skidded to a stop, eyes wide as he gazed up. "Is that a dragon?"

Asvoria whispered a command.

Brigg stumbled as the ground beneath him began to rumble. Tatelyn fell to her hands.

The soil near the Tatelyn's feet sifted and churned. Tips of claws and fingers appeared in the dirt, digging up from beneath. She gasped.

With a great explosion of dirt, the giant worm, its body lined with stolen limbs, burst from beneath the ground directly between the girl and boy.

Tatelyn shrieked.

"Watch out!" Brigg cried. He started to race toward Tatelyn, but the worm's stolen limbs clawed at his face, and he jumped back.

Tatelyn's hands shook. It appeared she was too frightened to move.

"Run!" the boy cried.

The worm lunged. The boy screamed.

And Asvoria laughed, as she watched the undead worm gorge itself on the unlucky boy.

Closing her eyes, Tatelyn fell face down in the dirt. She covered her head in her hands and let out a gasping sob.

Tilting her great head to look at the forest behind her, Asvoria watched as shadows emerged from behind branches and bushes. Mismatched creatures in all sorts of terrifying shapes and sizes trudged toward the village of Forestedge.

Her army would destroy them all.

Clambering to her feet, the girl start to run toward town. The giant worm waved its limbs at her as she ran past. She screamed.

Asvoria watched, silently, as the monsters trampled the small shoots and stomped on the farm animals, killing them. Tatelyn's warning shouts rang through the empty streets.

The screams began in the village, only a few at first, then more and more as people ran from their homes, fleeing for their lives.

They would soon find they had no escape.

"Everything is going exactly as I planned," Asvoria said, turning to look at Ophion. The shapeshifter nodded its feathered head.

Feeling a strange sensation, Asvoria turned her head and looked south toward the hills. She saw two people standing there, stoic and silent, watching. They looked young and human, one a boy and one a girl. Their blond hair whipped about their faces in the breeze as they observed the massacre from afar.

The boy's eyes flitted back and forth, taking it all in. A small smile appeared at the edges of his lips.

"Hmm," Asvoria muttered. "Appears we have some spectators."

Ophion tilted its head questioningly, but Asvoria shook her head. "No matter. Nothing can stop us now. Let's go."

Ignoring the two watchers, Asvoria flapped her great wings and hefted herself high into the air. Ophion at her side, she glided over the hopeless villagers of Forestedge and headed for her new mountain home.

14   The Messengers

Rina guided her friends west through the forest, following the trampled foliage left in the wake of Asvoria's army. Rina was the first to crest the hill and the first to see the carnage.

The village had once been large and full of life, that much Rina could tell. Grand houses that once stood as a proud testament to the village's wealth now blazed with flame. Smoke billowed from their remains, blackening the otherwise clear blue sky.

In the marketplace at the village's center, fruit and meat lay in piles surrounded by a fog of flies. Every cart and awning had been overturned.

Countless bodies lay along the dirt roads, in ditches, and on doorsteps. Just as many were already standing, raised by Asvoria's spell. As Rina watched, more bodies rose—new additions to the sorceress's army of the dead.

Flinching, the elf looked away and took several deep breaths. Such disregard for the sanctity of life was far beyond anything she could ever imagine.

"E'li help us all," she whispered.

Clomping human footsteps sounded behind her and Rina **107** blinked back tears. She turned to find Davyn and Catriona climbing the hill, the others trailing behind.

"Is it bad?" Davyn asked.

Rina could only nod.

For a long while, the small group studied the scene in silence. Glancing about nervously, Jirah was the first to speak.

"What do we do now?" she asked. The pale human girl bit her lip and inched forward to stand beside Davyn—terribly close, Rina noted.

Rina aimed her ears toward the lower valleys of the hills and listened. She could make out faint voices and the crackling of fire.

"There are survivors," she announced. "I can hear them setting up camp."

Davyn nodded, then looked back at the village. His eyes followed the smoke billowing into the sky before blowing away on the wind. "We should offer any assistance we can, and then find out what happened. Most importantly, we need to find out where Asvoria went."

No one argued.

With a nod, he started down the hill. Jirah trailed by his side.

Rina took in a sharp breath. Stop walking so close to him! her angry thoughts screamed.

Shaking her head, she tried to rid herself of such thoughts. These were petty matters, unimportant and childish when compared to the events at hand. Still, the sight of Jirah so near Davyn made Rina want to shoot an arrow deep into the other girl's heart.

Running ahead, Rina kept pace at Davyn's side. She placed a hand on his arm. "You all right, boss?"

He glanced at her. "I'm fine. Just worried about Nearra, and about those people."

"Always worrying," Rina said with a shake of her head. A

thick lock of golden hair fell into her eyes. Running her fingers lightly along her forehead, Rina tucked her hair behind her pointed ear. She offered another smile, one that never failed to dazzle.

Davyn walked on, noticing neither her smiles nor her hair.

Rina scowled, then caught Jirah's eye. With a smirk, the human girl pretended to stumble. Davyn offered his arm, and pulled herself up. Even though she regained her balance, she didn't let go.

Davyn didn't acknowledge Jirah, just as he hadn't paid attention to Rina. But he also didn't pull away.

I'm acting like a fool, Rina thought. Maybe Jirah is right. Maybe he doesn't need me now that we've found his other friends. Maybe—

Rina quickened her pace to take the lead, so she didn't have to see Jirah and Davyn holding hands.

The companions walked down the hill, untamed grass wisping around their legs. Rounding a boulder framed by scrub bushes, they came upon a makeshift camp.

There were more people than Rina had suspected would have survived Asvoria's attack, but they were still few compared to how many must have resided in the village. Lean-tos and small tents had been set up in a circle, around a great bonfire. The humans' clothes were torn, their faces stained with blood and tears. But they didn't speak or cry. The silence was even more disturbing than if the survivors had been sobbing.

"How do we approach them?" Catriona whispered. Red hair whipped about her head in the wind, and it seemed almost mane-like. Fitting for someone so lionhearted, Rina thought.

"I don't think we have to," Mudd said. He pointed toward a pair of young humans walking up the hill toward them. "Looks like we've been spotted."

The humans were young, maybe around Jirah's age. They

were both thin and about the same height. They looked similar enough to be twins, with identical sharp noses.

The girl carried herself with the air of someone used to leading. Rina decided that she must, in fact, be the older of the two siblings.

Both wore drab peasant's clothing, and both had blond hair. The girl's hung long and free down her back, the boy's was overgrown and unruly. His bangs covered the upper third of his face.

As they came closer, the girl bobbed her head in greeting. She held her head high and her hands behind her back. Her brother stood near her, shoulders hunched and eyes narrowed. His lips seemed stuck in a position that was neither smile nor frown.

"Good day," the girl called.

"*Good* day?" Jirah asked.

With a small gasp, the girl covered her mouth with her hand. "By the gods, I'm sorry. It's just habit."

The edge of the boy's lips twitched into a smile, then returned to their usually noncommittal expression.

"Hello," Davyn said, and nodded. "We've come to see if we can help."

"Wonderful," the girl said. "So have we."

Rina glanced at Catriona and met her eye. The warrior frowned. Though the boy was sullen, neither of the two humans seemed overcome with despair.

Finally reaching the group, the girl stopped before Davyn and took a deep breath. "I am Janeesa. This is my brother, Tylari."

Davyn quickly introduced everyone. Maddoc bowed and kept silent, his eyes stern, and Jirah seemed strangely jittery when he spoke her name. Sindri beamed and jumped forward to bow.

"A pleasure to meet you all," Janeesa said with a nod in their direction. Her eyes seemed to linger on Jirah and then on Rina. "Isn't it a pleasure, Tylari?"

As though waking from slumber, the boy turned slowly and looked at his sister. "Quite."

"You weren't from the village, were you?" Mudd asked. "You seem much too . . . well, you know." He grinned nervously, then ducked his head. "Never mind."

"No, it's fine," Janeesa said with a wave of her hand. "We aren't from around here. I must seem terribly heartless, but I find it hard to be broken up about the deaths of people I've never met, don't you?"

Rina didn't agree in the slightest. She crossed her arms.

"My brother and I are here with our father," Janeesa went on. "Or, well, we were. He's a messenger, you see, and he's already out to spread word of what happened here. We're going to wait with the survivors until he comes back."

"A messenger, huh?" Jirah said, then turned to look at Davyn. Davyn, in turn, glanced at Catriona, who shook her head and shrugged.

"Messengers!" Sindri cried, clapping his hands. "How delightful. Traveling the countryside, hearing new stories, and getting paid for it! If I weren't already a wizard, I think I might like your job."

Janeesa laughed. "Well, aren't you an energetic fellow?"

Sindri beamed. "Yes! I—" He started to say more, but his gaze wandered to the refugees behind the two young humans. His face fell and he looked down, his expression confused. "Nice to meet you," he mumbled, before retreating back to Maddoc's side.

"Yes, nice to meet you," Davyn said with a concerned glance at the kender. "We're on our way to offer help to the survivors. If we see you later, maybe you can tell Sindri some of your stories."

Though her eyes were cold, Janeesa smiled and nodded. Tylari nudged her.

"Davyn," Jirah said, tugging at his sleeve. "Maybe we could

use these two to spread word about what happened here. You told me stories about all you and Catriona and Sindri have done. Surely you have friends that could come help us fight?"

Before Davyn could say anything, Janeesa stepped forward and clapped her hands. "A marvelous idea. And we wouldn't mind in the least. We know all our father's connections, so it wouldn't be any trouble to give word to these friends of yours."

Catriona tilted her head and met Janeesa's eye. "Doesn't your father want you to wait here?"

Again Janeesa waved her hand dismissively. "Oh, he won't mind. He'd want us to do this."

Davyn shrugged. "Well, all right. We could definitely use the help. Thank you, Janeesa and . . . what was your name again?"

The strange boy sneered. "My name," he said between clenched teeth, "is—"

Janeesa gripped his shoulder. "Don't worry about our names. Everyone just calls us the Messengers." As she said the name, her eyes bored into Rina's own.

Rina furrowed her brow. There was something decidedly strange about these two, though she had no idea why the girl kept focusing on her. She'd never met these Messengers before.

Then, memories of Southern Ergoth flashed in her mind.

"The Messengers," she whispered and looked away, trying to remember the stories. There were three, she'd heard of them. But their actual names she couldn't remember.

Janeesa let go of her brother's shoulder and stepped forward. "Yes?" Her eyes still did not leave Rina's face.

"Oh," Rina said. Everyone watched her with various expressions of concern and confusion. "It's nothing," she went on. "I knew of three others who called themselves the Messengers, but we're far away from them. I thought it an interesting coincidence."

"Yes," Janeesa said. "But I admit, it's not the most original of names. So," she said, turning back to Davyn, "where are we to send word? We could have them convene here in the hills below the village? It seems safe enough for now."

"There are the clerics at the Temple of the Holy Orders of the Stars," Catriona said. "Good thinking," Davyn said with a nod. "They were certainly helpful against Slean."

"I'm sure there's lots of people back in Potter's Mill that'd help," Mudd added. "According to Sindri's maps, it's actually not that far from here."

They continued rattling off names, and even Sindri and Jirah joined in. But Rina could think of no one who would come to her aid. Instead she crossed her arms and watched as Janeesa took notes.

Tylari stood where Janeesa had left him. He watched the group, shoulders still stooped, mouth slightly open, a blank expression on his face.

Then, his eyes came alive and darted in Rina's direction. A shiver ran down her spine.

"Rina, is there anyone you can think of?" Davyn called to her.

She tried to ignore the unsettling feeling. With a final look at Tylari, Rina took a breath and walked to join the group.

15 MADDOC'S SECRET

And then I ran," Tatelyn whispered. "I ran and screamed for everyone else to run until I couldn't run or scream anymore."

Catriona watched the girl's eyes as she spoke. The reflection of the small fire glinted off her tears as she looked into the distance, remembering what had happened that morning.

"Tatelyn," Davyn said. "Do you remember anything else? Where the dragon went?"

Wiping her eyes with the back of her hands, the girl turned to Davyn and shook her head. Dozens of black braids rustled against her back.

"No. But people who did see said it flew up into the mountains. One of the men—Gregor, I think—he went after it. We tried to stop him, but . . ." She shook her head.

Davyn patted her on the back. "Thank you, Tatelyn. And . . . I'm sorry."

The girl said nothing. An old woman appeared at her side and touched her shoulder, and she reacted with a start. Then she stood and let the woman lead her away.

Night had fallen and the companions sat around their own fire on the outskirts of the refugee camp. They'd done nothing for the last half-day except tend to the wounded and offer whatever hope they could. All the while they tried to find out more about what had happened, but only Tatelyn had been willing to relive the day's events.

"So," Davyn said as he watched the girl and the old woman disappear among the milling people near the main bonfire. "We know Asvoria is in caves in the mountains."

"Probably caves near the village," Mudd said. "She probably killed them so she could add them to her army and keep anyone from coming after her."

"But someone did go after her," Rina pointed out. "That Gregor person."

"Maybe we can ask Gregor when he gets back how to get there," Sindri said. "I could draw a map."

Jirah rolled her eyes. "I don't think Gregor's coming back, Sindri."

"But . . ." Sindri's face fell and he looked away. "Oh."

Davyn paced in front of the fire, his arms crossed. "We know where Asvoria is, and we have the Messengers sending word to our friends that we need help. But there has got to be more we can do. We can't just wait for them to meet us here."

Catriona tilted her head back and looked at the stars. "If only we had a way to really hurt Asvoria," she said. "She's got the powers of a dragon and a sorceress now. That's going to be hard to beat."

Everyone fell silent. With a sigh, Davyn plopped himself down on a boulder and slumped his shoulders.

"Nearra's up there," he said. "For some reason Asvoria took her, which means she's still alive and we need to save her—"

"Stop talking about Nearra all the time," Jirah snapped.

Stunned, everyone turned to face her. Biting her lip, she stood and went to sit by Davyn. "I mean," she said as she grabbed his hand, "this isn't just about saving her. This is hurting more than just one person, you know."

Davyn shook his head. "I know. Catriona's right, though, Asvoria seems pretty unstoppable right now. But there's got to be some way."

"There may be."

Startled, Catriona turned to look at the shadowy figure crouching near the fire. It was Maddoc. Though everyone else had huddled around one end of the fire to be near each other, the former wizard had gone off to sit by himself and hadn't spoken since.

"Maddoc?" Catriona asked. "You know Asvoria better than anyone. Is there a way?"

Maddoc tilted back his head to meet Catriona's eyes. "My dear, there has always been a way," he said. "Just as the Daystar could act either as the key to Asvoria's ascension or a way to destroy her, so can one other item: the Aegis."

Sindri shook his head. "But Maddoc, don't you remember? We destroyed the Aegis, you and me together. I'll never forget what that felt like—"

"Yes, it was shattered." Looking away, Maddoc stood. "But I salvaged the pieces and reforged the sword. I put it in safe hands until we needed it. That time is now."

"You did what?" Catriona stood to face him, arms crossed. "Maddoc, when did you have time to reforge the Aegis or send it someone? How could you possible have reforged a sword like that without magic? And why didn't you tell us about this before we went to face Asvoria at her manor? We could have stopped her!"

Maddoc walked to Catriona and rested his hand on her shoulder. "My dear warrior, there are some things about me that you'll never understand. But know that my actions were only for the better good. If we brought the sword to Asvoria's manor, she likely would have taken it to use in her spell just as she did the Daystar. I couldn't take that chance."

Shoving Maddoc's hand away, Catriona stepped away. "But

you were willing to let Sindri face her with the Daystar, knowing he took on the very same risk. You're lying again!"

Davyn stopped pacing. "Do you think the sword can help save Nearra?"

He nodded. "I don't just think, I know."

Someone snorted. Looking up, Catriona saw Rina rise to her feet.

"Why should we trust anything you say? Catriona is right. You could have told us about this sword a long time ago and neglected to do so. Besides, you're the one responsible for this anyway! Has everyone forgotten?"

Maddoc regarded Rina with dark eyes, saying nothing.

Davyn took a breath and stared at the fire. "It may not have been entirely Maddoc's fault. Asvoria said things on the rooftop after she possessed Raedon. I think she may have used magic on Maddoc to make him do those experiments and release her. He may be just as much a victim of her as anyone else."

"Is this true?" Catriona spun around to face him.

Maddoc sneered. "Does it matter? Anything I say could be a lie."

Mudd shook his head. "This is all so confusing. First Maddoc's a black-robed wizard out to get you, and now he's a former black-robed wizard trying to help us because he was under mind-control spells?"

Maddoc let out a snorting laugh. "Who knew that a man my age would be so incapable of figuring out who he is?"

Everyone fell silent.

"Son," Maddoc said, clutching at Davyn's arm, "you have to trust me. Follow me and I will lead you to the Aegis's hiding place. We can get the sword, stop Asvoria, and save Nearra. And . . . and I may be able to restore Raedon's soul."

"What?" Davyn said, tilting his head.

Maddoc nodded. "That glass ball you salvaged from the roof, it contains Raedon's displaced spirit. I've been thinking about it, and we may be able to put Raedon back in his body. But the only way we can do that is if we get the Aegis."

Davyn turned and met Catriona's eye. She shrugged.

"I don't know what to think anymore," she said, her toe tracing a circle in the dirt. "But we have to try. Even if it means we have to trust him."

Maddoc tried to meet her eye, but she kept her eyes on the ground.

"Fair enough," he whispered.

"We need to work together now—as a team—" Davyn said, "and that includes Maddoc. We'll head out tomorrow. When we get back, our friends—I hope—will be waiting."

"And then," Catriona said, glancing at Sindri staring off into the distance, "we'll face Asvoria again."

Davyn turned to look at the vast mountains rising up into the dark night sky so near them.

"Yes we will," he said, his voice full of conviction. "Only this time, we will win."

"Beware all who cross this bridge," Mudd read the weathered sign planted beside the stone bridge. "For the Goblin Man lies in wait."

"Ooh!" Sindri cried. "A Goblin Man! I wonder what that means?"

Arching over a deep chasm, the bridge seemed carved from the mountain itself. Fog rose like steam from the rift, clouding the mountainface from view. Moss hung from the cliffsides like thick green curtains in some rich noble's house.

Jirah gripped Davyn's arm. "Are you sure this is safe?"

Davyn chuckled, and rested his hand on Jirah's. "Don't pay any attention to that sign. It's just another one of Maddoc's deceptions. He used to tell me all the time that the Goblin Man would come to get me if I didn't do my chores. But of course, no

Goblin Man ever materialized. It wasn't until I was ten that I realized there was no Goblin Man. It was just a story Maddoc told to scare me. I'm sure he put up this sign to scare people away from his secret path." Davyn gestured toward Maddoc. "Right, old man?"

But Maddoc was already making his way across the bridge. He did not turn around to reply.

They had left the morning after Maddoc's revelation. Under the shelter of the trees and hidden from Asvoria's monsters, they headed north.

When they emerged from the forest, they could see smoke billowing into the sky to the west, as yet another mountain village burned. They could only assume it was yet another of Asvoria's conquests. But there was nothing they could do, and so they moved on.

Somber quiet had resided among the group after that. But it wasn't long before boredom set in, and the mood turned strangely light. Someone or other had made a joke at someone else's expense, which caused hesitant laughter and, then, more jokes.

It seemed the farther away they got from Asvoria's death and destruction the easier it was for them to shove all that had happened into the distant corners of their minds. After all they'd been through, it was the only way any of them could deal with the task that loomed before them.

After several days traveling and sleeping beneath the stars, they booked a night at an inn where already there were rumors of the strange happenings to the south. The tales were told as stories to pass the time, and none of the villagers seemed concerned.

That morning, after a hearty meal in the inn's main room, the companions headed west toward the mountains. It was there that they came upon the chasm and the arching bridge that seemed carved from the very mountain itself.

That was when Mudd found the sign.

Catriona studied the writing and chuckled. "We just faced an entire army of zombie creatures and a sorceress in the body of a dragon. A Goblin Man hardly strikes fear into my heart."

"This doesn't look like Maddoc's handwriting," Sindri said, looking so closely his nose pressed against the weathered wood. He glanced back over his shoulder. "I think the Goblin Man is real!"

"Well, let's go and find out, Sindri," Catriona said. "You first." She winked at Mudd and he laughed.

Brushing her hair behind her ears, Jirah looked up at Mudd with her pale blue eyes and pouted. "Are we almost there?"

"The Goblin Man awaits," he said, then gestured with a flourish. Mudd noticed Rina's satisfied smile at Jirah's sudden fear.

After allowing the others to pass, Mudd stepped one boot onto the stone, certain that at any moment the ancient bridge would crumble and toss them into the chasm's unseen depths, or that the steam had made the way so slick he'd slip and fall.

That would certainly make Asvoria's job easier, he thought.

As he neared the center of the bridge, the cloud of cool steam became like a sheet of thin cloth thrown over his head. The others in front of him were nothing but smoky shadows and he couldn't tell how far away they were. But the bridge proved to be fairly sturdy. Soon, he found himself nearing one of the shadows.

It was Sindri kneeling on the bridge. He peered down into the chasm with awestruck eyes. Mudd got an idea.

Crouching next to Sindri's ear, Mudd clamped his hands hard on the kender's shoulders.

"Goblin Man!" he screamed.

"Where?" Sindri cried. Sindri leaped up at Mudd's touch, dangerously close to the edge of the bridge. His eyes were alight with excitement. His head looked left and right. After a moment, his shoulders slumped. "I don't see any Goblin Man."

Mudd chuckled. "Sorry Sindri. My mistake."

Together, they finally made it through the thickest of the steam and emerged on the opposite side. The cliff rose steeply into the sky above, and the path he stood upon seemed much too narrow. He inched closer to the wall.

Rina looked him up and down with a sardonic smile. "Who knew crossing a bridge could be such an ordeal?"

"Mudd thought he saw the Goblin Man," Sindri said. "Do you think the Goblin Man might be able to turn invisible? That would certainly explain what Mudd saw!"

"Yes, that would explain it," Catriona said, with a roll of her eyes.

"You find the thought of my existence humorous?" a gravelly voice said.

With a start, everyone turned to see a man standing next to Maddoc. Wearing the black robes of a dark wizard, the man stood no taller than Jirah. Beady eyes sat close on either side of his wide nose, and short gray hair receded from his squareish forehead. His jowls jiggling, he grinned, revealing yellowed teeth.

"Children, allow me to introduce you to my old friend"— Maddoc paused dramatically— "the Goblin Man."

16 The Goblin Man

"Tea?"

The Goblin Man loomed in Mudd's face, his lips pressed together in a toad-like grin. Tilting his head, he gestured toward a small pot on the table before him.

"Er, all right," Mudd said.

With little introduction, the companions had been rushed along the path to a hidden door. Passing through, they entered a craggy tunnel that seemed to lead deep inside the cliff. Then, finally, they reached the Goblin Man's home.

It was little more than a single room, but it was more than enough space to hold them all. It was filled to the brim with furniture and knicknacks. Plush armchairs were arranged in threes around misshapen wooden tables. Threadbare brown rugs covered the stone floor. Two fireplaces blazed with flame, and strange metal artifacts crowded their hearths.

Two doors were cut into the rocky walls. The rest were lined from floor to ceiling with wooden bookshelves. They seemed to hold thousands of dusty books and crumbling scrolls.

Ushering them into the armchairs, the Goblin Man—whose name they learned was actually Arvin Derry—had quickly produced the beverages, though Mudd hadn't seen from where.

Mudd reached for the teapot. It was cold to the touch, but that didn't mean anything. Maybe it was enchanted so as not to scald. Pouring the thin yellow-brown liquid into a cup, Mudd raised it to his lips, took a sip, and promptly spit it out.

"This isn't tea," he gasped. Fire rushed down his throat.

Coughing from where he sat beside Catriona and Rina, Maddoc forced himself to swallow the drink he'd taken from a short, clear glass. Meeting Arvin's eye, he frowned. "This would be the tea. It tastes about three days old."

Arvin reared his head back into a high-pitched laugh. Mudd could swear he saw his yellow teeth momentarily sharpen into fang-like points, but they were back to normal in an instant.

"Oh, my," Arvin said, wiping away a tear. "Seems I switched the brandy and the tea once again. My stupidity never fails to amuse me."

His thin lips curled into a snarl, and he whipped around. He pointed an accusatory finger at Sindri, who had been fingering the spines of the books.

"Touch nothing, kender!" he shouted. "Or I shall turn you into a gnat." Giggling, he dropped his hands and turned to Maddoc. "I know some magic." This sent him into yet another fit of laughter.

Watching in surprise, Sindri backed away from the bookshelves.

"How did Maddoc say he knew this man?" Mudd whispered to Davyn. The boy only shrugged.

"You'll have to excuse my old friend," Maddoc said. "His isolation has caused him to lose quite a bit of his sanity."

"Among other things," Arvin said.

"And yet you trusted him with the Aegis?" Catriona crossed her arms. "You might as well just have handed it over to Asvoria and been done with it."

Trembling, Arvin turned to face Catriona. His skin seemed to flush red in anger, but soon the red became much too dark to be a blush. His eyes blackened, his skin creased and drew tight, and his nose flattened. As his mouth opened to speak, Mudd once again saw twin rows of jagged teeth.

With a snarl, Arvin thrust his face near Catriona's and let loose a string of guttural goblin words. Spit flew in Catriona's eyes.

With a war cry, Catriona shoved the rabid man away from her and jumped to her feet, dragon claws suddenly in her hands.

Arvin stumbled backward. He thudded against one of the bookshelves. Dust rained upon his head—a head that was now back to its normal human shape.

Bowing, he looked up to meet Catriona's eyes. "My apologies," he said in a tone that seemed to Mudd to be entirely insincere. "I can never predict when I'll have a hiccup."

"So that's why you're called the Goblin Man!" Sindri clapped in glee. He plopped down to sit cross-legged at the strange wizard's feet. "How did this happen? Did someone do it to you? Can you change when you want?"

"Kender," Arvin said with a shake of his semi-bald head. Turning to Maddoc he jerked a gnarled thumb toward Sindri. "I never thought I'd see the day you'd travel with one of these creatures."

"There are many things I thought I'd never see, but time has proven me wrong." Maddoc gestured toward the other companions. "Go ahead. Tell the children your tale."

"We don't have time for this, Maddoc." Rina lifted her chin. "If you haven't already forgotten, we aren't here on a social call."

Jirah rolled her eyes and leaned over the back of her seat to meet Rina's eye. "Oh come on, Rina," she said. "While you were living in high Silvanesti society, the rest of us were already forced out into the hard world. May we be allowed a few moments to rest?"

Rina frowned, then waved her hand. "Fine. Go ahead."

"I don't feel much love from the Silvanesti," Arvin said, his eyes cold. "But I shall tell the story anyway."

"I can hardly wait," Rina muttered.

"All this began when Maddoc and I were young men studying to be wizards. We both chose the path of the black robes, though Maddoc, being Maddoc, passed the tests at the Towers of High Sorcery at an infuriatingly young age. I was never the greatest at anything, so I stayed by his side. We discovered the volumes about Asvoria together, didn't we, Maddoc?"

"That we did," Maddoc said with a nod.

The Goblin Man began to pace the room as he spoke, the twin fires casting long shadows in every direction. "Asvoria was never very well known, which was a shame. She first started her wonderfully bloody reign over two thousand years ago, while what used to be known as Ergoth was in a period of upheaval. Unfortunately, she was but one of many emperors vying for control and her doings were mostly lost to time after that Solamnus fellow had his divine vision and decided to set things back to order.

"For years we followed her exploits as best we could with what little there was written about her, all the while expanding in our magical knowledge. We ran out of steel before long and started hiring ourselves out to earn more. We made quite a living, doing certain . . . things."

He stopped for a second, his gaze meeting Mudd's. A shiver ran down his spine. Mudd wasn't certain of much, but he did know he never wanted to know what those things were.

"Maddoc claimed Asvoria as his obsession," Arvin went on, "and so I turned my attention elsewhere: her familiar, Ophion. While Maddoc tried to learn Asvoria's secrets of necromancy and soul displacement, I set about learning all I could about this strange shifting creature and, more specifically, the act of changing one's form. After Maddoc purchased Asvoria's keep and found that old tapestry, his obsession grew a hundredfold and we parted ways. I found myself here, in this cave, doing my own experiments. I wanted to do what Ophion could—I wanted to shapeshift."

"But that's easy," Sindri said, then shrugged. "Well, or so I hear. You've been at this a while, couldn't you have just cast a spell?"

Grinning his yellow teeth, Arvin chuckled deep in his throat. "Ah, kender, but I wanted more. I didn't want simply to shape-shift, I wanted to become a shapeshifter. I wanted to have that power in me, to change at will without mumbling words and mussing with spell components. I did experiments with a few unfortunate goblins, and the result is what you see today." Stepping back, he flung out his arms to present himself. "The Goblin Man."

Jirah nodded, her expression unreadable. "It didn't quite work, did it? You don't have control of it."

Arvin leered at the girl, then leaned back against a bookshelf. "As I've said, I'm hardly the brightest man. So, no, it didn't work out the way I wanted. And alas, my ability to be a wizard seems to have suffered for it. But being a Goblin Man hasn't been all bad. Keeps most visitors away."

"So that's why Maddoc sent you the Aegis," Davyn said, nodding. "He knew he could trust you and that you'd know what the sword meant. He also knew no one would come looking for it here."

"Astute young man," Arvin said, peering at him closely. "Davyn, was it? You're Maddoc's adopted son, if I recall the missives he sent. I remember your parents. Painfully honest, those two."

Davyn's brow furrowed. "Thank you."

Tilting back his head, Arvin laughed. "It wasn't a compliment."

Before Davyn could react, Rina stood. "So we know your tale. Now we'd like what we came for."

"Oh, the Aegis?" Arvin said with a tilt of his hand. "It's down below, protected by magic."

"Well, can you go get it?" Davyn went to Rina's side and crossed his arms.

"I'd love to," Arvin said. "But, you see, I wanted to ensure that no one would be able to take the sword. I erased the memory of how I protected the Aegis should Asvoria find me and try to make me retrieve it." He strummed his fingers against one another. "I'm afraid I'll be absolutely no help."

Catriona frowned. "Do you mean we're going to have to figure out how to get this sword ourselves?"

Arvin's lips parted into a sick smile. "You're going to have to fight for your prize. I can't remember the obstacles and couldn't get rid of them if I wanted to." He gestured at one of the doors with a hand that quickly shriveled into a red goblin's claw. "The Aegis lies through there. Have fun!"

Falling back in a fit of insane giggles, the Goblin Man collapsed into the nearest free chair, tears streaming down his face. No one could do anything but stare.

Sindri watched his friends huddle by the fireplace and discuss what to do next, but he stayed sitting in the shadows. His mind was consumed by other matters.

After revealing the sword's location, the Goblin Man had wished the others well (though Sindri was fairly certain he didn't mean it) and then retired through the right-hand door. Maddoc still sat in his chair, legs crossed and sipping at brandy he had poured from the teapot.

Aside from himself, only Jirah hadn't joined in the conversation. Instead, she hid around a corner in a shadowy alcove. Again she had her little mirror out, and again she spoke to her reflection.

One day I really will have to ask her about that, Sindri reminded himself.

His eye had caught one of the thick tomes on the shelf next to him. Its spine read "Spells of Destruction, Volume 7." He fingered the lettering.

"Yes," he whispered in glee, then shook his head. He wasn't sure why he'd said that. But, then, his thoughts had been so strange lately. They insisted on circling back to the images Asvoria has thrust into his mind. And with the images always came the echo of the repulsive joy Asvoria had made him feel at seeing his friends die.

Jumping to his feet, Sindri walked to Maddoc. With a leap, he plopped himself into the armchair next to the one the former wizard sat in. He sank into the overstuffed seat and imagined for a moment that he was sitting on a red- and green-patterned cloud.

"May I help you?" Maddoc asked. He took another sip of his brandy and closed his eyes as he swallowed.

Sindri leaned over the armrest and nodded sagely. "Yes," he said. "You're going to stay up here and study how to restore Raedon, right?"

"That I am," Maddoc said, glancing over at Davyn.

"I'm staying too," Sindri said. "I've decided something."

"What's that?"

Sindri took a breath. "Asvoria did something to me. And I don't much like it. I changed my mind, Maddoc. I want to stop Asvoria no matter what. I want you to teach me dark magic."

Raising an eyebrow, Maddoc set his glass on the low table in front of him. "Are you certain?"

"Of course!" Sindri said, nodding vigorously.

"Well then," Maddoc said. "I suppose lessons could be arranged."

Sindri leaned back in his chair, satisfied. Looking deep into the fire that blazed nearby, he remembered the black moon that seemed like someone had torn through the sky. His heart pounded, though he didn't know why.

"Good," he said. "When do we start?"

CHAPTER

17

INTO THE CHASM

"I still say we need someone who knows magic to come with us," Jirah said as she followed Davyn and Mudd through the door and into the dimly lit stone hallway. "We're stupid to do this without Maddoc or, gods, even Sindri."

"We can handle it," Rina said, following behind her. "If not, then we can always go back for Sindri."

Jirah snorted. "Are all of you elves so arrogant? Maybe if you didn't think you were the greatest race in the world less people would be dead right now."

Rina took in a breath despite herself. The thorny words left a stinging cut, and her anger bubbled up. "Why are you such a—"

"Jirah!" Davyn called back. "It's all right. Sindri just needs a rest. He's been through a lot."

The pale human girl's lips widened into a smile. "Of course, Davyn." With a little jump in her step, she quickened her pace to walk between him and Mudd.

"That girl," Rina seethed. The door shut behind her and the hallway was thrust into shadow. Flickering light from twin torches carried by Davyn in the lead and Catriona in the rear pierced the darkness.

"What was that about?" the warrior asked as she came by Rina's side.

The elf shrugged, unwilling to confess her feelings.

They followed the two boys and Jirah down the sloping tunnel as it descended deeper and deeper within the rocky cliff. Rina could sense the trail winding but she couldn't tell how much. Water dripped down the craggy walls and pooled at their feet, leaving slimy, moldy trails. Even with her night vision, the shadows left by the torches seemed to twist and move as though alive. Rina's heart fluttered.

"Do you feel ready for whatever it is that man set to guard the Aegis?" Rina whispered to Catriona as they walked.

Catriona showed no emotion. "I try always to be ready."

Rina nodded. "Oh, me too. I'm definitely ready. Just wanted to know if you were."

Catriona chuckled. "Don't worry, it's all right to be afraid." She started to say something, then shook her head.

"What?" Rina asked.

"I was just going to say," Catriona said, steeling her face again, "that you don't always have to put on such a show. I'm often afraid, myself. I've failed too often to be too confident."

"That can't be true," Rina said, carefully making her way around a boulder in the path. "You've handled everything we've faced so far with grace and honor."

Catriona shrugged and looked down. "I suppose. But I can't help but think of myself as a failure, even now." Her eyes scanned Rina's face. Then, with a breath, she turned away. "The reason I'm on this journey is that I failed to save my aunt from being killed by bandits. I was her squire, and it was my duty to stand by her side. Ever since then I've promised to protect everyone who needs protecting. So far it seems I've done nothing but fail them."

"Do you still feel that way?" Rina asked. "Davyn told me stories of your exploits, and everything I've seen you do has shown you to be nothing if not tremendously brave."

Catriona smiled sadly. "Every time I fight, I remember my aunt. The look she gave me even as she told me to run away. . ." Catriona closed her eyes and let out a breath. "She couldn't keep the disappointment from her eyes. I'm afraid all the time, Rina. But I keep fighting because I must. Her look will never leave me, nor will my shame."

"I knew nothing of shame," Rina said. "Nothing of disappointment or hardship. My life was simple. Even with the war and the exodus from Silvanesti to Southern Ergoth, I was kept sheltered from everything. I could have stayed in Southern Ergoth or gone back to Silvanesti and lived happy for the rest of my years, I suppose."

"Then why did you leave?" Catriona asked.

"My father died in the war. After he died . . . there was a boy." Rina fell silent for a moment. "His name was Fiernan. He was different than everyone else. Even though I never saw a dragon or had to fight, he taught me more about archery and combat than my father had ever dared to teach me, just so I could feel safe as the War of the Lance raged on. I needed to fight once Father was dead, to help destroy the enemy that had taken him from us." She shook her head and sighed as memories came back to her.

"Fiernan had ideas," she continued. "Strange ideas. When we trained together, we had many long discussions. I started to see things differently. I began to wonder if all the things my parents and my grandparents had always taught me about the races of Krynn were true. So I decided I needed to find out truths on my own instead of accepting what I was told."

"What happened?" Catriona asked.

"As soon as the war ended and we grieved for our losses, I figured the first thing I should do was find my half-brother and find out for myself who he was while we still had time in our lives to do so. My mother never spoke highly of Elidor, and my father always told me he was dirt, a half-breed. It just didn't seem right, though. To hate someone for something they had no control over. I needed to speak to him myself."

Catriona nodded sadly. "But before you could find him—"

Rina looked down, remembering. "We received a package the day I planned to leave. It contained Elidor's belongings and . . . and it had a letter." She sighed. "I felt so much rage when I learned of his death, Catriona. First Father, now Elidor. It was so unfair, and I had never known 'unfair' before. At least, not anything beyond simple childhood notions of the word. That's why I'm here now. I needed to hurt those who hurt me. Everything outside of my home is so different. Sometimes it's hard to take. But I'm trying."

"I never would have known," Catriona said. "You seem to hold your own with us as well as Elidor always did. Maybe even better."

Rina smiled. "I'm good at faking it."

"I suppose I am too." Catriona met Rina's eyes. "It hasn't been all bad, has it? Between all the fighting with monsters, that is. Are we non-elves truly that bad?"

"Well," Rina said without thinking, "you do have this strange smell." She put her hand to her mouth and gave Catriona an apologetic look.

The warrior let out a small laugh. "Oh really?"

"I apologize," Rina said, lowering her hand. "I didn't mean—"

"No," Catriona said. "It's all right. What else?"

Shaking her head, Rina went on. "You all eat with gross disregard to etiquette. Your males grow hair on their faces, stiff and brittle hair with no discernable purpose. Your language is crude and unruly. You lumber about like animals, wild and ungraceful. And," she said staring hard at the side of Catriona's head, "your ears are *round*."

Catriona let out another small laugh. "Is that all?"

Rina shrugged. "Those are my family's words. You're just

different. Humans aren't all bad." As she said the last part, her eyes darted forward to glance at Davyn in the lead.

"You love him, don't you?" Catriona asked softly.

With a start, Rina turned back to look at Catriona and promptly stumbled over a pile of rocks. For a moment she was entirely ungraceful, but soon she caught her balance.

"How did you know?" she asked, trying to regain her composure.

"You and Jirah had your claws bared from the moment we met," Catriona said. "And yet I'm the one everyone calls Cat."

Looking ahead, Rina saw Jirah playfully grab at Davyn's arm, and she had to take a deep breath.

"It is forbidden. I know this. I know this!" Rina hung her head. "I just can't help the way I feel. And then, there's Jirah, who's always going on about how Davyn doesn't need me and, from what I've seen, maybe she isn't all wrong. And even if Jirah weren't in the picture, there's Nearra. He acted as though he no longer loves her, that he has closed himself off from the feelings. But the feelings are still there. They'll always be there, won't they?"

"What is it about Davyn that's so attractive?" Catriona asked. "Everyone falls for him."

"He's just . . . Davyn," Rina said. "I'm not sure I can explain it. Maybe if I could, it would go away and I could stop acting like a stupid child."

"It's not stupid," Catriona said. "But I know what you mean. I remember being jealous of Nearra a little, but not because of Davyn. I wanted to forget everything just like she had. I wanted to start fresh. Maybe then I could be the person everyone expects me to become."

Rina didn't know what to say, so she only nodded. The two girls walked on in silence. The only noise was the sound of their footsteps and the crackling of the torch's flame. Shadows burned away as pale white light seeped from around a corner. With a look at Catriona, Rina quickened her pace to join the others as they rounded the tunnel's bend.

Davyn, Mudd, and Jirah huddled around a wide cave opening filled with misty daylight. Blinking her eyes, Rina stepped beside them.

The tunnel opened up into the chasm they had crossed over. Looking up, Rina could see a sheer cliff rising high up to the bridge, which was nothing but a small shadow. The cliff stretched far below into hazy mist, making it seem as though it went down forever.

White steam billowed up from the chasm's depths and rose in an endless sheet that spread out in both directions, completely obscuring the other side of the chasm. Wet droplets splashed from the cloudy mist as it rushed by.

"All right, then." Mudd was quiet for a moment. He shrugged. "Maybe we made a wrong turn?"

Davyn shook his head. "There were no other turns. But why would Arvin build a tunnel opening up into the chasm? It doesn't make sense."

"It does if he were just playing with us." Rina scowled, as she peered into the chasm's eerie depths. "That man was—"

Before Rina could finish, someone shoved her from behind. With a gasp, the elf stumbled forward, pinwheeling her arms.

The stone path at her feet began to crumble.

Screaming, Rina lost her balance and slipped into the wide chasm.

CHAPTER

18   THE AEGIS

"R ina!" Catriona dropped to her knees at the
edge of the cliff. She looked down, expect-
ing to see the elf girl tumbling into the chasm's depths.

Instead, she found Rina clinging against the rocky wall, head
facing down and arms clutching at any crevice her fingers could
find. Her back heaved as she gasped for air.

"Give me your hand!" Catriona called.

As the warrior lowered her hand, it seemed to grow heavy
and pull against the wall. She barely noticed as Rina started to
stand.

"What in the Abyss?" Mudd gasped from above her.

Her feet still against the chasm's sheer wall, Rina stood—
sideways. She jutted out from the cliff's sheer wall like a lone
tree branch, though doing so was clearly impossible. It was as
though the wall had suddenly become the ground.

"Catriona?" She twisted to look back at the others. Her eyes
grew wide. "What's going on?"

"A spell." Davyn sighed with relief. "Arvin must have put a
spell on the wall. Good thing, Rina, or you'd be gone."

Rina's eyes narrowed. "I'm sure that's exactly what Jirah had
planned, isn't it?"

135

Catriona spun around to see Jirah raising her hands defensively.

"I didn't!" she insisted, lips trembling. "I would never. I—"

"Come on, Rina," Davyn said, crossing his arms and looking down at her. "Jirah would never want to see you hurt. You know that."

"Are you deaf and blind, Davyn?" Rina snapped. "She's been trying to get rid of me for weeks."

"Now, now, ladies," Mudd said, coming to stand beside Davyn. "Let's just thank the gods Rina is all right and get back to finding the Aegis."

"Right," Davyn said, though he looked confused. "The Aegis."

Stepping to the edge of the hole, Catriona looked down at Rina still standing sideways on the cliff wall. The elf had turned her attention to surveying the surroundings.

"I think I see something up ahead," she called back. "I mean, farther down. Oh, this is confusing."

"Maybe we should follow her," Mudd said, peering down past Rina. "You go first, Davyn."

"I'll go first," Catriona said, gently pushing through Davyn and Mudd.

Though her heart thudded in her chest, Catriona forced herself to look straight ahead, her face expressionless. Then, she stepped forward.

It was as if the whole world were spinning around her. For a moment Catriona wondered whether the spell hadn't worked. But then her foot hit solid ground and suddenly the cliff wall became a plain of stone, the rising steam an expanse of writhing storm clouds, and the bottomless pit a dark cave ahead.

She slid her other foot forward and put her arms out to hold herself steady. The shift in scenery was entirely disorienting, and she felt a bit nauseous. *Sindri will be upset he missed this,* she thought.

Davyn, Mudd, and Jirah were quick to follow.

"Wizards." Mudd closed his eyes and shook his head to get a handle on the shift. "I wonder if you're required to be a bit crazy in order to study magic."

"I think it's clever." Jirah lifted a slender hand to touch the flowing steam. "Who would think to walk down the wall?"

"You said you saw something?" Davyn asked Rina.

"Yes!" The elf pointed toward the wall of mist. "Something glittering green."

"The Aegis," Catriona said. "Come on!"

She raced ahead with Davyn at her side. Their boots pounded against the stone and muffled echoes sounded from behind them. It wasn't long before they grew near the tiny dot on the false horizon and saw that it was, in fact, the Aegis.

The sword lay suspended in air. Its point barely touched the stony expanse and its glittering malachite hilt was aimed toward what now seemed to be the sky. Like a stained glass window in a temple, hazy light reflected off the emerald shards embedded in the steel blade. Pale green shadows flickered at their feet.

"It's magnificent," Jirah whispered in awe.

"It's the sword Asvoria used to murder who knows how many people." Davyn's face was stern.

"I can't believe it's here," Catriona said. "We saw it shatter."

"Maddoc did a good job putting it back together," Davyn said. "But Arvin didn't exactly do a good job of hiding it."

"Are we just going to stand here or is Catriona going to grab that thing?" Mudd said. "I don't like the feeling of standing on this wall. The faster we get off of it, the better."

Davyn put a hand on Cat's shoulder. "Are you sure you want to do this? We talked about what the sword did to you last time you held it. And Maddoc said that no one could take it away from you. It could corrupt you."

Cat stared at the sword. "I'm sure. And I'm willing to take

the risk to save Nearra and Raedon, and to stop Asvoria."

With a nod, Davyn let go of Catriona's shoulder.

Anxiety climbed up Cat's spine. It couldn't be this easy. Not after all they'd gone through to get rid of the sword in the first place. Not after Elidor lost his life to help keep Asvoria from regaining it.

Without a word, she stepped forward. The steam coursed like a river above her head. Dark shadows passed behind it like fish swimming in its expansive depths. Above where the Aegis hung, the steam curled in on itself in a spiraling whirlpool.

With only three steps to go, she reached out a hand to grab the sword's hilt. Just as her fingers grazed the cool metal, the whirlpool in the air reacted. Quicker than Catriona could blink, the swirling steam pulsed and began to spin into a maelstrom of magic fury.

With a whoosh of wind and water, the whirlpool formed into a screaming tornado that shot down toward the Aegis. Catriona barely had time to pull her hand out of the way before the tornado swallowed the sword, enveloping it in its smoky interior. With a roar of rushing air, the whirling steam suddenly became much more solid.

Where the Aegis once lay, a giant serpent stood. The outline of its body seemed to be constantly shifting as though it were still made of the steam itself. Flaky green scales flowed over the beast. Its blood-red eyes blazed on a diamond-shaped head. Its mouth opened to bare twin pairs of arcing, poison-tipped fangs. The sword was gone, trapped inside the belly of the beast. The whirlpool in the false sky was gone as well.

With a hissing screech, the serpent lunged.

"Watch out!" The cry came from Rina, but she needn't have worried. With a well-practiced sweep of her arms, the dragon claws were in Cat's hands in seconds.

With a yell, the warrior brought the top sword down on the serpent's snout before quickly bringing the lower one around to jab it in its exposed belly. The creature snarled and swept past Catriona, though her blows seemed to have no effect.

"I don't think it's solid!"

Davyn pulled his sword free. The serpent lunged forward and Davyn brought the weapon up in a graceful swing. Ivory teeth met hard steel with a clang that echoed between the rock and the steam. Startled at this failure, the misty beast reared back for another go.

With a small scream, Jirah turned and fled back for the top of the chasm. No one paid her any mind. Mudd pulled free his own short sword and tried hacking at the creature's tail, to no avail. Meanwhile, Rina had pulled two small throwing knives from her boots—just like Elidor, Catriona thought—and circled warily, her eyes full of concern.

With a steeling cry, Catriona swept the dragon claws forward. Its jagged edges tore through serpent's flowing green scales. Any other beast would have been sliced in half, but the creature's skin only rippled as though she had done nothing but throw stones into a lake.

Ignoring Catriona's attack, the serpent still lunged at Davyn. The boy blocked the savage blows, but the creature whipped its head back and forth so fast that it managed to carve its teeth deep into his leather armor. Rina screamed, but he was fine, save for two deep lacerations along the front of the green leather covering his chest.

"How do we stop this thing?" Mudd cried as yet another one of his strikes went right through the creature's tail and slammed against the rocky cliff wall.

In response, the serpent smacked Mudd in his middle with its tail. The boy flew backward and landed on his back with a small thud.

Catriona let out a shout and bashed her swords against the serpent's mouth. Several small teeth broke off and scattered at their feet, misshapen white pebbles.

Hissing, the serpent turned its attention from Davyn and shot down toward Catriona's neck. Then, with a garbled screech, it pulled back. Thick green liquid oozed down its face. The hilt of a dagger protruded from its eye.

"Good shot!" Davyn called to Rina. The elf girl responded with a dazzling smile.

The serpent thrashed wildly. Its head butted Davyn in the gut, sending him flying to the ground beside Mudd. Catriona barely managed to jump over its tail.

There has to be a way to stop this thing, she thought. Fighting isn't doing anything.

That was when she saw the Aegis, floating within the creature's swirling green skin.

She had an idea.

Reattaching the dragon claws to her belt, she leaped over the snake's tail and ducked beneath its head. She outstretched her hand and kept her eyes focused only on the sword. Without stopping to think, she plunged her arm through the serpent's body and into its hot, watery innards. It continued to hiss and thrash.

Catriona had to leap around to keep up with the serpent's movements, and the hilt of the sword kept sloshing out of her reach. Her fingers grazed the sword several times but always the serpent moved at the last minute.

There was only one thing Catriona could do.

Whispering a quick prayer to Paladine, the warrior held her breath and dived into the snake's belly.

19   CATRIONA'S OATH

The world turned a hazy green blur as the serpent's watery insides enveloped Catriona. It was warm and thick, like floating in watered-down honey. It was, in fact, the strangest feeling Catriona could ever recall.

But she had to get the sword.

Inside the beast, she could barely feel its movements. Vaguely it felt as though she were once again caught in a swelling wave like the one that had once carried her overboard a ship. Sounds were muffled and distant. The loudest noise was the constant rush of blood pounding past her ears.

She kept her eyes open, pinwheeled her arms, and thrashed her legs. It felt more like climbing than swimming. The sword lay suspended in front of her, still shining brilliantly even inside the creature's unnatural body.

At last, her fingers encircled the cool malachite. As soon as the hilt was gripped firmly in her hand, the sword came alive.

Sparkling lightning coursed over the Aegis's blade, lancing out in all directions like wiry vines. The emerald shards glowed with an inner light.

In a flash, warrior and sword were connected. The sword

pulsed with each beat of her heart. It reacted to each glancing thought that passed through her mind. The magic flowed through her body like a warm drink on a frosty night, and for the first time in a long while Catriona's mind felt complete and utter clarity.

Then her lungs began to ache.

The burning in her chest pulled her away from the sword's power. Spinning her arms, she tried to push herself through the creature's skin and free herself, but the snake was beginning to solidify, its watery insides gelling and hardening.

She was trapped.

Frantically, she clawed at the inside of the snake's skin, her need for air growing as pain lanced in her head.

But the sword in her hand seemed to speak to her, soothing her. The pain in her chest seemed distant and unimportant. Her mind cleared. She could see clearly what to do. In the pearly green depths ahead of her, she saw the inside of the serpent's thrashing head. Floating between its eyes was a swirling red orb that hadn't been visible from outside.

She aimed the Aegis straight up. Without even having to think about it, she thrust forward. The tip of the sword plunged deep into the crimson ball and lightning flashed. Muted screeching met Catriona's ears. The watery void around her began to vibrate.

And then, the serpent exploded.

Catriona collapsed to the stony ground. Soaked head to toe with goo, she gasped for air. The stench was like clay mixed with cow dung, but Catriona didn't care. She could breathe, and they had the Aegis.

"Catriona!" Davyn, Rina, and Mudd raced toward her. Rina landed on her knees beside her and grabbed Catriona's slime-coated shoulder.

"Are you all right?" she asked.

Spitting out the foul liquid that had slipped between her lips, she ran her free hand through her slick hair and sat up. "Yes." She looked at the glowing sword in her hand and smiled. "Yes, I am."

"That was good thinking," Davyn said, kneeling beside her. "I never would have thought to go inside the serpent."

"Well, it seemed like the thing to do," Catriona said, climbing to her feet. "Do you suppose Arvin has a bath?"

"Uh, Cat . . ." Mudd began.

"I don't know," Rina said, crinkling her nose. "But you certainly need one."

"You smell like a cattle pen," Davyn said. "It's not the worst thing I've smelled . . ." He grinned. "But it's close."

"Davyn, Cat, Rina . . ." Mudd started inching his way toward the dark hole above them. "I think we need to get off this wall, and fast."

"What is it?" Rina asked.

He didn't have to answer. They all felt it.

The serpent's remains began to drip past their feet as the whole world lurched. It felt as though the ground was heaving beneath them.

That was when they all realized the same thing—whatever magic had enabled them to walk on the wall was going away. Fast.

Without a word, the four friends turned and raced toward the hole. Catriona's boots slipped on the sheer cliff-face, and she scrambled to find handholds to pull herself forward. With each second that passed, the ground became more and more of a wall, and gravity began to pull her backward.

Rina, Davyn, and Mudd were ahead of her, and she saw Mudd dive into the hole. Her slime-coated feet slipped. She fell to her knees. With her slick fingers, it was too hard to grab hold of any cracks.

She should have felt fear. She always felt fear. But the strength of the magic sword wouldn't allow her anything but the strongest of convictions. It was for that reason she didn't call out for help as she started to fall.

"Cat!" someone cried, or several someones, but Catriona couldn't see. All she could tell was that her friends were standing in the hole above her and she was tumbling backward, spinning and twisting as she plummeted into the chasm's depths.

Unafraid, she held the Aegis straight out and plunged it forward.

The blade met the cliff's wall with a clink and a shower of green sparks. Catriona jerked to a stop. The sword quivered from where it had embedded itself in the stone. Catriona clung to its hilt with all her strength.

For a long moment, Catriona hung in the air, her feet dangling miles above a rocky death. She closed her eyes and breathed deeply. Her shoulders ached, her fingers felt as though they'd slip from he hilt at any moment, but her heart did not pound. She felt nothing but a deep certainty that she'd find a way out of this and be completely fine.

Then, the pain in her shoulders eased. Opening her eyes, she looked up to see two tiny hands sticking out from the hole in the cliff's wall. A silver ring glinted from one of its flickering fingers. Catriona began to slowly float up toward the sky.

Pulling the Aegis from the wall with ease, the warrior let herself drift up into the cave. Sindri watched her with sweat flooding down his face, but his focus did not waver. Catriona landed on the cave floor in a crouch, unharmed.

Sindri's hands dropped and he gasped for air.

As Cat landed, the Aegis clattered to the ground. In that brief moment, a surge of fear flooded Catriona's system. Without hesitation, she grabbed the sword, once again letting its insidious power take control. Immediately her body relaxed, and her head cleared.

Davyn and Rina stood on either side of Maddoc, who kneeled at Sindri's side. Jirah smirked beside Mudd, her arms crossed.

"I ran to get Sindri," the girl said. "I was right that we needed his magic."

Catriona nodded, barely noticing Rina's glare. "It seems you were."

Certain Sindri was fine, Maddoc came to Catriona's side. He raised an eyebrow as his eyes fell on the Aegis. "I see you retrieved the sword."

"Oh, it was nothing," Mudd said. "Walking down an enchanted cliff wall, battling a serpent made of watery goop, almost plummeting to our deaths. All in a day's adventuring."

Maddoc ignored him. "Perfect. Meanwhile, Sindri and I found a way to save Raedon and Nearra." Meeting Catriona's eyes, his features tightened. "Catriona, its success relies entirely on you."

Catriona sat in one of Arvin's armchairs. Sticky flakes covered her skin where the goo had crusted and dried. The stomach-heaving smell still lingered in the air, and her hair was plastered against her neck, stiff and brittle. But she didn't care. Her eyes could not leave the Aegis. She cradled it in her lap like a newborn child.

The green sword continued to flicker with mystical currents, sending jolts of energy zipping through her limbs. With each second that passed, she could feel its power become more and more in control of her. It erased her fears, eradicated her doubts. Her conviction gave the sword its power, but it, in turn, gave her the strength to feel in complete control.

It was a perfect union, but deadly in its own way. A weapon like this would corrupt even the most honorable Solamnic knight. Catriona knew this. But at that moment, after feeling afraid for so long, after not trusting herself, and after being unable to move past these emotions no matter how hard she tried, she didn't care what the Aegis did.

Many lives were on the line now. She was weak without the sword. Magic consumed her mind. It took away the memory of old failures and replaced it with a sense of unabashed pride.

She welcomed the magic. Let it corrupt me, she thought. It will be worth it to put this to rest, once and for all.

"Cat?" Sindri shook her arm and she snapped out of her daze.

She smiled. "Thanks again for saving me."

"Of course!" he said. "I barely remember falling myself, but I know it was quite exhilarating. But it would probably have hurt a lot if you'd hit the ground."

Maddoc sat in the chair next to her and placed a heavy tome on a table between them.

"Raedon," Davyn said from behind him. Crossing his arms, he leaned against the armrest of Catriona's chair. "You're certain you can save him? And Nearra will be free of whatever control Asvoria still has over her?"

Maddoc nodded and flipped the pages of the book. Flickering shadows from the fireplace shrouded the text in darkness, but the former wizard didn't seem to notice. After finding what he was looking for, he held the pages flat and turned the book so Catriona could see.

On the left page was tiny, blocky text written in a language Catriona couldn't understand. But that didn't matter, because the illustration on the opposite page spelled things out in deadly clarity.

Sketched in perfect detail was the figure of a man laying on his back, arms outstretched. Eyes closed and mouth slack, he appeared to be dead. Etched on his arms, legs, and chest were several different symbols.

"This is the spell Sindri will perform with my instruction," Maddoc said. "And these symbols are what you will need to carve on Asvoria's dragon body so that we can put Raedon's soul back in place. This will destroy Asvoria, and Nearra will finally be freed. The only difference is that, unlike the figure here, she will be alive while you do this."

"Wait," Rina said, raising her hands. "You want Catriona to face Asvoria alone and try to cut all those symbols on her? How is that possible?"

"I trust she will find a way," Maddoc said.

"This is crazy," Davyn said. "You're sentencing her to death!"

"That may be," the wizard said. He stood up and paced in front of the fire. "But Catriona made an oath to me. In exchange for showing Sindri how to destroy Asvoria, she promised to place herself in my service. The time has come when I must take advantage of that."

Mudd threw up his hands. "But you failed to teach him! Sindri didn't stop Asvoria!"

"I almost did," Sindri shouted. "It wasn't Maddoc's fault."

The former wizard held up his palm. "It doesn't matter. This is the only way. Don't you want to save Nearra and Raedon?"

"Maybe Davyn should do it," Jirah said, clutching at his arm. Davyn tried to wiggle from her grip. "That is, if Catriona is afraid."

"As much as I want to be the one to hurt Asvoria," Davyn said as he finally managed to wrench his arm free, "only a woman can take advantage of the Aegis's full powers, and it's likely only the Aegis can harm Asvoria. Normal swords can't hurt dragons."

Rina and Mudd raised more protests, trying in vain to convince Maddoc to find another way, to not put Catriona in harm's way. But the warrior ignored them all. She could not tear her eyes away from the Aegis. The more she looked at it, the more she felt connected to a power greater than herself.

"I'll do it," she said. Conviction made the words unwavering, and they hung in the air solid and final. Everyone fell silent.

"Catriona, are you sure?" Davyn asked.

She nodded. "It's the only way. And I will not go back on my oath." Turning to Maddoc, she met his eyes. "Show me the symbols."

Maddoc bowed his head slightly. "Of course."

Ignoring the concerned glances Rina, Mudd, and Davyn gave one another, Catriona studied the book as Maddoc pointed to the symbols and explained how they must be etched. For a moment, she couldn't help but smile. Only hours ago the thought of their plan resting entirely on her shoulders would have set her on a path of self-doubt that could have proven enough to incapacitate her.

But that time had passed. She had the Aegis now, and nothing could stop her.

CHAPTER

20

AN EXAMPLE

The world was upside down.

No, Asvoria thought. I am.

Snorting at the thought, she climbed farther up the sloping roof of the large mountain cave.

Spiderwalking was an ability inherent to all copper dragons, and it meant they were able to scale walls with ease. Delighted at having discovered how to do this, Asvoria clung to the stone and waited for her guest to arrive.

Hanging upside down with wings flapping and feeling rather like a bat, Asvoria arched her neck down and studied her new throne room. It wasn't quite the way she intended it to look, but it would be soon.

There had already been tunnels carved through these caves where another dragon had once lived, but he must not have cared about décor. The main room had consisted only of the rock walls and an indent on the floor where the great beast had once slept.

Now, Asvoria's handiwork could be seen everywhere. Like twin tusks, two great stalagmites had originally jutted up from the front of the cavern. Using her own magic and that of her dragon body, she'd carved shapes into the stone pillars.

149

One stood as a testament to her original human body, slender with angular features and a gown befitting only a queen. The other was of a dragon soaring up into the sky, wings pressed flat against its back and mouth open wide in a triumphant roar. Glimmering purple jewels stood in for eyes.

In the center of the cavern she had raised a great dais and added a back that curved up like half of a smoothed shell. A dragon-sized throne. Piles of old gold from the original dragon inhabitant were melted with her magic and spread into a thin coating. Beneath the yellow metal she had raised the stone into figures of dragons in flight. In the shimmering daylight flowing from a hole in the cavern's ceiling, they seemed almost alive.

Against the back wall, she'd spent much time etching in a large symbol of the letter A. A slender dragon arched through the hole in the letter's center, its tail wrapped protectively around the lower slant.

An old symbol, to be sure. And the statues and throne were hardly dragon-like—they were remnants of her old human tastes, if anything. But now they were larger than life, like her. She might be a dragon now, but she would always be Asvoria, and no one would ever forget her name.

The girl, Nearra, lay on an outcropping of rock beneath the A symbol, flat on her back and hands crossed over her chest. Her eyelids fluttered as she dreamed or, maybe, as she saw through Asvoria's eyes.

Nearra had been silent ever since they'd left the manor, not even whining as Asvoria sent her army to attack the village. Either she was saving up strength or she'd already spent all she'd had to use. Didn't matter either way. Ophion was off searching for ways to sever the dragon well's connection. Once the shape-shifter found the way, Asvoria would make a meal of the girl and be rid of her forever.

Asvoria tilted her great copper head and regarded a stalactite

JEFF SAMPSON

jutting down from the ceiling. That won't do, she thought.

Whispering a spell, she sent the rock formation on a path of heightened erosion. Solid rock broke into pebbles that crumbled into dust until there was no sign it had ever existed.

"Much better," she rumbled.

"Milady?" The voice, vaguely male, echoed throughout the cave.

Narrowing her eyes, Asvoria saw Ophion. The shapeshifter was once again in humanoid form, skin shifting like some sort of magnifying glass as it passed by the walls and replicated their coloring.

"Dragon Queen," Ophion called again. "Are you here?"

Chuckling to herself, Asvoria gripped the stone and slithered across it. Her scales rustled and the sound echoed throughout the cave. Ophion's eyes darted about, trying to find the noise's source.

Asvoria dropped behind him, using her wings to drag at the air and land gracefully.

Lowering her head to her oblivious familiar's ear, she whispered, "What have we here?"

The shapeshifter's skin bubbled up as though bugs climbed beneath the rubbery flesh. In one swift move, Ophion spun around into a low bow. "Milady."

"What have you found?"

"Your guest is on the way." Peering up at her with shifting blue eyes, Ophion frowned. "And there are people gathering in the hills below."

Asvoria snorted and leaned back on her haunches. Of course people would come upon hearing tales of the attacks. And she knew that the children—the girl's friends—would come to try to save her, as they fancied themselves heroes. But her army sat still, as harmless as scarecrows as they guarded the two villages she'd already destroyed. Connections coursed between each of the undead beasts and herself, and she could feel them all, like distant, phantom fingers stretching throughout the countryside. She could flex her magic and bring them to life in an instant, but the energy it would take . . .

She'd been resting, as much as she would allow herself. But a battle was coming. Of course she'd expected this, had known her new reign would not come without a fight. Raising the initial army and the actual dragon possession itself were only early steps in her plans, and relatively easy steps compared with what lay ahead.

Snorting, Asvoria turned her massive body and leaped at the wall. Her curved claws clung to the stone with ease. She looked back. "Did you find out how to sever the connection?"

"No, milady," the shapeshifter said, head bowed. "But I have leads."

Asvoria growled and climbed up the stone. "We haven't much time. I don't doubt we can defeat Davyn and the others, but once word spreads, more will rise against us. I can't be saddled with the girl when that happens."

"Yes, my queen."

A great roar echoed from the sky high above the cavernous throne room and a vast shadow passed over the floor. Wind rushed by with the force of the creature's wings.

"Looks like our guest is finally here," Asvoria said with a satisfied smile.

A great red blur of wings and claws burst through the hole in the ceiling and landed on the floor with a furious boom. Without missing a stride, the creature—a small red dragon as red dragons go—stormed toward Asvoria where she clung to the wall. Ophion slipped into the shadows, unnoticed.

"Explain yourself, Copper!" the red dragon demanded. "How dare you claim space on my mountain!"

"Ah, Magmus," Asvoria cooed. "So glad you could join us."

With a bellow of rage, the red dragon opened his mouth and let forth a burst of fire. Flames licked up the cave wall, blackening the stone with smoke, but Asvoria stood calmly. She had put up a protective spell in anticipation of this.

"Now, now," Asvoria said as the flames died away. "Is that anyway to treat the Dragon Queen?"

Cocking its head, the red's eyes fell into a look of confusion. "What Dragon Queen? Where?"

"Right here."

The young red snorted with laughter. "But you are male! Shouldn't you claim to be a Dragon King? And that still doesn't explain why in the Abyss you're on my territory!"

Growling, Asvoria leaped from the wall and landed snout to snout with Magmus. Baring teeth, she leaned forward. "I assure you, I am most decidedly female. And this is no longer your territory, dragon. A new reign is about to begin."

"You think you can take me on?" Magmus said with an angry flap of his wings. "You don't know who you're dealing with!"

Asvoria leaned back on her haunches. "And neither, apparently, do you."

Bunching up her muscular hind legs she leaped into the air and landed near her statues. Without looking back, she walked out of the stone room and into the outer caves. "Follow me."

"I will not!"

Asvoria stopped mid-step and turned her head slightly. "It wasn't a request." She stomped her great clawed foot on the cavern floor, sending a mystical jolt of energy coursing through the stone toward the red dragon. Jagged pieces of stone flew through the room and bounced off the red's hard scales.

Snarling, Magmus raced to follow with his mouth wide open. A burning inferno flared deep within the blackness of his throat. Unconcerned, Asvoria turned and continued her stroll through the outer tunnels.

She rounded a corner and entered another cavern, only slightly smaller than her throne room. There was no hole in the ceiling to allow light in here, and the cavern was filled with inky blackness. Ragged breaths sounded from the center of the room. Asvoria sunk into the shadows.

The enraged dragon scrambled through the caves behind her, blasting fire. In a flurry of flame and wing, he charged into the cavern and skidded to a stop. His head darted about, searching for Asvoria.

"Glad you decided to follow," she said as the red's eyes finally found her in the darkness. "I have something I want to show you."

Before Magmus could move, Asvoria whispered a spell, and torches all around the room flared to life. The cavern itself was stark, undecorated. But even if it had been covered in gold and jewels, it was unlikely anyone would have noticed. Instead, their eyes would immediately have been drawn to the black dragon tethered to the center of the room.

"What is this?" Magmus hissed.

The ancient black lay in the cavern, eyes half-open and gasping for breath. Hundreds of stone chains stretched from the floor and the ceiling to bind his wings tightly against his back and force his immense head to lay at an odd angle against the floor. Blinking in the sudden light, the black's hate-filled eyes met Asvoria's.

"Have you come to finish me, Sorceress?" he wheezed.

Asvoria didn't answer. Instead, wings held taut at her sides, she strolled to stand between Magmus and the black.

"This is Victant," she told the red. "He decided he didn't want to join me. And so I have decided to make him an example."

Magmus's eyes narrowed, but he didn't respond.

"As I tried to say earlier, my dear Magmus," Asvoria growled, "I am the Dragon Queen. I have more power than any dragon that's ever existed on this planet. Now, all I want is to bring our races together as one exalted species. But naturally there are those of us who won't want to join in. Like Victant here."

She lashed out with a back claw and kicked Victant in his unprotected belly. The ancient dragon winced.

"As with all creatures on Krynn, the gods have limited the dragons to certain traits that bind us," Asvoria went on. "And Magmus, you've proven thus far to be an exemplary red dragon. However, unless you care to share the fate that is about to befall Victant, I suggest you do some rethinking about your place in the world."

Magmus growled, but still he didn't speak.

Whispering a magical word, Asvoria turned to Victant. The chains uncoiled from his massive body and slithered across the cavern's floor before disappearing into the stone from where they had come.

Slowly, limbs trembling, the black lifted himself to stand his full height.

"I told you that you'd regret your dissension, dragon," Asvoria hissed as she rounded on her opponent.

Victant's features were hard, but his eyes betrayed an uncertainty that told Asvoria he wanted to flee. Typical black dragon, she thought. Never wants to fight someone he's not certain he can destroy.

Rage flooded Asvoria's thoughts. How could such a weak creature treat her with such condescension! Before she could stop herself, she reared back her head and let forth a stream of steaming acid.

The acid flowed, harmless as water, from Victant's scales. He laughed. "For someone who fancies herself a Dragon Queen, you don't know a lot about dragons. I am immune to acid."

Behind her, Magmus joined in Victant's laughter. "This is your example? Ha! I could destroy this black in seconds. Besides, I still don't understand why you call yourself a queen when you are most definitely male."

"I am FEMALE!" Asvoria roared and she leaped in the air. She slammed on top of Victant's back like a boulder. Unable to hold her weight, he collapsed to the floor. He snapped his head back and forth, trying to nip at her neck.

Digging her claws deep into the black's scales, Asvoria whispered an old spell. It was one she had created long ago, one that drew its power from a substance of which there was an abundance at the tip of her claws: dragon's blood.

Victant choked and he clenched his eyes closed. His whole body thrashed. Wings flapped, legs scrabbled against the stony floor, tail and neck whipped back and forth. Still Asvoria whispered.

Red and violet light shone beneath the dragon's scales. First a little and then more and more until his scales shuddered like leaves caught in a heavy wind. Victant's choking turned into guttural screams as he bucked up and down, trying to throw Asvoria off of him. Still the sorceress held on, still she cast her deadly magic.

Then, Victant shuddered. Scales exploded off his flesh, exposing muscle and bone. Blood seeped from his closed eyes and from his nostrils. Muffled bursting sounded from deep inside his belly.

After a moment, the light faded away. The black dragon collapsed to the cavern floor, dead.

Asvoria stayed clamped to the black's back, her wings flapping slowly. Then, cocking her head, she met Magmus's eye.

"Could you have done *that*?" she hissed.

The red dragon said nothing. Eyes narrowed, he backed slowly toward the cave's exit.

"You are unnatural," he said. "You are a demon dragon."

"Perhaps," Asvoria said. Pulling her claws free from Victant's back, she climbed off and stalked toward the red. Blood dripped from her claws, leaving a gory trail. "But I am to be your new ruler."

Grumbling deep within his throat, Magmus looked back and forth between Asvoria and the dead black dragon. "We shall see, Copper," he said. "We shall see."

Forgetting his territorial rage, the red dragon turned and left. Asvoria chuckled and shook her great head.

"That was quite the show, milady," Ophion said. Seeping out from the shadows, the shapeshifter came to stand beside Asvoria and bowed its head.

"He'll be mine," she said. "They'll all be mine."

"You are truly awe-inspiring, Dragon Queen."

"I know." Tilting her head, she regarded her shapeshifter with flashing violet eyes. "I am feeling confident, Ophion," she said. "I want to get this over with as soon as possible. I would like you to head down to the hills and integrate yourself in with those who would try and stop me."

"Yes, milady."

"Until then, I have much to do," she said. She turned to face the dead dragon and narrowed her eyes. "This is going to be a battle they'll never forget, my dear familiar. And it will be the last one they'll ever live to see."

With the force of her magical will, a connection coursed between herself and the dead dragon. His claws grasped at the air, his wings shuddered. Eyelids snapped open to reveal dark, empty sockets.

Asvoria smiled. "I will never be defeated."

21   A Gathering of Heroes

With each passing day, more dread filled Davyn's heart.

They had set out for the hills near Forestedge as soon as they could. After a quick stay at an inn so Catriona could wash and they could all have a good meal, they began their trip back south. Whatever laughter had been in the group drifted away as they neared the remains of the second village Asvoria's army had destroyed. Even though several days had gone by since they first passed, the smoke from the decimated villages still hadn't faded away. Twice as many undead creatures stood as eerie soldiers to guard the broken streets. Decaying skin fell from their yellowed bones. They did not move, but Asvoria's monsters still seemed much too alive.

Davyn had made them ignore the awful sight, but he knew it was all any of them could think about.

After a day's travel farther south, they finally reached the woods outside of Forestedge. But no one was in any hurry to leave the shelter of the trees. Instead, they set up camp for one last night before heading out to begin the final battle.

Davyn sat alone that night, keeping watch and staring at the sky. The field of stars was framed by the craggy shadows of the trees towering above him. He inhaled crisp air tainted with just a hint of fire smoke, taking in the scent of earth and leaves. He felt at home in the woods, safe and protected. The mingling smells brought back memories of his youth, and he clung to those images with all his might.

Beside him, a journal lay open. It wasn't his own, and in fact belonged a man that was long dead—Heiro Viranesh, the last descendent of Captain Viranesh to bear the title of Dragon Knight. He'd read the journal many times, and always he found nothing new, nothing that could help. But as the time to face Asvoria grew near, something told him to take another look.

The most he'd discovered was that the sword he wielded had some sort of magical power. There was discussion of its properties to unbind spells, but his eyes were weary and he found he couldn't concentrate on the sprawling letters.

"Davyn," someone whispered. Jolted from his thoughts, the ranger turned from the dark forest. A slender shadow passed in front of the glowing embers of the dying fire. Jirah.

"Hello," he said, then turned back to watch the woods. Adrenaline flooded his system, waking him.

"I'm sorry if I scared you," the girl said in hushed tones. Sitting down next to him, she scooted to be at his side.

"It's all right." Davyn scanned the trees for anything out of place. "Couldn't sleep?"

"No," she said. "I'm just worried, is all. And . . . I wanted to ask you something."

"All right."

Hands fidgeting, Jirah looked down. Her black hair shrouded her cheeks. "I think we're going to save Nearra. I really do. I know you can do it, that we can all do it. But I'm afraid what will happen afterward. I don't know if Nearra will be well enough to break the curse."

"Oh?" Leaves rustled, and Davyn's hands tensed on his bow.

A small white rabbit leaped from a bush and he relaxed.

"Will you come with me?" Jirah said, her hand suddenly on his, her eyes boring into his own. "Will you promise to help us? For . . . for me?"

Davyn met her pleading eyes.

"First things first, all right? With Nearra out of commission, Asvoria can't use the Trinistyr to gain access to the gods' powers, even if she knew about it. We can worry about the rest, once . . . once we've won."

"All right." Shivering, the girl got to her feet. Her fingers climbed up her arms to hug herself. "I think I'm going to go lay down."

"Sleep well."

With a quick wave, Jirah wandered off and Davyn turned away from the fire. Someone snorted behind him.

"Yes, Maddoc?" Davyn said.

Robes rustled as the old man rose, but Davyn did not turn around to face him. "I know after everything that has happened you're likely never to trust me again. But perhaps I can offer some fatherly advice before this battle is done and we part ways."

Davyn said nothing.

Maddoc went on, his voice low and gravelly. "You're starting to get in over your head. Something all young men are apt to do, I suppose. Be a bit more observant, son. You're good at finding tracks, hunting beasts, and fighting with enemies, but friendship and love is still new to you. From what I've seen, your emotional ties could prove to be your undoing. Be wary."

Again Davyn said nothing. He heard the old man sigh and lay back down.

After a moment, Davyn shook his head. "Thank you for the advice," he whispered.

Steady, rhythmic breathing was his only response. Fingering his bow, Davyn turned back to watch the trees.

Writing like restless spirits, a thick fog swirled between the hills. Davyn led his friends out of the trees and past scrub brushes and boulders. The fog hid the remains of Forestedge from view. Davyn thanked Paladine for small favors.

Heavy clouds covered the high peaks of the Vingaard Mountains. Scavenger birds flew low over the unseen village, cawing in their hunger for carrion.

Sindri scrabbled to Davyn's right, using his hoopak to help him climb. Catriona strolled at his left, Aegis unsheathed and clenched tight in her hands. Hazy, distant shadows floated between indistinct tents and he could just make out the glow of shrouded fires.

"There you are," a familiar voice said. As though appearing from the shadows, the two Messengers approached. Janeesa smiled and Tylari scowled, the same as before.

"We've been waiting," Janeesa went on. "How did your mission go?"

"Good," Davyn said. "I am glad to see you are well. Did you get messages to our friends?"

With a flip of her hair, Janeesa gestured behind her with a flourish. "Why don't you ask them yourself?"

"Ah, if it isn't my old nemesis, Sindri Suncatcher."

The voice was deep, booming, and instantly familiar. Davyn felt a rush of hope.

Appearing from the mist behind the Messengers came a figure seven feet tall. Robes as black as the short, glossy fur that covered his muscled body hung from his broad shoulders. Baring white teeth on a wide, bull-like face in what Davyn hoped was his version of a smile, he stopped before the companions and bowed.

"Jax!" Sindri cried and clapped in glee. "It's been so long! Remember when you thought I stole your money, or when we fought Slean and almost died? Oh, those were good times."

"Seems like you Messengers worked out after all," Mudd said, coming to Davyn's side as Sindri rounded on the minotaur, positively bouncing in excitement. "Did everyone else come?"

"Most," Tylari muttered. His eyes darted back and forth, as though searching for something.

"Thank you," Davyn nodded his head toward Janeesa. "You have been a great help."

"It wasn't a problem. But we must run, our father is around here somewhere and he's expecting us." She grabbed Tylari's arm and the two Messengers disappeared as quickly as they had come.

Davyn ran to shake Jax's thick hand. "Glad you could make it."

"I fought by your side," Jax said. "You saved my life and helped me find my destiny. I owe you friends a great debt. Even if my fellow clerics had declined to come, I would have come myself." Using his axe to point, he gestured in the direction the Messengers had disappeared. "Strange children, those two. But they have earned my respect for traveling so far on your behalf."

"As honorable as ever," Catriona said.

"That he is." A pretty young woman with a gentle smile stepped out from behind him. Brown hair fell to her neck, around which hung a silver pendant shaped in the looping form of a figure eight laying on its side—the symbol of the goddess of healing, Mishakal. Light blue robes flowed to her feet and she held a long staff.

"Nysse," Davyn said. "It is wonderful to see you again."

"Oh, yes!" Sindri cried. "How is everyone at the Temple of the Holy Orders of the Stars? Did many other clerics come? Did Slean's body rise from the dead? That seems to be happening a lot lately."

Nysse chuckled. "We are doing fine, my children. We will have to discuss this at a later time, however."

"Aww," Sindri pouted.

Davyn quickly introduced Rina, Jirah, Mudd, and Maddoc. After calming Jax down enough to explain that Maddoc was no longer sending dragons and goblins after them and was, in fact, helping them, the man-bull sheathed his battleaxe and listened to the rest of their tale.

Nysse in turn explained what had happened since they'd left the hills to find the Aegis. As promised, the Messengers had sent word of the impending battle. Nysse wasn't sure who had come, but tents had sprung up almost every night since she'd arrived. In the meantime, she and her fellow clerics had kept busy offering prayers to the gods to help the refugees in their time of need. She'd done nothing the past several days except heal the wounded using the powers Mishakal granted her.

"Jax and I left the temple as soon as we heard word," Nysse went on. "We brought some of the younger clerics with us. Feandan is making plans back at the temple with Gunna and Pedar. More clerics may come if the need is great."

For the first time, Davyn actually felt true hope. Jax and Nysse had come, as had others, and they had the Aegis. His mind raced.

"Let's head into the camp," he said. "We can find out who else is here and start getting ready."

Nysse and Jax led the way, with Sindri still pestering them for their tales. Mudd raced to Davyn's side, a wide grin on his face.

Makeshift tents seemed to sprout up around them as they walked deeper into the foggy valley. Patched with colorful cloth, the tents seemed like the canopy of trees in fall. There were more traditional tents further back and several lean-tos scattered here and there. Between it all were small bonfires that did little to pierce the gloomy fog around them. Pigs roasted on spits above their embers, filling the air with hearty smells.

There were far more people here than when they had left. Survivors from the attack farther north had migrated down here, and there seemed to be a lot of people from other villages who had come to help. The outer circle of tents housed heavily muscled men and stout women armed with pitchforks and axes, the inner tents the young and the elderly. Some nodded in recognition as the companions passed.

Past these tents they reached the camp of the outsiders.

"Hey, it's Noxon and Petrie!" Mudd shouted as he recognized old friends from Potter's Mill. "And Goddard and Whedon. I wonder if Set-ai came?"

"I doubt it," Davyn said. "Shemnara probably made him stay home. But I bet he had a hand in rounding up so many of these people here."

"I'm going to go talk to them, see who's in charge so we can get organized," Mudd said.

"I'll go with you," Catriona said. Without looking back, she strode forward to the camp of Potter's Mill's heroes.

"Davyn, look," Rina said as she came to his side. "Is that who I think it is?"

Standing next to one of the bonfires, hands on his waist and laughing maniacally, was a tall man with unruly black hair. From a distance he looked normal enough, but Davyn knew close up his eyes would betray a not so small amount of insanity.

"Cirill," Davyn said. "I'm surprised he came."

"I'm not," Rina said. "You saved him and the freeholders from a lifetime of imprisonment. Seems to me they owe you a bit of a debt."

Davyn studied Cirill's men, his eyes falling on a young man with straw-colored hair. He couldn't recall the man's name, but he recognized him as the surgeon that had amputated Set-ai's arm.

"We should go talk to them, too," Rina said. She started

strolling toward the group. Davyn was about to follow when he caught a flash of chestnut-brown fur.

"Jirah, you go with her," he said. "There's someone I need to see."

Jirah frowned, but did as she was told.

Davyn waded through the milling people toward the centaur trying her best to hide between the tents. A beautiful mix of equine body with a slender female torso arching up where a horse's head would normally be, she took in the scene with calm blue eyes. She flipped her brown hair out of her face and dug into the dirt with one of her front hooves.

"Ayanti," Davyn said as he came to her side.

"Finally, a familiar face." Flicking her tail, Ayanti leaned down and placed her hand on Davyn's head. "You're getting so tall! If I didn't know any better, I'd think you were a man and not the boy who was my old partner in crime."

Davyn's cheeks burned, and he looked down. "It's good to see you, Ayanti. I wasn't sure you'd come."

She shrugged. "I wasn't sure I was going to, either. I'm not a fighter. But when the Messengers told me about Raedon . . ." She shook her head. "I had to come and help."

"You left your beasts at home?"

Ayanti nodded. "They're in good hands."

Taking her hand, Davyn led her out from her little alcove. "Come on, we can talk as we go. I need to start speaking with some of the leaders here, make plans."

Her eyes darted back and forth as Davyn lead her out. "That's exactly what those knights have been doing. Maybe you should talk to them?"

Davyn furrowed his brow. "Knights? What knights?"

She pointed past a group of would-be soldiers practicing fighting techniques, and Davyn saw him. Tall and imposing, with a body as broad as the side of a house and covered head to toe in decorated plate armor, was a Solamnic knight. Etched on his breast plate was a symbol of a crown, and he held his helmet in his hands. He nodded sagely to a woman he was in deep discussion with. Long brown hair flowed free and a thick moustache quivered above his lip as he spoke.

The knight turned to the side, revealing the woman. A fur-lined robe hung from her delicate shoulders, smooth white-blond fell hair to the small of her back. Sharp features regarded the knight from a pale face as he spoke. Her eyes were an icy blue.

Vael. The baroness of the long hidden village of Tarrent. Elidor's beloved.

With Ayanti at his side, Davyn made a path between the milling villagers straight toward the baroness. Only then did he notice that some of the men and women around them weren't entirely human. Their eyes, their ears, their builds revealed the influences of ogre and elven ancestry, among others Davyn couldn't quite place.

"Vael," he said as he approached. The woman's eyes widened in surprise, but the rest of her features remained calm. Resting a hand on the knight's shoulder, she moved to greet Davyn.

"We have come," she said.

"I am glad for it," Davyn said with a respectful bow. "I know it must have been difficult to convince your people to leave the shelter of the village to come and fight."

Vael nodded, white hair an icy stream flowing past her shoulders. "We knew Asvoria would come for us in the end. We are the desscendants of her old slaves and she would not suffer to let us live. And . . . I could not stand back while Elidor's murderers went free."

Davyn sighed. "The Messengers gave you word of his death, then."

Hand trembling, the baroness closed her eyes. Then, with a breath, she opened them to meet Davyn's gaze. "They did. And now we are here to help as we are needed."

"Ahem."

Behind them, the knight crossed his arms and raised an eyebrow appraisingly. "Shall I be introduced? But only if you wish it, Baroness," he added quickly and respectfully.

Shaking her head, Vael stepped aside to let Davyn and the knight meet face-to-face. Davyn heard Ayanti shift from hoof to hoof behind him, but she said nothing.

"Of course," Vael said. "This is Sir Christoph uth Witdel of the Solamnic knights. And this is Davyn."

The knight's other eyebrow raised. He tilted his head. "Davyn. I've heard much about you and your companions the last few days. We've come to help and, apparently, clean up the mess you've made."

Before Davyn could register the insult, Christoph brushed past him. "Come on, young adventurer," he said with no lack of sarcasm. "Gather your friends. We've got much to discuss."

22 BATTLE PLANS

Davyn had rounded up the leaders of the various groups, and now Sir Christoph uth Witdel led the way. Catriona and Davyn, Vael and her imposing half-ogre guard, Cirill and a representative each from Potter's Mill and the destroyed villages followed. The knight took them to the outskirts of the camp, where Catriona saw an awning atop the highest hill acting as a makeshift outlook. Two small red and gold flags fluttered in the wind at its sides, the symbol of the kingfisher emblazoned upon them.

A Solamnic knight wearing dented plate armor leaned over a table that sat beneath the awning. Stroking a thick black moustache, he studied a map spread out before him. His hair lay matted against his skull, and his helm sat askew at his feet. A shield with the symbol of a crown etched across it leaned against the table's leg.

"Raynard!" Christoph called as they neared. "Any news?"

The knight at the awning stood up straight and then shook his head. "None, sir. There's been no activity since the two dragons flew into the mountains several days ago."

"Thank you, Raynard." Sword clanking against his metal-clad legs, Christoph went to the awning and studied the map laid out on the table. Lopsided stones had been set on its corners, but its free edges still flapped in the wind.

"Go back to the camp," Christoph commanded Raynard. "Tell the others I will want to see them later this evening."

Raynard nodded and did as he was told. Picking up his helmet and his shield, he raced down the hill, his eyes meeting Catriona's for just a moment as he passed. Recognition flashed on his face, but he didn't stop to say anything.

"Come, take a look," the older Solamnic knight said. Bowing respectfully to Vael, Davyn let her go first, then followed at her heels. Catriona stayed by his side as the others crowded around the map.

"This is where we are," he said, pointing to several small half circles meant to represent the hills. "Here is the river between the two villages that have been destroyed. We've been studying the mountains for days and the only activity was the arrival of the two dragons."

"Was one of them copper?" Davyn asked.

Christoph shook his head. "One black, then a day later a red. The red left shortly after it arrived, the black is still there, as far as we know. But we believe this place to be the location of the dragon that attacked these two villages."

"Not a dragon," Catriona said. "A sorceress."

"Yes, I've heard tales." Christoph leaned back on his heels and regarded Catriona with appraising eyes. "Interesting sword you have there."

She nodded.

"You look familiar," the knight went on. "And I don't believe I've known many striking, six foot tall women warriors in my time. Have we met before?"

Catriona shook her head. "No. But you may have met my aunt. People used to tell us we looked like sisters."

Stiffening suddenly, the knight's eyes hardened. "Leyana. You're Leyana's niece."

Catriona nodded.

"I was there at your trial," he went on. "I'm surprised to see you fighting."

"With all due respect, sir," the man from Potter's Mill said, "Catriona has proven to be a great warrior. She helped rid our town of a vicious beast and she personally killed the bandit king that was sending it after us."

Rounding on the man, the knight peered at him down his nose. "What is your name?"

"Blucas, sir."

"Well, Blucas," Christoph said, "I'm not one to make up my mind on the basis of rumors." Without waiting for a response, he turned back to Catriona. Some feeling flared within her chest, something deep and pounding that threatened to overtake her conviction. Opening her mind, she let more of the sword's power flow in to force it back down.

"I was told of a Catriona Goodlund being offered a chance to rejoin the knighthood after doing some great deed in Palanthas," he went on. "I suppose that's you?"

Catriona nodded.

"Interesting," Christoph said, stroking his moustache. "Usually when a squire fails so miraculously, a second chance isn't granted."

Anger started to flow through her limbs. The Aegis pulsed in her hand.

"Davyn," Catriona said, ignoring the knight. "I think I'm going to go back down to the camps. Come get me when you're done discussing things."

Turning on her heels, she stormed away from the awning. A deep urge to plunge her sword deep into Sir Christoph uth Witdel's heart threatened to overwhelm her, but she pushed it down.

The murderous impulse had came from the sword, she knew. At that moment, she couldn't find it in herself to care.

"Once the last symbol is carved into Asvoria's chest, then you'll begin the spell. Don't forget to enunciate the last syllable of this word here." Maddoc pointed to the spellbook and Sindri nodded. "If you emphasize the first syllable the spell may still work, but not as fast, and we need to be quick."

"I understand." Sindri squirmed beneath the older man's watchful eye. "We've been over this a million times already. I want to go talk to Jax some more."

Maddoc sighed and leaned back against the boulder they'd sat beneath. "Don't you think this is a bit more important?"

Of course he thought so, but Sindri only shrugged, eyes darting about. He felt restless, his limbs full of so much energy he was quite certain he could do a dozen back flips if he wanted to. He was about to get up and try when he saw Catriona storm down from the hills where the knight had led Davyn and a bunch of other people. Her face was stone, her eyes flared with anger. The Aegis flashed green in her hands.

Rina ran to greet the warrior as she made her way through the villagers, but Catriona didn't seem to notice and brushed past. For a moment, the elf girl stood and watched her go, shaking her head in confusion. Then Jirah came up behind her, whispered something in her ear, and walked on to be swallowed up by the crowd. Rina's head darted back and forth, trying to find the black-haired girl, but she was already gone. Her head fell and her eyes flashed with hurt.

Sindri looked away, not understanding what he had just seen. The anticipation for the upcoming battle was enough to drive him insane and he couldn't concentrate on anything for more than a few moments.

He still saw flashes of the spell Asvoria had cast on him in those final moments before she tossed him from the balcony. He still felt a deep anger at that betrayal, and he wanted to hurt her, badly. He couldn't remember ever wanting to hurt anyone ever in his whole life, but now it was almost all that he could think about.

"Maddoc," he said. "I want to look at the dark spells again."

The former wizard raised an eyebrow. He started to speak, then quickly looked down as several men clad in makeshift armor marched by. Motioning Sindri closer, he pulled another book from his pack.

"Of course," he said in a low voice. "What sort of spell are you interested in?"

Sindri swallowed and thought for a moment. "I want the one that will cause the most damage," he said. "And I want it to hurt."

Unreadable emotions flickered in Maddoc's eyes, but he said nothing. Instead, he smiled and opened the book to a page in the middle.

"I think," he said, "that I know the perfect one."

Davyn clenched his teeth as Christoph droned on. The knight seemed unwilling to listen to anything he had to say.

". . . As soon as we have done this, we will report to the council and give our findings. They'll then decide how many knights to deploy to take care of the situation. At that time, we will be outfitted with dragonlances and will be able to handle the dragon with ease."

They sat in a circle near the awning. Christoph leaned forward on his knees, gesturing to emphasize his plan. Cirill, Blucas, and the two men from the destroyed villages listened intently. Vael leaned back against her stoic half-ogre guard, fanning herself as she stared at the gray sky.

The man from Forestedge nodded vigorously. "That sounds like it could be for the best. Everyone below is prepared to fight the monsters, but if it can be avoided . . ."

"No," Davyn said, his hands clenched at his side.

"I agree," Christoph went on, ignoring Davyn. "This would undoubtedly lead to the least amount of casualties."

"No!" Davyn said again.

"I beg your pardon?" Christoph said, rising to his feet. He glared at Davyn. "As I already said, we are here to clean up your mess, young man. You would do well to listen to your elders."

Davyn stood almost nose-to-nose with the knight. "You don't know anything that's been going on." His hands trembled, but his voice held steady. "We don't have time to get more knights here. We have what we have. Any moment now Asvoria could decide to attack. She has a shapeshifting familiar, did you know that? It could be right here, right now, spying."

Everyone peered at one another, suddenly suspicious. Cirill made a show of scooting away from Blucas.

"Not even as one of us," Davyn went on. "It could be a bug crawling on a blade of grass. Doesn't matter. What does matter is that every day Asvoria is left to her own devices is another day that she learns more about her powers. She's undoubtedly growing stronger by the minute."

Forcing himself to calm down, Davyn leaned back. "I have friends held captive up there. One is the dragon you want to slay with the dragonlances. He's a kindhearted dragon whose body was stolen by Asvoria. The other is an innocent girl. My friends and I can save both of them, and we can destroy this army at the same time. Despite what you think of us or of me, we will stop this." Davyn lifted his chin, his lips tightened into a line. "And we're going to fight through those monsters and go in, whether you help us or not."

Davyn took in a slow breath. On the ground, Vael adjusted her robes and sat up straighter. A small smile twitched at the edge of her lips.

For a moment, the knight could do nothing but stare. Then his eyes narrowed. "You would have me lead an army of untrained villagers against a horde of monsters so that a bunch of children can rush into a cave to fight a possessed dragon? Are you mad?"

"I guess I am," Davyn said.

"I—"

He didn't get a chance to finish speaking. Shouts sounded from below, and the group turned to find the knight from earlier racing up the hill.

"Sir!" the knight called. Huffing for breath, he came to Christoph's side and pointed toward the village. "Something's happening."

Davyn turned to follow the knight's pointed finger. The fog had burned away as mid-day came upon them and he could see that the mismatched monsters and the corpses of the villagers had moved. Instead of staring with no awareness and standing still in the abandoned streets and between the blackened shells of the buildings, now they had shifted to face south.

They began to march.

"They're coming to the hills," Vael said, her voice unwavering. "They're coming to destroy us before we can attack them. Davyn's right, we can't wait for the Solamnics to come and save us."

Rounding on Christoph, Davyn grabbed the older man's arm. "With all due respect, sir, there's no more time to argue."

"I say—" Christoph started to say, but Davyn gripped his arm harder, shaking it.

"No, listen to me!" he demanded, his voice firm, his eyes hardened. To Davyn's surprise, the knight fell silent. "You're right. The knights are better trained for this than I am or will likely ever be. If we had time to bring in a cavalry of knights, I'd let them come. But only my friends and I can actually stop Asvoria. You and your knights round up the people who want to fight. Work with Vael, Blucas, Cirill and the others to organize a defense with their people and the villagers. Protect the clerics so they can heal the wounded. No matter what, my friends and I have to get through that village and into the mountains."

The knight scoffed. Blue eyes opened wide, his moustache quivered. "You're giving me orders?"

"I guess I am," Davyn said.

Shaking his head, the knight let out a bitter laugh. "Fine, then, young ranger. Looks like we have no choice if we don't want more innocent people to die. Get your friends ready. I will corral the rest. We will meet at the bottom of the hills as soon as possible. And may Paladine help us all."

Nodding, Davyn let go of the knight's arm, and they both turned and ran down the hill. Someone raced to match his pace, and he turned to find Vael's ice-colored eyes watching him with interest. Her half-ogre guard took wide steps behind her.

"For a long time my opinions of Elidor were clouded by hurt," she said as they raced past boulders and neared the camp. "But the both of you proved me wrong when last we met. I think he'd be proud of you."

Davyn nodded, but said nothing. He appreciated her words, but deep down he knew the truth. Christoph was right—it was his fault Elidor was dead and all this was happening. He was just trying to clean up the mess he made before too many more were hurt. Before Nearra was lost forever.

They reached the camp and separated. Vael went to her people and Davyn raced to round up his friends.

This was it. The final battle was about to begin.

CHAPTER 23

THE DEAD VILLAGE

The makeshift army stood in long rows at the foot of the hills. Ahead of them on the misty plain, between the hills and the village, the undead army stalked forward. The mismatched beasts were now joined by the scarred, mutilated, walking bodies of the fallen villagers. They moved forward, unhurried and steady, their footsteps beating out a constant, inhumanly perfect rhythm.

It wouldn't be long before the two sides met and the battle began. Only they weren't going to wait for the monsters to get to them first.

Sir Christoph uth Witdel rode back and forth in front of the makeshift army on a proud brown steed. The fighters stood in groups behind their respective leaders. The refugees' skin was dirty, their clothing torn, but their faces held the most resolve of anyone's. Davyn, Catriona, Jax and the others stood together in the center, with Vael and her people to their left and Cirill and his men to their right. The Solamnics, the only ones with horses, stood between the groups, heads high and polished armor glinting in the hazy light.

Despite being against this plan, Christoph dived into the role of a general with gusto. He shouted out commands and words of encouragement, but Davyn couldn't pay attention. His breathing and his pounding heart were all he could hear.

"Most important of all," Christoph shouted as he brought his horse before Davyn and the companions, "is that these people be kept safe. It is vital to our success that they reach the mountains unharmed. Our job is not to kill these unkillable monsters, but to help those with the power to destroy their creator."

Taking in a calming breath, Davyn turned to his left and met Vael's eye. The baroness stood in front of her guards and volunteer soldiers, a long, thin blade resting in her slender hand. She nodded gravely and turned back to listen to the knight's commands.

Heavy footsteps sounded on the soft grass behind him, and Davyn turned to find Ayanti standing near, her hands crossed in front of her. She bowed her head and looked down.

"Davyn, I want to help," she said.

"You don't have to." Near them Catriona flexed the Aegis and studied the sheet of parchment with the mystic symbols. Rina nocked an arrow, her face firm and unreadable. Mudd clenched his sword and muttered to himself, his chest rising and falling in quick bursts.

"No, I want to," she said. "I don't want to fight, but there's got to be some way I can help, something I can do for you."

Jirah paced back and forth in small circles, her hands fidgeting with her clothing and her hair. Sindri stood next to Maddoc, the two whispering their own final plans. Beyond them Jax raised his battle-axe high, Cirill and his men their swords.

Davyn's pack weighed heavy on his shoulders, and he realized how Ayanti could help.

"Here," he said. Resting the Dragon Knight's sword in the grass, he opened his pack and pulled free the glowing green orb. "This holds Raedon's soul. I was supposed to carry it up the mountain, but it'll be easier to defend myself if I don't have the pack weighing me down."

"You want me to carry Raedon's soul?" Ayanti asked.

"It seems fitting," Davyn said. "And it'd be a great help."

With gentle hands, Ayanti reached out and took the glass ball. Caressing it with her fingers, she stared deeply into its smoky green interior. "Thank you," she whispered. "I won't let you down."

"I know you won't." Davyn handed her the pack. She put the orb back safely inside and looped the straps over her shoulders.

Davyn tensed and turned to look forward. Like a swarm of insects, the black forms of the monster army trudged forward, closer and closer. Still Christoph rode in front of them calling out instructions.

"As soon as I give word," he shouted above his beating of his horse's hooves, "you are to fall back and protect these hills. Once those who are going to the mountain are safely through, there is no need to be on the battlefield. Retreat, friends, and pray that this ends well. We are watched over by Paladine, and he will see us through."

A murmur bubbled up from the crowd. Silver sword held high, Vael stepped from the front line. Turning, she faced her people.

"People of Tarrent!" she called. "Descendants of Asvoria's slaves! Raise your weapons!"

The mixed-race warriors hefted their swords and axes and let out a roaring cheer. Following Vael's lead, Cirill leaped from the crowd, his own sword aimed skyward.

"Freeholders, ready!"

More shouts and hollers. Blucas stepped forward to do the same, the two leaders of the destroyed villages close behind. People let out cries of war and stamped their feet, trying to shake off their nerves and find it within themselves to battle these fearless foes.

Davyn found himself raising his voice in this chorus of defiance along with everyone else. He raised his sword high, and out of the corner of his eye saw his friends do the same. Catriona's sword sparkled and a jolt of green lightning shot into the sky, its crack booming throughout the hills.

"Solamnics!" Christoph cried last, his deep voice thunderous even over the roar of the crowd. "Ready!"

The cries of war reached a crescendo as the handful of knights joined in.

"Attack!"

The crowd surged forward, an immense wave rushing to flood the open land. Grunting and shouting surrounded Davyn. The smell of sweaty flesh and churning dirt filled his nostrils. Unable to see anything but his fellow warriors, he let himself be carried forward.

For a long moment, all he could hear was the labored breathing of those around him and the thumping of hundreds upon hundreds of boots. Then, distantly, he heard a clang of steel against bone, and someone shout in pain. Then, more clangs, more shouts. The unearthly yowling of the zombies soon roared as loudly as the villagers' cries of war. Davyn swallowed, tried to ignore the sounds, and pressed on.

Christoph rode his steed through the crowd, shouting orders above the noise that Davyn couldn't hear as he lanced down with his sword. Someone nearby started crying and tried to run back through the current of warriors, a losing battle in and of itself.

"Davyn!" Ayanti's voice wavered with fear, and he turned to find her wide-eyed behind him. Rearing onto her hind legs, she clutched the pack tight. "DAVYN!"

"I'm here!" Gripping her around her back, he led her forward. "Don't worry, I'm here. Keep moving."

Someone screamed and Davyn turned to see the Urkhan worm rearing back from the crowd, a man clutched in its mismatched claws. Towering above them, it carried the terrified man up its body. The slits of its mouth opened and closed in anticipation.

"No!" a woman shouted. "Help him!"

Davyn turned away, trying to focus on moving forward, trying not to flinch as the man's screams ended much too soon.

Frantically, he turned left and right, but he couldn't find his friends. All he saw were brown clothes and flashing swords and monstrous claws. All he heard were grunts of effort and shouts of triumph and the howls of the attacking dead. He shoved through, leading Ayanti forward, trying not to be swallowed by the crowd.

"Davyn!" Looking up, he saw the outpost knight forcing his steed through battle. "This way!"

"Come on!" Davyn called to Ayanti, and they shoved past two men trying to hack apart a goblin. They leaped out of the way as a giant bird missing half its feathers landed heavily against a woman's chest, knocking her to the ground.

Then, ahead, he saw Catriona. She let out a war cry and lashed out with the Aegis. The sword sliced through several of the monsters at once with ease. It flashed with light. Beside her, Jax raised his battleaxe and chopped with steady precision.

Davyn and Ayanti pushed their way through the falling bodies and saw Rina, Mudd, Jirah, Maddoc, and Sindri already there, standing on the border where field grass met stone street. Christoph rode up beside them, with several of his knights surrounding him.

Suddenly, it seemed, broken walls rose around them and jagged glass crunched beneath their boots. Gaunt, unseeing faces of zombie villagers stared out from blackened windows. Opening bloodstained lips, they moaned and started forward to attack.

"Papa!" someone cried from behind them. "No, Papa! It's me!"

"Ayanti, just focus on walking," Davyn said. "I'm going to be right here."

The centaur nodded, her eyes wide with fear, and Davyn raced past Mudd and Jirah to come to Catriona's side.

The redheaded warrior snarled and hefted her blade back. With one quick move, she stabbed it forward, deep into the chest of a young woman whose face had been horribly burned. The zombie woman's eyes stared, glassy and doll-like, and she continued to moan as she tried to move forward. Disgusted, Catriona let out a shout, hefted her sword free, and shoved the woman aside.

"The person responsible for this deserves a swift and painful death," Jax said. With a grunt, he swung his axe to decapitate an attacker.

Davyn nodded. "I agree." He sliced backward with his sword, impaling what had once been an old man but was now little more than an envelope of skin covering brittle bones. He let out a yell and flipped his sword forward, throwing the zombie into the side of what had once been a pub.

"Here, Davyn," Christoph said, slowing his horse to match his pace. He reached out a hand. "Come up."

Taking the knight's hand, Davyn placed his boot on the horse's flank and hefted himself atop its back. Hanging onto the sides of the older man's belt, he looked ahead.

Up ahead was the center of the town, the devastated market. Stacks of vegetables had rotted into a sick green paste. Beyond the mess stood a tall brown arch. Painted across its top were the words "Forestedge Pass."

"Through there is the trail leading up," Christoph called back. "That's where we have to go."

Davyn nodded and started to say something, then shouted as clammy hands clawed at his leg. Looking down he saw black eyes glaring up at him out of a fleshless face, stringy black hair hanging from its scalp like dead seaweed on an ocean-side rock.

He thrashed with his boot, but the creature would not let go. Another hand grabbed him, pulling at his trousers, wrenching his leg back and forth as though trying to tear it from his body. Lashing out with the sword, he knocked one of the former humans away, but more came. They clutched at the horse and the steed whinnied.

"Whoa, girl," Christoph said, but the smell of the dead creatures had disturbed the horse and she bucked up before rearing back. Davyn lost his grip and fell into the waiting arms of Asvoria's zombies.

The creatures descended, smothering him with their putrid flesh. They scratched at his cheeks and his arms. Davyn yelled, his throat scraping with the noise, and he swung his sword in wild arcs.

"Davyn!" someone cried. Past the swinging arms he saw Rina trying to dive through the monsters to reach him.

"No!" he said. "Go! Leave me, I'll be fine!" It was a lie, he knew it, but if he were to die he didn't want to take Rina with him. Not after her brother had already been lost.

Rina seemed to disappear and a strong, gauntlet-covered hand reached through the monsters and grabbed his own. Hefting him forward, the hand pulled Davyn free of his captors.

"Thank you," Davyn said as he gasped for air.

The owner of the hand, Christoph, nodded, his face stern. "We're almost there."

Shoving past more undead villagers, Davyn followed Christoph through the market. Rotten meat squished beneath his feet. He leaped over fallen carts. Ahead he saw Catriona shout in anger as she sliced through poles holding up awnings, dropping the cloth onto her foes and incapacitating them. She was almost to the arch.

Rounding corners and ducking between the arms of his attackers, he was there himself. Miraculously, so were his companions, some of the knights, and Jax.

"Up, up, up!" Davyn cried as he neared. "Go!"

Christoph was at his heels, his armor clanking as he ran.

"Retreat!" he called over his shoulder. "We made it! Call back to retreat!"

Davyn and Christoph raced through the arch to follow his friends. Davyn was relieved to see Ayanti there as well, making her way up the stony path at Jax's side.

Not daring to look back, Davyn climbed up the slope to where Asvoria lay in wait.

CHAPTER

24   THE DRAGON'S LAIR

Asvoria opened her eyes and gasped for air.

The magic flowing through her dragon body was intoxicating. It flooded her mind with waves of pleasure. At the same time, her energy began to ebb.

The battle raged on below. She could feel her army winning. It was almost as though she'd killed the enemies herself. She felt her undead army's claws tearing into flesh. She cackled as the blood flowed.

And now, the fools were retreating back to the hills, fleeing from her advancing creatures. "There will be no escape," she hissed.

Her head snapped to attention. She stopped and listened. Voices echoed deep within her caves. A dozen heartbeats pounded in her ears. She sensed magic.

There was something else, too. A warm, familiar presence.

Turning to look over her golden throne, she regarded the girl who still lay motionless and corpse-like. "Looks like your friends have arrived," Asvoria whispered. "But I have a few surprises in store."

Flapping her wings in contentment, she settled on her

haunches atop the cool metal of her golden throne, closed her eyes, and sent a surge of magic to the most recent addition to her army.

No one dared breathe as they entered the cave.

The tunnel was wide and tall, though narrow by dragon standards. Stalactites jutted down from the cavernous roof and stalagmites rose from the stony floor like rows of giant, shredding teeth.

The companions walked slowly through the cave's opening, weapons held ready. Davyn, Catriona, and Christoph were in the lead. Behind them, Davyn heard Jax's heavy, snorting breath and Ayanti's clip-clopping hooves.

They strode forward in silence. Gray light faded away as they walked deeper and deeper into the tunnel, their shadows long and thin in front of them. Cool air wound past the natural stone pillars, drying the sweat that coursed down their cheeks.

Then, just as the natural daylight began to fade away completely, they rounded a bend in the tunnel's twisting path. Ahead, the light of dozens of orange flames flickered, waiting.

"Do you think that's her lair?" Jirah whispered.

Davyn shrugged.

Gesturing with his head for them to follow, Christoph led the way.

The light came from a wide, empty cavern. Unlike the tunnel, the stone was devoid of any natural pillars. In fact, it seemed smoothed to an unnatural perfection. Metal sconces were embedded in the stony walls all around the cavern, holding torches that blazed with orange flame. The shadows of the companions danced behind them. Davyn swallowed as he saw trickling trails of dried blood near the center of the room.

"There's nothing," Mudd whispered. "Maybe she isn't here."

The crackling of the torches and the companion's labored

breathing was all anyone could hear. Davyn's heart beat so loud he was certain the noise was echoing around them.

Then, in the shadows, something rustled.

"What was that?" Jirah yelped. The knights shushed her and she bowed her head.

Quiet and tense, everyone listened. For a moment, there was nothing, then, again, a rustling of hard scales against stone, a clacking of claws against a hard surface.

"She's coming," Rina said.

"Back up," Christoph commanded. "Everyone back up toward the outer tunnel. We want to give her the least amount of space possible to attack us."

Without a word, everyone complied. Not daring to run lest they catch her attention, they took slow, silent steps. Ayanti's hooves continued to make tiny, echoing clomps and she winced with each noise, her eyes pleading with them to forgive her.

Then, just as they stepped back into the safety of the tunnel, the creature appeared.

The black dragon seeped out of the darkness and strode to the center of the cavern. Its claws clicked with each step, its wings shuddered at its side.

"The black dragon," Christoph whispered. "It's the black dragon we saw fly in here several days ago."

Something was terribly wrong with the dragon. Patches of its scales were gone, revealing gray muscle that tensed and stretched with each step. Its black eyes were dim and dark.

No, Davyn realized. Its eyes weren't black at all. The creature had no eyes, just two empty hollows where eyes should be. Blood had dried on its cheeks like fallen tears, showing up flat and dull against its glossy black scales.

"It's another zombie." Catriona said. Her face was tight and focused.

"What sort of creature has the power to kill a dragon and raise it from the dead?" one of the knights whispered, incredulous.

"Asvoria," Davyn said.

"How are we supposed to get past?" Mudd asked.

"We will destroy it," Jax said, his voice gruff and full of conviction. "It will fall to our blades."

"Now, let's not be rash," Christoph said. Turning to Maddoc, the knight studied the old man head to toe. "You are a mage?"

Maddoc's lips lifted into a partial smile. "Of sorts."

"I'm a wizard," Sindri announced.

Christoph ignored him. "Is there something you can do to get us past this beast?" he asked Maddoc.

"My kender friend and I can try," Maddoc said with a respectful nod. "But it will take time."

As they spoke, Jirah wandered farther and farther away from the cavern and the zombie dragon. Davyn saw her back around a pillar, her arms shaking, her eyes glinting.

Then she screamed.

Immediately everyone raised their weapons and the black-haired girl ran back. Stumbling into Davyn's arms, she pointed behind her, eyes wide and fearful.

"They're coming through the caves!" she cried. "They're coming to trap us!"

They heard it. The sound of hundreds of feet scuffling against the tunnel's floor echoed above them. Spiny legs skittered, and an unearthly voice cried out.

Panic rushed through the group, a feeling so thick it was almost alive and tangible. Davyn could taste his friends' fear. Only Sindri and, strangely, Catriona seemed unafraid. The red-haired warrior leaped to Christoph's side.

"Hold steady!" she shouted. "We can handle this!"

A swarm of undead rounded the stalagmites. Their eyes shone blank in the torchlight. Their mouths were opened wide into snarls. Humans, with gray skin puffy and rancid, reached out bony hands and raised weapons. Around them were more of the mismatched creatures, the goblins and ogres and furry beasts that had been Asvoria's first additions to her army. Giant insects skittered along the wall, their beady eyes shining like hundreds of black opals.

There seemed no end to the army as they surged forward. Their eerie moaning echoed around them.

"Oh no," Jirah muttered. "Oh no, oh no, oh no."

"By the gods," Ayanti whispered.

Davyn said nothing. Taking a steely breath, he held his sword ready. Near him, Jax and Catriona did the same. Rina nocked an arrow as Maddoc pulled Sindri back from the front of the group, where he'd come to stand with his hands outstretched and ready.

"Knights, at my call," Christoph said, his voice low and serious. The knights nodded, not having to hear more.

The line of monsters reached them in seconds. And, with Christoph's cry, the knights leaped forward.

A sneering man with terrible gashes running through his face and his chest hefted up a shovel and brought it down in a killing blow.

Davyn sliced through the wooden handle of the shovel with his sword, sending the metal end flying back into the oncoming creatures. With Davyn's sword in the air and his feet slightly off-balance, the zombie man shoved Davyn's chest.

Stumbling backward, Davyn hit against someone. Turning, he saw Mudd trip and sprawl backward into the cavern. The boy landed with a thud and, groaning, he started to get back to his feet.

That was when the undead dragon flared to life.

"Mudd!" Davyn cried. Forgetting the monster army, he ran to aid his friend.

Mouth opening wide in a hollow roar, the dragon's wings flapped. His nostrils flared. With one giant leap, he landed with a resounding boom near Mudd's feet. Like a snake, his head shot down. His massive jaws clamped around the black-haired boy's leg, wrenching him off the ground.

Davyn jumped up to grab Mudd's outstretched hand. But their fingers only grazed each other. Mouth open in a silent scream, his terrified eyes bore into Davyn's own as he disappeared up to the dark, cavernous ceiling.

Enraged at the thought of losing another friend, Davyn screamed and raced to attack the dragon.

"Aargh!"

Sindri heard the guttural scream and turned to see Davyn race toward the undead dragon's flank, his sword swinging wildly. The dragon's head was high in the cavern, shrouded in shadows, but Sindri could make out something—or someone—dangling between his teeth.

Davyn's sword lanced off the dragon's scales harmlessly, but still he attacked. Unable to see the fight with the zombies over the wall of knights and his friends now that Maddoc had pulled him from the front line, he turned and raced to see if he could help Davyn.

"What is it?" Sindri cried. "What are you doing?"

"He got Mudd!" Davyn cried.

Mudd screamed. Davyn resumed his useless strikes against the dragon's leg.

"Stand aside!" a girl's voice cried. Sindri turned to see Rina. The battle in the outer tunnel was a blur of bleeding flesh and glinting swords behind her. Her slender legs stood apart, and her eyes narrowed in focus. A white-shafted arrow was nocked in her bow and aimed at the dragon's head.

With a twang, the arrow let loose, soaring toward the ceiling. There was a crack as the metal arrowhead met hard dragon teeth. Something that looked like a white pebble tumbled to the ground.

189

Without hesitation, Rina let loose several more volleys of arrows. Though Sindri couldn't see into the heavy darkness above the radius of the torchlight, the elf girl's night vision let her see her foe as clearly as if she had been fighting in broad daylight. As Mudd's screams grew louder, her arrows met their mark and more teeth crumbled from the blows.

Then, with one final arrow, the last tooth holding Mudd split. The boy tumbled through the air on a crash course with the hard stone ground.

"Sindri!" Davyn shouted. "Use your magic, quick!"

Sindri grinned. Though Davyn no doubt intended him to use the ring that granted him telekinetic magic, he had a spell he'd been waiting for the perfect time to use.

Lifting his hands, he wiggled his fingers and shouted, "*Pfeatherfall!*"

Mudd's descent slowed. His face was twisted in agony, and he clutched at his mangled leg. But he landed safely near the edge of the cave wall.

Davyn and Rina immediately ran to Mudd's side. Neither noticed the dragon open its jaws and shoot its head down, straight toward them.

"No!" Sindri shouted. Raising his hands again, he mumbled a spell. Red and orange light flared as a tiny ball of flame shot from his outstretched fingers.

The flaming ball met the dragon's snout and exploded, causing as much harm as a mosquito bite on a giant's hand. Still, the dragon's head stopped its rapid descent. Cocking his head to the side, he seemed to study Sindri.

Slow and steady, the dragon started walking toward Sindri, his lips raised into a snarl.

Sindri backed away from his friends and the battle in the caves as the dragon grew closer. He found himself moving deeper and deeper into the cavern. For a moment he wondered what it would be like to be eaten by an undead dragon. Then, deciding he'd rather not find out, he raised his hands and hoped he remembered the spell that Maddoc had taught him.

His first black magic spell . . .

CHAPTER 25

SURROUNDED

"Mudd, are you all right?" Rina kneeled at his side and gently touched the wound.

"No, I'm not!" he yelled. Tears coursed down his cheeks. "My leg just got chewed on by a dragon and—OW!"

"Sorry." Rina winced and pulled her hand back. She wished Mudd would stop moaning and just let her take care of it, but she figured it was best not to tell him that.

Davyn hovered above them, pacing back and forth, his sword swinging from his hands like a pendulum. He looked back at the battle that was slowly being pushed backward into the cavern, then back to Rina and Mudd.

Without saying a word, Davyn bounded off to rejoin the fighting. As he ran, he passed a small, dark-haired figure.

"Mudd!" Jirah cried. She dropped to her knees and skidded to his side, her hands immediately running over Mudd's wound with practiced and gentle precision. He seethed through his teeth but did not cry out.

"I'm handling it," Rina said.

Jirah rolled her eyes as she pulled a small pouch of herbs free from her belt. "You want him to lose his leg like Set-ai lost his arm?"

"I know what I'm doing." Rina hopped to her feet. Behind her she heard the clicking of the dragon's claws and the shuffling of Sindri's feet, but she paid it no mind. "You're a little girl," she went on, "a little girl with a crush. Davyn obviously thought me capable since he left me here to take care of Mudd."

"That's not what he said when he passed me just now." Spilling the herbs into her hand, Jirah poured water from a skin over Mudd's wound and rubbed the herbs into the cleaned flesh. He yelped.

"Davyn didn't say anything," Rina seethed. "And you know it."

Jirah shrugged, intent on Mudd's wound. He continued to writhe in pain. "Believe what you like. He told me to make sure you stayed back here so you wouldn't get hurt, and that I should take care of Mudd."

"You're lying!" Rina said, "and I know it."

Looking up from Mudd's leg, Jirah tilted her head. "Then why is it that Davyn hasn't been talking to you? Why is it that he reprimanded you down below when you tried to help him? He's starting to see through your little act. I know because that's exactly what he said when we talked last night."

Rina clenched her fists. "Why, you—"

"Stop!" Mudd shouted. Arching his back, he tilted his head back and clenched his eyes closed in his pain. "Just stop! Is this really the time—OW!"

"Rina," Jirah said as she started to bind Mudd's leg. "We're in the middle of a battle. I know it probably hurts to hear the truth, and I'm sorry. But you're going to need to deal with it. We have to save my sister and that dragon."

Behind them the sounds of the battle grew louder as their friends were pushed farther back into the cavern. Unearthly howls and the sound of scrabbling feet echoed around her, but Rina didn't care. Hands trembling, she could only stare at Jirah's head. By E'li, she hated her so much.

"Watch out!"

At Mudd's shout, Rina spun around to see a beast charging toward her on all fours. Fumbling with her bow, she tried to nock an arrow and aim, but she knew there was no time.

With a bellow, Jax leaped forward, axe held high. He brought it down in a heavy blow, cleaving the creature's head from its shoulders. Still it charged forward, but it ran blind, curving away from them. It ran into the cavern's wall with a heavy thump and landed on its side, its paws clawing uselessly at the air.

"You are hurt," the minotaur said to Mudd, who was clutching at the wall behind him, his chest heaving. "I will protect you."

"Please," Mudd said.

With a sudden cry from one of the knights, the battle in the caves burst into the cavern. In seconds the undead beasts coursed around the knights, Catriona, and Davyn. Creatures with snarling faces and bony hands raced toward Jax, Rina, and Jirah.

"Ladies," Mudd wheezed, "I think now is the time to set aside your differences and fight. Please!"

Rina said nothing. She just took a breath and raised her bow. At her side, Jirah raised her sword. Though her lip trembled, she brought it down at the nearest beast with as much strength as her young arms could muster.

Rina let off shot after shot, trying to ignore the thoughts of jealousy and doubt racing through her head.

Catriona slashed at the approaching ogre and its arm flew. Another slice and a gaping wound opened on its chest. Unfazed, the beast lumbered forward, its eyes open wide. Its stained teeth parted to reveal a swollen tongue.

The warrior backed up, unable to do anything else. Around her she saw her companions do the same. The knights fought, but the onslaught of zombies forced them slowly but surely out into the cavern.

With a cry of frustration, Catriona thrust her sword deep into the ogre's chest. It continued to walk forward, slicing the sword deeper and deeper into its body with a sick squelch. It raised its giant fists, knuckles rubbed raw to the bone, and tried to punch in her skull.

"Not this time," she seethed. Twisting the sword, she let out a grunt. The blade sparked and the ogre's gray skin blazed with flame. Catriona twisted the sword further, willing more magic to consume her foe. The acrid scent of burning flesh filled her nose as magical fire ate through the monster's body.

Catriona's fist thrust through the beast's middle, pushing the sword all the way through. With a groan of disgust, she pulled the sword free and stood back to watch as the creature combusted into nothingness.

Catriona laughed, harsh and cold.

Raising her sword to go back and join the fray, she felt a strong hand clutch at her arm. Shouting, she spun to attack this new foe.

Maddoc let go her arm and raised his hands. "It's me."

Catriona stopped mid-swing, though her expression did not change.

Gripping her arm once again, Maddoc pulled her away from the fighting. He led her into the shadows beneath two torches then gestured toward a dark tunnel.

"Now is your chance, Catriona," he whispered. "Go. Find Asvoria. Begin your task."

"But the battle—" she started.

Maddoc grabbed her shoulders and shook her. "It is time. You have to go now, Catriona," he said. "The knights will take care of the monsters. We'll be there to finish the spell soon."

Nodding, Catriona lowered her sword. Without looking

back, she turned and ran toward the pitch-black tunnel that no doubt led to Asvoria's true lair.

Electric currents snapped between the emerald flecks on the Aegis and again Catriona smiled. Soon Asvoria would be the one fighting for her life.

Spittle flew from between the creature's snarling lips and landed on Davyn's cheeks. The saliva was cold as ice and smelled like rotten meat

The beast leaped for Davyn's throat and he hefted the Dragon Knight's sword, slicing the creature through its middle. With a yowl, the beast fell into two halves beside him. Not stopping to revel in this small victory, he walked past the severed creature. Its head still darted about and nipped at his heels.

In a shadowy corner, he saw a flash of chestnut fur disappear into a dark alcove. Ayanti.

Shoving past the sickly cold monsters, he raced through the fighting to follow her. An undead man leaped in front of him, but his sword sliced through him with ease. The zombie flew backward.

"Ayanti!" Davyn called, skidding into the alcove. "Are you all right? Were you hurt?"

The centaur stood in the center of the small cave, Davyn's pack slack on the floor beside her. Glowing green, she held the orb in front of her face, staring into its enchanting depths. Flickering orange light and clawed shadows danced across her face.

"I'm fine," she said. "In fact, I'm more than fine."

Blue eyes darting to meet his own, Ayanti smirked. She unfurled her fingers and released the glass ball.

Davyn could only watch as the orb that housed Raedon's soul spun heavy through the air. It landed against the stone floor with a sharp crack and rolled in front of Ayanti's hooves.

Davyn let out a sigh of relief. Though a white crack snaked along the orb's side, it was mostly unharmed. Raedon's soul was all right and—

In one swift motion, Ayanti lifted up her front hoof. Resting it on top of the glass ball, again she met Davyn's eyes, again she smirked. Then she stomped on the orb.

It shattered into a million pieces around her black hoof. The green smoke that had been housed in its interior drifted up and faded away.

Ayanti's bright, glowing blue eyes opened wide in mock embarrassment. "Oh, dear. What have I done?"

26 DAVYN'S TEST

Davyn couldn't speak.

Ayanti stood still. A devilish smile seared her cheeks. The shards of the glass ball were scattered about her hoofs.

"Raedon," Davyn whispered. Sounds of the fighting behind him faded away. His limbs trembled.

No. Not Ayanti. It couldn't be Ayanti.

"I'm so terribly clumsy," the centaur said, her hand fluttering to her chest in a false show of sincerity. Her voice echoed through the alcove above them, its singsong tone repeating over and over like a chorus of taunts.

Davyn's jaw clenched.

"Yet another fallen comrade," Ayanti said with a sad shake of her head. Her hoofs crunched the glass as she walked over the remnants of the orb.

"What did you do with Ayanti?" Davyn demanded. "You didn't—"

"No, I didn't," the creature said. Its tone started to change, it sounded deeper and male. "She didn't show up. Can you blame her? With your track record for failing your friends, you might as well have just killed her yourself instead of asking her to come fight your little battle. Just like you killed Elidor."

"Don't you dare speak of him!" Davyn said, knowing now that he had been tricked. Gazing into the deep blue eyes of the creature that looked like Ayanti, he raised his sword high. "You were the one that killed him."

"That I did," Ayanti said.

Before Davyn could protest, the false centaur let out a horse-like whinny and reared back on its hind legs. With two loud slurps, its front legs sucked back into a torso that started tightening and compacting into a well-built chest. Its hindquarters deflated into two thin yet muscular legs. Its hooves flattened and splayed out into feet.

Blond hair fell to the creature's broad shoulders, parted behind its pointed ears. The chestnut fur of Ayanti's centaur body shuddered and smoothed into a plain gray tunic designed to blend into the background of crowded city streets. The skin of its lower legs darkened and bulged out into black boots, with twin daggers strapped to their sides.

Cocking its head, the creature's lips parted into a familiar lopsided grin.

Davyn couldn't breathe.

"It's been a long time, brother. Why haven't you written?" It was Elidor's voice. A voice that had been forever silenced months and months ago.

Finding his breath, Davyn stepped forward. "How dare you."

Ophion flexed its arms and slender hands and looked down at its new body. "What's wrong? Don't recognize your old friend Elidor? Really, has it been that long? Most people find it hard to forget someone as charming and clever as me."

"You killed him," Davyn repeated. "Not me." He stepped backward and began to circle the shapeshifter. Like ghosts from the Abyss, fanged shadows from the battle in the cavern flickered in the alcove. Darkness shrouded Ophion's features.

"Wait, are you saying I'm dead?" Ophion cocked its head. *Elidor's* head. "Yes, that's right. I did die. You couldn't kill Asvoria because you loved the girl who used to have her body. So I had to do it for you. Except, I did it just as I was about to kill Ophion. So, in fact, if you had only had the strength to kill her, I could have killed the shapeshifter and, well, things would have been a lot different now, wouldn't they?"

"No."

"Yes, I'm sure of it." Rubbing its chin thoughtfully, Ophion furrowed its brow. "You could have killed Asvoria, and I'd be alive today. Which means those villages down there would never have been destroyed and Raedon"—he gestured at the glass shards—"would be alive and well and tricking gully dwarves. Yes, I do believe that makes this all your fault."

Davyn's whole body trembled as though an earthquake were raging around him. His heart pounded in his ears.

It's true, Davyn thought, unable to keep old wounds from reopening. I am worthless. If only I had been truthful from the beginning. If only I had killed Asvoria when I had a chance. If only I hadn't run away. If only . . .

Elidor—no, Ophion, Davyn reminded himself, it's Ophion!—laughed a good-natured laugh. Holding up a hand, he looked at Davyn and grinned. "Remember this?" he said. A cut appeared in the center of its palm, red blood trickling down its wrist. "Remember when we became brothers? I think that means we were supposed to always be there for one another. I suppose it didn't quite work out that way. But what could I expect? There's no honor among thieves."

"How do you know about that?" He meant to shout, but his voice would only come in a hoarse whisper.

The shapeshifter's smile fell into a sneer, its eyes narrowed into furious slits. "I know everything. I know your deepest wishes and your most hidden fears. I know that you want to be a hero, Davyn, but that you know you'll never be. You are nothing but a pitiful orphan, after all, meant to be used as a pawn in events greater than you could ever imagine. You are nothing but a failure at every task ever set before you. You wanted to help Maddoc and failed. You wanted to save Nearra and failed. Elidor, Raedon, all your friends out there, you have failed them all. When you aren't running away from your problems, you are a dark soul whose only purpose in life is to help bring about misery and death to anyone you come in contact with."

Taking a step forward, the creature's sneer widened into a deadly grin. "And you know it."

Davyn couldn't speak. He knew this was all trickery and deceit, that Ophion was playing a game, manipulating his emotions. But it felt as though some giant hand were clutching at his insides, pulling him in on himself. A shudder passed through his body.

I have to fight this, he thought. I have to fight.

Ophion's hands reached down and pulled the two daggers from his boots. Holding both out, the shapeshifter took a step toward Davyn, then another. Davyn forced himself to raise his sword high, but all he saw right then were Elidor's eyes pleading with him, wanting to know why he had been allowed to die.

Thudding footsteps echoed through the cavern and a shadow darker than the rest flowed past Ophion's face.

"Davyn, Ayanti!" a girl's voice called. "We need you and—" The girl gasped, and both Ophion and Davyn spun to look at her as she entered the alcove.

"Rina," Davyn whispered, his voice still scratchy and raw.

The elf girl watched the two of them with wide eyes, her bow held slack.

"Elidor! It can't be! We thought you were . . ." She shook her head. "What's going on?"

Ophion ignored Davyn, stepping closer to Rina. "Sister!" The shapeshifter's face widened into a broad smile. "I haven't seen you in years. I'm surprised you came."

"Elidor," she whispered, her eyes confused. "No, this isn't real. You're not Elidor."

"No, you're right," Ophion said, shoulders slumping and face falling. "I died saving your friend here. Only, wait, what's this?" The shapeshifter tilted its elven head. "Why, you want him to be more than a friend? Isn't that a twist. But don't you know he only has eyes for Nearra? And you, well, you're just a spoiled Silvanesti child trying to pretend she knows her way around the world. That's quite amusing, I think. Funny you'd fall for a human boy, especially one who doesn't want you around in the first place."

"No," Rina said, her limbs trembling with anger. "What are you talking about? You don't know anything!"

"I know plenty," the shapeshifter sneered. Stepping closer to her, Ophion lowered its voice. "Shame Jirah never got a chance to kill you. She'd have done the whole world a favor. One less self-centered Silvanesti around to banish the half-breeds and condemn them to death."

Ophion raised the knives high. "You could have saved him. Too bad."

Tears welled in Rina's eyes. Hand shaking, she let out a cry of despair, raised her bow, and fired.

"You are lying!" she screamed as she nocked another arrow and shot. "I did nothing!"

The shapeshifter stood still, and holes appeared in its rubbery body. The arrows passed right through Ophion and clattered against the cave wall.

The shapeshifter laughed. "Stupid, worthless girl." Then, with a snarl, it leaped.

Rina screamed and backed against a wall. Her bow fell to the stony floor. Quickly she reached for her daggers, only managing to pull one free before Ophion was upon her. The creature attacked with rapid, unrelenting jabs to her gut, her chest, her neck. Rina blocked as best she could, but one of the daggers met

JEFF SAMPSON

her neck and left a long cut. Bright red blood oozed from the wound. She screamed in pain.

The scream met Davyn's ears like a slap to his face.

Davyn felt the doubt and despair flow free from his body. Raising his head high, he raced toward Ophion and Rina.

"Leave here alone!" Davyn shouted. "She's not important. It's me you want."

Ophion ignored him, consumed with its task. With a cry of righteous anger, Davyn swept the Dragon Knight's sword toward the shapeshifter's back. Ophion wasn't prepared. He did not shift his flesh to keep it from being severed. The sword met the shapeshifter's right shoulder, sliced deep through its torso.

Davyn held the sword ready to strike Ophion one more time. The shapeshifter coughed and sputtered. Features creased with shock, it turned to look at Davyn. It still wore Elidor's face, but Davyn didn't notice. All he saw were those terrible, glowing blue eyes.

Clutching at its sides, Ophion backed away from Rina. Its legs shuddered and it stumbled, falling backward at Davyn's feet. The two halves of its body parted as it smashed against the ground with a loud, wet smack. Black blood pooled on the floor.

Ophion let out a high-pitched scream. Its features melted and softened. Any trace of Elidor's form disappeared as its skin turned gray like the stone he lay upon. Then, its flesh blistered and blackened.

With one final shudder, the shapeshifter's screaming stopped. All that was left was a steaming husk in a vaguely humanoid shape, surrounded by a pool of black blood.

Davyn watched Ophion die, his face devoid of emotion. Somewhere deep in the caves, a dragon's enraged roar echoed. For a moment the fighting in the cavern stopped, then just as quickly began again.

Standing still, Davyn watched the body on the floor, not believing that Asvoria's vile familiar was actually dead. But the husk did nothing but shrivel in on itself, smaller and smaller, as the pool of blood spread farther into the alcove.

After a long moment, Davyn let himself breathe.

Gasping cries sounded from the wall. Davyn snapped his head and saw Rina still crouched there, head covered in her arms, sobbing. Blood dripped down her shoulder as she rocked back and forth.

"Are you all right?" Davyn asked. Sliding his stained sword into its scabbard, he turned to her.

"E'li help me," she sobbed. The elf's usual beauty and grace was gone, made ugly and twisted by her despair. Her curly gold hair hung limp, stained from the blood oozing from her wound.

"He's dead," Davyn whispered. "Here." Ripping a long strip from his cloak, he folded it up and gave it to Rina to press against her neck and stop the bleeding.

"It's all true," Rina whispered. Her body trembled. She seemed so young right then, her confidence and friendly mocking erased in the wake of Ophion's taunts. "Everything was true. I'm just a stupid, worthless child." Meeting his gaze with hurt eyes, she swallowed. "Unimportant."

"That's crazy . . . " Davyn started to say.

"There you are!" Jirah ran into a room, almost slipping on Ophion's blood. "What happened?" she asked, her eyes flicking from the shapeshifter's crumpled corpse to Davyn and Rina against the wall.

"Ophion was posing as Ayanti," Davyn said. "He destroyed Raedon's soul, then tried to kill us."

"Oh no," Jirah whispered.

"Rina, come on," Davyn said, kneeling down and shaking her gently. "We have to go. We still need to fight."

Rina's eyes met Jirah's and again the elf girl trembled. "I can't," she whispered. "I . . . I can't."

"Come on, Davyn, we have to go!" Jirah said. "If she doesn't want to help, just leave her here."

Shaking his head, Davyn got to his feet and walked to Jirah's side. An ocean of bodies writhed in battle outside the alcove, the yowling loud and unbearable. Davyn could see a few of the knights hacking through the undead monsters. The knights' faces were masks of resolve. Not even their moustaches quivered.

"Stay here," Davyn said to Rina, his voice more stern than he intended.

He noticed Jirah's eyes were still on Rina, a small smile on her lips. Jirah quickly looked away. "I'm glad you two are all right. I was worried."

Nodding, Davyn pulled his sword from his scabbard. It came free with a sick squelch. Blood splattered to the floor and onto his leg.

He turned to Jirah. "Let's go."

27   CONNECTIONS

An anguished roar blasted through the caves. The sound reverberated in Catriona's ears, threatening to deafen her.

"No!" a deep voice howled. "Ophion!"

More screeching roars sounded as Asvoria—for that was only who it could have been—began thudding about her cavern. "I'll kill them all!" she raged.

Holding the Aegis high, Catriona felt a new surge of strength enter her muscles. With a smile, she reached into the top of her breastplate and pulled the folded parchment free. She studied it one last time though she now knew it better than even Maddoc and Sindri.

She crumpled the paper in her fist and started forward.

She could see dim gray light up ahead. Something big and glittering rustled behind the stone. Flashes of gold glinted behind it.

Two massive statues towered above her. One was of a woman. A cruel expression creased her otherwise lovely face. The other was of a deadly dragon sweeping up into the sky. The gems of their eyes refracted the dim light, casting violet shadows on the walls.

Sword held at the ready, Catriona rounded the statues and entered the cavern.

Asvoria thrashed wildly about the room. Her tail whipped back and forth, hitting the cave walls with heavy thumps. Clouds of dust rained from the cavern's ceiling. Beyond a large hole in the ceiling, gray clouds seethed.

A massive golden throne took up the center of the room, completely hiding the back wall from Catriona's view. She couldn't see Nearra.

Was she even here? Catriona worried. Perhaps they had arrived too late.

The dragon continued to thrash in wild rage, not noticing the young warrior standing between the statues. "They will pay for this!" she thundered, her voice tainted with human emotion.

Catriona was certain that somehow Ophion had been killed. Smiling with satisfaction, she gripped the Aegis hard and walked into Asvoria's line of sight.

"Hello, Asvoria," she said. Her voice was cold and for a moment Catriona was startled to realize the words had come from her own lips.

Asvoria skidded to a stop and turned to face Catriona. Her chest heaved, the Daystar symbol contorting with each breath.

"You," she hissed. Then, opening her mouth wide, she spewed forth a stream of deadly acid.

Catriona leaped to the side, and the foul liquid splashed behind her. It hissed as it ate into the stone.

Catriona sprinted past Asvoria, putting the massive and gaudy throne between the two of them. Her mind raced. How, exactly, was she going to cut the symbols into the dragon's flesh without dying first?

Behind the throne, lying on her back beneath the towering symbol of a letter *A*, was Nearra. Catriona heaved a sigh of relief. The girl seemed unharmed, but her skin was pale, her cheeks gaunt. Blond hair splayed around her head like a faded halo.

"You can't escape!" Asvoria called. "I can hear your heartbeat, girl. You were a fool to think you could fight me."

"Yes," Catriona called. "But I'm a fool with your sword." Turning from Nearra, she raised the Aegis high.

Asvoria crouched back on her haunches and leaped into the sky. She hovered directly above Catriona and opened her mouth once again. This time, a steaming cone of copper-colored gas whooshed out. Again Catriona leaped out of the way, covering her hands and nose so as not to inhale any of the poisonous cloud. It was slow gas, and if Asvoria managed to spray her with it, she'd be virtually frozen in place. Asvoria would kill her in an instant.

So blinded with anger and emotion, Asvoria didn't notice Catriona was no longer in her line of fire. She continued to belch the slow gas, her wings flapping to keep her aloft.

Catriona saw her chance.

She gripped onto the dragon jutting from the side of the throne and hefted herself up. Asvoria hovered directly above her head. Jaw clenched, Catriona raised the Aegis high. Emerald shards glittered in anticipation.

With one swift slice, Catriona brought the sword down to make the first line of the first symbol. Sparks of mystical energy flew as the enchanted sword met the copper-and-black scales. Asvoria screamed, dark blood seeping from her flesh.

Catriona brought the sword up to make another cut before Asvoria could move.

But then she noticed Nearra.

The human girl shuddered, her mouth opened in gasps as her arm flopped wildly at her side. A deep cut had appeared on her pale flesh, in the exact same place as the cut made to Asvoria.

"Oh, no," Catriona whispered. There was a fatal flaw in their plan. Asvoria and Nearra were still connected, and it seemed every wound inflicted on the sorceress would appear on the peasant girl as well. Though a dragon could surely handle the wounds Catriona intended to inflict, Nearra would never survive.

Catriona leaned backward and stumbled, falling off the throne. She managed to land in a crouch, but the fall had been enough to catch Asvoria's attention.

Snarling, the dragon turned mid-air and caught the warrior's eye.

Catriona ran. Dust and flakes of broken stone swirled. Her hair whipped around her face. Hot breath that stunk of dead animals washed over her. She could almost feel the pinpricks of razor sharp claws meeting her unprotected back.

Ahead were the two statues. If she could just reach them, she could use them for protection while she regrouped. She dared to look back. Asvoria was close, much too close, and bright red light flared between her front claws.

She was casting a spell!

Catriona forced her aching muscles to pump faster. She was close to shelter, just a few more steps . . .

With a whoosh, a ball of flame burst toward Catriona. Heat washed over her, so intense it singed her eyebrows. For a moment she was certain she would be incinerated, but the Aegis glowed and the fireball shot past harmlessly. It crashed against the base of the female statue.

The stone exploded. A cloud of dust and black smoke unfurled into the sky, shrouding everything in darkness.

Coughing, Catriona raced through the dust. Something creaked to her right and moments later the broken statue crashed to the ground with a resounding boom, so close that the tip of Asvoria's nose grazed her back.

Catriona hid herself in the shadows and tried to figure out what to do next.

Staring at Sindri with its empty eye sockets, the dragon stalked forward. Broken scales fell from his back. His claws clinked against in the stone in a steady rhythm.

Ignoring the fighting around him, Sindri raised his hands high and tried to chant. But still his own excitement got the better of him and he found himself stumbling over the words.

The undead black dragon came closer. Its lips parted to show a mouth full of jagged teeth.

"Sindri," Maddoc said, coming up behind him. "Cast the spell! Why haven't you cast the spell!"

"I can't!" he cried. "I've been trying, Maddoc, but I can't do it!"

Maddoc gripped Sindri's arms from behind and held them straight. His mouth directly near the kender's ears, the former wizard spoke, his words low and slick. "Yes you can, Sindri. This is new magic to you, but you can do it. Do it with me, all right?"

Sindri nodded.

As one, kender and wizard spoke the words to their destructive spell. The phrases came out in intricate patterns, curling in on themselves in unexpected ways. The syllables were harsh to Sindri's ears. They felt hot as they left his tongue, but he pressed on.

Then, Sindri felt it. A warmth deep inside his belly. Gasping, he almost stumbled over the words, but Maddoc tightened his grip and he regained focus. Where Maddoc's fingers met his arms, Sindri felt a tingling, like bugs crawling over his skin, but he ignored the sensation.

Red mist flowed from Sindri's hands and, as the first tendrils of the magic met the approaching dragon's body, it stopped.

"Finish it, Sindri," Maddoc hissed in his ear. "Feel the power."

Consumed by the energy filling him from the tip of his stunted toes to the ends of his hair, Sindri couldn't respond.

The magic was in control now, raging through him.

In front of him, the dragon stood still as a statue. Its skin seemed to ripple and then, where the scales had already torn away, its flesh began to peel backward.

Sindri couldn't help but stare in fascination. Layer upon layer of the undead dragon's body fell away. Muscle slackened and let go of bone, veins dropped into piles like coils of rope. Blobby, fleshy shapes fell from deep within its cage-like ribs and plopped to the floor.

Within moments, the dragon was reduced to a steaming pile of flesh and bone. The only recognizable feature was its triangular skull. The smell, Sindri thought, was fascinating in a horrendous sort of way.

Elated in ways he'd never thought possible, Sindri clapped his hands. "That was—" He started to say, but a wave of exhaustion flooded his system. He collapsed at Maddoc's feet.

"Good, Sindri," the former wizard whispered as he held the kender up. "You did very well. But don't stop now. We still have much to do."

Though his head spun with wooziness and his eyes longed to close, Sindri nodded and stood. As he did, he saw Jirah and Davyn racing toward them from a small cave. They both stopped to gape at the black dragon's remains. Jirah covered her nose.

"Where's Ayanti?" Sindri called. "Is she all right?"

Davyn swallowed and looked away from the aftermath of Sindri's spell. "It wasn't her. It was Ophion and he—it—destroyed Raedon's soul."

"Is Ophion dead?" Maddoc asked.

"Yes," Jirah said. "Davyn killed him."

Echoing from the bowels of the cavern, there came the sound of an explosion and then a massive boom as something crashed to the floor.

"Cat!" Sindri cried. "She's fighting Asvoria. We have to help her!"

"Come on!" Davyn shouted.

Though still weak, Sindri forced himself to move toward the dark tunnel from which the black dragon had originally emerged.

If he'd looked back, he would have seen the disturbed look on Davyn's face as he raced past the dragon's remains.

He would have seen Maddoc's small but triumphant smile.

28 SEVERED SOULS

"Come out, warrior!" the dragon bellowed. "Face me with my sword!"

The dust from the explosion settled around Catriona and she held back a cough. She pressed her back flat against the cool stone of the dragon statue towering above her. Asvoria paced back and forth in her throne room, her head whipping back and forth.

"You think you can cut my flesh and live!" she roared. "Come out and die!"

Catriona clenched her eyes closed and willed her hands to stop shaking. The fallen statue of Asvoria stared at her with its glimmering amethyst eyes, judging her. The Aegis's crackling lightning faded as her resolve and conviction wavered. The whole plan rested on the spell to restore Raedon's soul. But how could they do it if it would kill Nearra? After all they'd been through, how could they just let her die, even if it was stop someone like Asvoria? Hopeless, it was all hopeless . . .

No! I will not fail! I refuse! I REFUSE!

A rush of strength surged into her mind and the Aegis flared with green light. Her face tightened. Her muscles relaxed. She could figure this out. She had to.

"Cat!" Davyn Sindri, Jirah and Maddoc raced toward her. Davyn's sword was held at his side. Black blood dripped from its point.

Davyn gripped her arm. "Cat, don't worry about the spell anymore. Ophion tricked us. He posed as Ayanti. He destroyed Raedon's soul."

"No!" Cat cried. She clenched her fist. "I'll kill him!"

"Too late," Jirah said. "Davyn already did."

"What do we do now?" Sindri asked. He tiptoed to the edge of the dragon statue and peered around, his eyes wide with wonder. "Wow, she looks upset."

"I can't kill her," Catriona said, spit flying in the anger with which she spoke the words. "Any damage I do to her happens to Nearra, too. They're still connected."

"I can hear you, warrior!" Asvoria called. "And I know your friends are there. Who should I eat first, the kender or the sister? Take your pick."

She stamped her foot and stone exploded to their left. With a yelp, Sindri leaped backward. "How did she do that?"

Davyn shook his head. "Raedon's dead. We have no choice now. We have to kill her." His voice was flat.

"We can't!" Jirah shouted. "What about Nearra?"

"We will save Nearra," Catriona interrupted. "I refuse to settle for less. You four, figure something out. I'll go distract Asvoria."

"But Cat—" Davyn started.

She shook her head. "The Aegis will protect me from her spells and I can dodge everything else. Just do it. Find a way."

Before anyone could protest further, Catriona ran out from behind the statue. "I am here, Asvoria. Do your worst."

Asvoria's lips pulled back into a hideous sneer. "With pleasure . . ."

Davyn paced, his hands clenching and unclenching at his sides.

Sindri watched Davyn in concern, not sure what to say. He racked his brain for answers, but he was so tired. All he wanted was to lie down and sleep.

Over in the corner, Jirah clutched her little silver mirror and whispered to her reflection. A moment later, she shoved it into her pack and raced back to Davyn's side.

Clutching at the ranger's sleeve, she took a breath. "I have an idea," she said. She flinched as an explosion rocked the cavern and dust rained on their heads. "If there's a magical connection, maybe it's something more physical, something you can cut." She gestured toward the ornate hilt jutting from the scabbard on his belt. "You know, with your sword."

"The Dragon Knight's journal did say something about unbinding spells," Davyn said. "But how can I cut what I can't see?"

Rubbing his chin, Maddoc nodded as he came to Davyn's side. "I can't believe I didn't think of that. Though unseen by most eyes, magic energy is very real. It courses all around us in currents. If you could see it, you could look at the sky at night and see it streaming from the moons like a rain of silver and blood."

"Sounds lovely," Davyn muttered. "Is there a way to see it? If so, we can sever the connection and Asvoria can be killed without hurting Nearra. Maybe this is the chance I was supposed to wait for."

Maddoc leaned over and gripped Sindri's shoulders. "We need to cast one more spell, Sindri. Do you have the energy?"

Sindri nodded. "Just give me the words."

Once again holding Sindri's arms straight, Maddoc whispered into Sindri's ear. As he spoke, the kender repeated his words. Again the magic flared within him. Again he felt intense pleasure as it pumped through his limbs. Only this time, a wave of exhaustion made his legs wobble. The words stopped coming. His hands went slack. But Maddoc held him up as he spoke the final words. Power coursed around Maddoc's hands.

Maddoc had finished the spell. Sindri desperately wanted to know how he had done so considering he wasn't supposed to have any magic power, but he found he didn't have the energy to do ask. Unable to keep himself aloft any longer, Sindri let his heavy eyes close and he collapsed to the cavern floor.

The world flowed with light.

As the final words of the spell were spoken, Davyn dared to blink. Everything swirled with currents of magic, glowed with auras of every color imaginable. Near him Sindri's fallen form shone like a beacon, his aura as bright as his Suncatcher name. Beside him Maddoc shone as well, though his light was darker and pulsing.

Bright green flashes threatened to blind him, and Davyn reeled back. Turning to look round the statue, he saw Catriona deflect Asvoria's magic blow, protecting them with the Aegis. Only now Davyn saw the scene in a series of awe-inspiring explosions.

"Davyn!" Jirah cried next him. Blinking, he met her eyes. Her glow was almost non-existent. Looking at her allowed him to focus.

"Do you see it?" she asked.

Davyn scanned the cavern. Everything was bright and moving, constantly moving. But then, yes, he saw it. A single strand of purple light no thicker than a strand of rope. It snaked from Asvoria's chest to behind the golden throne, and pulsed with a steady rhythm, like a heartbeat.

In his hand, the Dragon Knight's sword flared with warmth. The blade shimmered with light.

It was the sign he had been waiting for. He knew what he had to do.

"I'm coming, Nearra," he whispered. Raising his sword high, he raced forward.

Orange and purple light cascaded from Asvoria like a torrent of spears, crashing around him and sending rock flying up with the force of their explosion.

"Catriona, keep fighting!" he called as he raced past her, but the girl paid him no mind. She let out a cry and hefted her sword high, smacking Asvoria across the nape of her neck and causing the sorceress to cry out.

Davyn leaped past her claws and ducked beneath her tail. The mystical purple bond glistened in front of him. Nearra flinched as Catriona made yet another blow to Asvoria's head.

Davyn stopped and closed his eyes. In his mind he saw Raedon and Elidor. Focused, he raised his sword high. The silver light pulsed as bright as Solinari.

The Dragon Knight's sword sliced through bond as easily as though Davyn had done nothing but swing the blade through the air. But for one brief moment when steel met magic, Davyn's mind flashed with images.

Asvoria, a raven-tressed queen cackling in dark glee on the steps of a building Davyn recognized immediately as his old home, Cairngorn Keep. In front of her, walking forward with stoic resolve, a knight clad in black armor, a bronze dragon emblazoned on his chest. No, not just a knight, Davyn realized. Though this was an image from another time, the knight wore Davyn's own face.

Then, the image shifted. Nearra, smiling slightly as she looked at him over a cup of tea in the darkened kitchen of Dog's trading post. He was there, too, his hand on hers. She reached out a slender hand to touch him back and a strange feeling flared within his chest.

Both scenes existed somehow side by side in his mind.

Then, suddenly, the women's faces contorted into screams and the vision shattered. The edge of the Dragon Knight's sword clanged against the stone ground, snapping Davyn back to reality.

The mystical bond withered. One half flowed back into Nearra's chest, the other into the Daystar scar on Asvoria's chest.

Asvoria's roars stopped. She shook her head in confusion and backed away.

Nearra's back arched and she gasped for breath. She heaved forward, her arms falling to her sides.

Davyn let his sword fall and ran to Nearra's side.

Asvoria backed farther and farther away from Catriona, her plate-sized eyes blinking as though adjusting to a sudden light.

"Something is wrong," she muttered, her limbs trembling. "My mind . . . Ophion is gone . . . my magic has been divided . . ." She whipped her head against the wall as though she were unable to control herself. "What have you done!"

"Catriona!" Maddoc called. "Kill her! Do it now while she is weak! Nearra is free!"

She didn't need to be told twice. Her heart beat slow and steady. She walked toward the dragon, raising the Aegis.

"No!" Asvoria cried. "This isn't how this is supposed to go! This is wrong!"

Without a word, Catriona stood beneath Asvoria's wide copper- and black-scaled chest. Lightning flared between the gemstones embedded on the Aegis's blade. Aiming its point directly at the vast scar, she plunged the sword upward.

Bright green light flashed. Asvoria roared. Catriona twisted the Aegis, forcing it deeper into the dragon's chest, plunging it deep into her evil heart. The roars turned to high-pitched screams.

Then, Asvoria shuddered and fell silent. She tipped onto her side and collapsed on the cavern floor with a thunderous boom.

Glazed over and confused, Asvoria's violet eyes met Catriona's. Her lips parted as though intending to speak. Instead, the Dragon Queen trembled once more and died.

29   MEMORIES

Tears filled Mudd's eyes and he let out an angry shout. An undead villager loomed over him, eyes bone white and unseeing. It raised a bloodstained scythe, ready to come down and end Mudd's life.

It wasn't fair. He couldn't die.

The minotaur Jax hollered as his axe chopped through the neck of a decaying goblin with a serpent's tail whipping from the base of its back. Consumed with battle, there was no way he could reach Mudd in time.

Cradling his injured leg, Mudd closed his eyes and continued to yell, trying to drown out the terrified screaming in his head. He waited for the rusted blade to meet his chest, ending his life once and for all.

The blade never reached him.

Mudd continued to yell until his throat was hoarse. It wasn't until a rough hand shook his shoulder that he stopped to gasp for air.

"Stop that," a gruff voice said.

Mudd opened his eyes and found Jax looking down at him. The man-bull's nostrils flared with annoyance, but he gestured behind him with his stained axe.

What once had been a scene of roiling violence was now frozen in time. The undead monsters had stopped mid-attack and stood still, waiting. The villager with the scythe was exactly where Mudd had seen him last, its weapon still raised high.

The knights looked around in confusion as Jax helped Mudd to his feet. One reached out a hand and pushed over a dog-like beast. It promptly fell to its side.

Then, deep within the caves, they all heard a thunderous boom. Seconds later, every remaining zombie creature collapsed.

For a moment, Mudd didn't dare to breathe. "Is it over?" he whispered.

Jax nodded his head. "It would seem so."

With a sigh, Mudd's limbs lost their strength and he collapsed.

Jax hefted Mudd back up and held him close to his side. The minotaur carried him out of the cavern and down the tunnel. Fresh air and gray light met them as they reached the end of the tunnel and looked down over the destroyed village of Forestedge.

Deep in the foothills, the combined forces of several villages, including those from Tarrent and Potter's Mill, had fought alongside Cirill and his warriors. Though they'd fled from the dead village at the command of the Solamnic knights, it appeared that Asvoria's undead creatures had followed. Nysse and her clerics rushed to pull the wounded from the front lines and pull them back to the camp, where they busied themselves with prayers to the gods to heal those fighting a good fight.

But the monster army had stopped moving.

The battle cries of the villagers slowly died out as they realized their foes were no longer attacking. Confused, they pulled back, weapons held wary.

Whatever magic that had given the undead the power to walk now suddenly was torn from their limbs. The creatures collapsed in heaps, leaving nothing behind but the horrific stench of their rotting flesh.

For a moment, no one said anything. Then, Vael—unmistakable even from this distance with her stark white hair—raised her sword high. "The Dragon Queen has been defeated!" Her voice echoed over the village and up the mountain face.

As one, the villagers raised their voices in a cheer. Men and women raced through the crowd to find one another, falling into each other's embrace, laughing and crying all at the same time.

Mudd let out a short laugh, then looked up at Jax. "I think I've had enough adventuring. Can I go home now?"

For a long moment, Catriona stood and watched Asvoria's body. No thought flashed through her mind, no emotion welled in her chest. She held the Aegis slack at her side, its glimmering brilliance now forever snuffed out by the blood of the Dragon Queen.

Raedon's blood.

Feelings of strength and power continued to surge from the blade into Catriona's soul, but it felt different now. It felt invasive and overwhelming, as though she were being possessed by some otherworldly force. Lingering rage was all she felt at that moment. A voice deep within her screamed that this was all wrong, that the sword was corrupting her.

Though her body protested, she somehow managed to loosen her fingers. The cool malachite hilt of the Aegis slipped from her grip and clattered to the floor. The sound echoed through the cavern.

Cat's heart flooded with pain and, unable to contain it, she let out her next breath in a gasping sob. Tears welled in her eyes.

So much death. So much loss. It was too much.

Her first instinct was the find the sword, to let it back in. But,

JEFF SAMPSON

somehow, Catriona found an untapped well of inner strength deep within her soul and forced herself to resist. She breathed in and out in long, slow breaths.

It was over now. Finally, it was over.

"I must admit," a deep male voice said from behind her, "I never thought you children would succeed. But you have proven me wrong."

Wiping her eyes, Catriona turned to face Sir Christoph uth Witdel. Behind him she saw Davyn leaning over Nearra near the giant A symbol etched into the wall.

Catriona had no words. She looked down, ashamed that the knight had seen her cry, ashamed to show even a moment of weakness in his presence.

The knight's eyes softened and he reached out a gentle hand to Catriona's shoulder. "It's all right. I know how it is, all this business of war. Sometimes we win. Sometimes we lose. But all we ever remember are our mistakes."

"I've made so many mistakes," Catriona whispered. "So many."

"And yet it seems you fought on despite them." He cupped her cheek and lifted her face to look up at him. "I knew your aunt, Catriona, better than you will ever know. We fought side by side during the War of the Lance, after her family had been slaughtered. I personally helped Leyana become a knight despite all opposition. And I can tell you now, no matter what you may think, she would be proud of you. I admit, my own feelings clouded my judgment when first we spoke. But I was wrong about you. Truly, you redeemed yourself today. In the eyes of mortals and gods alike, you are a knight through and through."

Gulping, Catriona looked into his blue eyes. Where before they had seemed condescending, now she realized he had just been a man trying to make the best of a horrible situation. And she saw something else there—complete and total sincerity.

Deep down, she knew it was true. She had redeemed herself for her failure two years ago, over and over again. That failure had driven her for so long, had consumed her with its passion for perfection, that now that it was gone she felt a deep, empty hollow deep in her gut.

"Thank you," she said. "Truly, thank you."

Someone called out for Christoph. Bowing his head, he turned to run back through the caverns. As he did, Jirah rushed by. For some reason she had been hiding behind the statues, and now she was running toward Davyn and Nearra.

Catriona grabbed her arm as she passed, and Jirah turned to look at her, her eyes guilty.

"Rina," Catriona said. "Where is she?"

"She was with Davyn in the cave, where he fought Ophion," Jirah said. "S-she should still be there."

Nodding, Catriona let the girl go and turned to race back through the caverns. Armor stifled her, her underclothes were damp with sweat, and she felt she couldn't breathe. Grunting, she hefted off her breastplate and flung her helmet to the ground with a heavy clang.

"Rina!" she called as she ran. Her heavy boots echoed through the caves. "Rina!" Up ahead she could see Jax leading Mudd outside, could see the other knights hefting up one of their own who had been injured.

Soft crying sounded nearby. Stopping, she found a dark opening. Red-black blood seeped from out of the darkness, staining the floor.

"Rina?" Catriona said softly. Peering into the shadows of the cave, she saw only a shriveled husk surrounded by blood. Then, looking to the left, she found the elf girl. Rina sat on the floor. Her knees were pulled tight against her chest. Her limp hair draped over her face.

"Are you all right?" Catriona fell to her side and saw that the elf had a bloody bandage tied to her neck.

Slowly, Rina looked up. "I'm done, Catriona." Dirty streaks glistened on her face. "Elidor's murderer has been killed. I'm going home."

"You've been hurt," Catriona said. "You can come with us, we'll make sure you're taken care of."

Rina shook here head. "I can't look at them. Davyn and Jirah. Everything that girl said, everything Ophion said, was true. I'm not made for this. I was just pretending. None of you need me around."

"That's not true," Catriona said, putting her hand on the elf girl's shoulder. "I'm your friend. I don't know what Ophion said, but that thing existed only to lie."

Rina furiously wiped at her eyes and shook her head again. "Don't worry about me. I'll be fine. What about you? You had to fight a dragon. Are you all right?"

"I'm fine," Cat whispered. "Christoph told me I was redeemed for my aunt's death. That I was a true knight."

"Oh, Catriona," Rina said. "That's wonderful."

"I don't know. I . . . I'm not sure I even want to be a knight anymore."

Again Rina swallowed, and she looked down. "I'm not sure about anything anymore."

Cat sighed and looked away. Soldiers shifted in the cavern, the orange torchlight casting long shadows. "Me neither," she said.

"Sindri." The voice was distant and muffled. Sindri searched through the darkness to find its source but saw nothing. That only made him all the more curious.

"Sindri!" the voice went on. "Sindri!"

"Hold your horses! I'm coming!" Sindri cried. "I'm—"

With a start, Sindri awoke. Coughing, his eyes darted around the cavern. Catriona was gone. The Daystar Dragon lay lifeless.

Davyn and Jirah were crouched near Nearra behind the giant golden throne.

Above him, Maddoc sighed with relief. "You're all right."

Rubbing his forehead, Sindri sat up. "Am I?" he asked. Then, thinking for a moment, he nodded. "Yes, I am. That's good."

Maddoc smiled. Crinkles appeared at the corner of his eyes, like little bird footprints. "You did beyond well, Sindri," Maddoc said. "You truly are a wizard."

Sindri ran his hand through his hair and felt through his cloak. Everything was in place. "Told you I was," he muttered. He tried to stand, but a wave of nausea rolled over him and he had to sit down.

"But, you are too," Sindri said. "I saw you. You finished the spell. I think maybe you've been doing spells all along, with me."

Maddoc leaned back and crossed his arms. "You saw that?"

Sindri nodded. "Of course! I don't miss much."

Searching Sindri's eyes, the wizard hesitated before speaking. "Perhaps you can understand why I kept my powers secret. Your friends would not have let me live, let alone let me help save Nearra, had they known the truth."

"I think they would have, Maddoc," Sindri said. "But I don't understand how you could not do magic! Casting spells is amazing. It feels so . . . so . . . "

"Indescribable?"

"Exactly!" Beaming, Sindri studied the doting forms of Davyn and Jirah. Nearra still lay sleeping. "They'll never know what it's like," he said, a sudden feeling of sadness washing over him. "What the power feels like when you speak the words and make things happen . . ."

Maddoc rested against the statue. "They won't, it's true."

"I don't know if I can keep traveling with them," Sindri said. "There's so much I still need to learn. Maybe I can go back to the Greeves Academy. Do you suppose Raistlin might like to hear my stories?"

Maddoc tilted back his head. "I doubt it. But, you know, Sindri, perhaps you should come back to Cairngorn Keep with me. It doesn't seem you fit in very well at the school, and my keep still holds untold secrets. Perhaps the two of us together could discover them, and I could teach you more."

"Would you really teach me?" Sindri asked, eyes open wide. "I mean, Asvoria is gone and we saved Nearra, you don't need to anymore."

"I think you've shown great potential," Maddoc said. Then bowing his head, he sighed. "That is, if you would have me as your teacher."

"Oh, I will! I definitely will!"

Again Maddoc smiled. "Perfect. But I think if we agree to this, it must be under one condition."

"What's that?" Sindri asked, tilting his head questioningly.

"Your friends must not know of my power," Maddoc said, resting his hand on Sindri's shoulder, his eyes boring into the kender's with passion. "If they do, they will never let you come with me. Do you agree?"

Sindri looked down, silent. He glanced back toward Nearra, Jirah, and Davyn, then at Maddoc.

After a moment, Sindri nodded. "I agree. I won't tell anyone. When can we go?"

"I think she's stirring."

Davyn waited, not daring to breathe. Jirah fidgeted behind him, pacing back and forth. He wanted to tell her to hold still, but he understood her anxiety.

Finally, Nearra opened her eyes. Her blue eyes.

"Davyn?" Her voice was strained. She coughed then clenched her fist on her injured arm. "Thirsty," she managed to whisper.

"Here," Jirah said. She handed Davyn a half-empty water skin and he poured the liquid into Nearra's parched lips. She gulped greedily. Davyn winced as he noticed the bruises rapidly forming on her cheeks and arms.

Sputtering, Nearra reached up a bony hand and pushed the skin away. She looked into Davyn's eyes and smiled. "Thank you."

His heart thudded and untold emotion rushed through his body. But Davyn only nodded.

After a long moment, Nearra groaned and tried to sit up. Turning her head, she gasped. "Jirah?"

Jirah stammered, her hand running self-consciously through her jet-black hair. "You remember me?"

"Well, you cut your hair," Nearra said, her voice still strained. "But of course I remember you." She gasped again. "Oh! I remember you!"

Davyn laughed and pulled her into a hug. Nearra winced, but patted him gently on the back. Letting her go, he couldn't contain the smile. "We did it! We saved you. You got your memories back."

Closing her eyes, Nearra took in a breath, then flexed her hands. "Just like you promised." Then, opening her eyes, her head darted back and forth, much too quickly as she studied her surroundings. Her gaze came to rest on the fallen dragon body of Asvoria and for a brief moment, a dark look flashed through her eyes.

"She violated me," Nearra whispered.

In that moment, in those seconds, memories flashed through Davyn's mind. He'd seen that look of rage and heard that angry whisper before. Shaking his head, he tried to rid himself of the thoughts, but it was that brief lapse into expressions he'd long since attributed to Asvoria that erased every bit of unrepentant joy from his heart.

Despite every rational thought in his head, when Nearra's lovely eyes turned back to meet his own and her gentle smile returned, all he could see was the face of the woman who had murdered Elidor.

"It's over now, Nearra," Jirah said, dropping to her knees and scooting beside her. She took her sister's hand in her own. "You're saved, and now we can save our family."

"What?" Nearra asked.

Jirah shook her head. "We'll talk about it later. But say it again, will you?"

"Yes," Davyn said, forcing back his unwanted revulsion. "Yes, Nearra, say it again."

Smiling through joyful tears, Nearra let out a small laugh. "I remember."

30

SEPARATE PATHS

Catriona stood at the window of her room and looked over the courtyard of the Temple of the Holy Orders of the Stars. Early morning light streamed through the shutters, highlighting her unmade bed and the single chair in the corner. Jirah's bed was empty.

Outside, bright blue birds flitted between flowering cherry trees. The pink blooms rustled in the light breeze. A few clerics walked among daffodils and primroses that now painted the courtyard with color.

With a sigh, Catriona lay down on her bed. She gazed up at the stone beams criss-crossing the ceiling and let her thoughts wander.

It had been a week since they had fought through Asvoria's monster army and freed Nearra. Only a week since Catriona had plunged the Aegis through Asvoria's heart and felt the hot blood of Raedon's stolen body flood over her fingers.

At first they'd stayed to help the survivors of Forestedge and the neighboring village begin to rebuild, but it was quickly decided that the companions had already done much to help them and they deserved rest. They almost had to be forced onto the wagons heading northeast to the temple, where Nysse had sent messengers ahead to prepare her fellow clerics for the arrival of badly wounded.

After the clerics healed his mangled leg back in Forestedge, Mudd had headed home with the fighters from Potter's Mill.

"I think," he had said, "that I've had enough fighting, at least for a little bit. I'd like to see Hiera again and Shemnara and Set-ai."

Jirah had accompanied Catriona, Davyn, Sindri, and Maddoc to the temple. Nearra had slept the entire way. She'd only managed to gain consciousness for a few moments at a time. Rina had started back with them, but she disappeared one day with a note telling them not to worry, that she felt she needed to return home as well. Before she'd gone, she and Catriona had several private discussions.

Those talks . . . Catriona sighed and rolled onto her side. Her red hair fell into her face, a thin curtain blocking out the rest of the room.

Something in the warrior had broken the moment she killed Asvoria. It was almost as though there had been a wall around her that had been pierced along with the Dragon Queen's heart, and that tiny wound had started the wall crumbling.

What had once been shrouded in shadow now seemed painfully clear. And now she had a choice to make.

Tiny rappings sounded from the door, and Catriona jerked up her head.

"Cat!" Sindri's muffled voice came from the other side. "She's awake and wants to see us!"

Catriona stretched her arms and sat up. "I'm coming!" Someone had filled a bowl with fresh water on a low table next to the bed and she splashed her face.

The stone floor was cold beneath her bare toes as she walked to the door and met Sindri. The kender grabbed her hand as soon as he saw her. He dragged her out into the hall.

"Come on," he said. "She may fall asleep again any moment,

and I want to know what it was like having someone else's soul in her body!"

Catriona let the little wizard pull her down the corridor to the room at the end of the hall. Pillars bearing the symbols of the gods lined the walls, and fires flared in small braziers above them. The door to the private chamber was slightly ajar. Sindri bounded through without bothering to knock.

"We're here!" he announced.

Surrounded by a sea of blankets and fluffy pillows, Nearra sat up against the backboard of an overstuffed bed. She smiled as they entered, but her eyes were rimmed with dark circles and her blond hair hung limp. Her right arm was bound where the cut had appeared and cradled in her hands was a steaming mug.

Sitting on a stool at her bedside was Davyn, his hair cut short and manageable. Arms crossed, his eyes were cast down and away from the peasant girl. He looked up and offered a brief smile as Catriona and Sindri came to Nearra's bedside.

"You're awake," Catriona said. Kneeling at her side, she grabbed one of Nearra's hands and squeezed it.

"I am. Finally," the blond girl said. Squeezing Catriona's hand back, she lifted up the mug and took a sip. "How are you two doing?"

"I'm—" Catriona started to say, but Sindri leaped on to the bed beside Nearra and sat cross-legged.

"I'm wonderful!" he said. "We saved the world and my magic helped. Only thing is, shouldn't there be parades and feasts in our honor? Or at least a party?"

"We didn't save the world, Sindri," Davyn said.

"Well, you never know," the kender said. "Just because Asvoria never got to build a huge army and spread all over the continent doesn't mean she wouldn't have if we weren't there."

"She's gone now," Catriona said. "And so are countless villagers, and heroes, and . . . and Raedon."

Everyone fell into an uncomfortable silence. Pulling her hand from Nearra's, Catriona leaned against the edge of the bed.

"How are you feeling, Nearra?" she asked after a moment. "What you went through must have been terrible."

"Yes, terrible!" Sindri said. "I can't wait to hear all about it."

Nearra shook her head and offered a weak smile. "It wasn't pleasant. But it's over now."

"And your memories?" Catriona asked. "You remember everything?"

"I think I do," she said, then looked down at the mug clasped in her hands. "It's all so confusing. I thought when this was all over and my memories came back it'd be so simple, like they'd just reappear and everything would be better. But it's overwhelming. I'm still sorting everything out."

"That sounds wonderful," Sindri said.

Nearra laughed. "It is, a little. It's like I'm meeting someone new, only that someone new is me. I see my past and then I see how I acted when I met all of you. I'm starting to realize that I'm not quite the same person all of you know, not entirely. And then there's . . . well, there's. . . ."

"What is it?" Davyn asked. He reached out a hand before quickly pulling away.

"When you severed the connection between Asvoria and me," Nearra whispered, "I think something was left behind. A piece of me in her, and a piece of her in me. I . . . I can feel this power in me, and I don't know what it is or what it means. It's frightening, a little."

"She's gone," Davyn said. "Anything left in you from her is you now. She has no control."

"I hope so," Nearra whispered.

Nodding thoughtfully, Catriona went to stand in front of Nearra's window. A different view could be seen here than from Catriona's own room. Jax stood stoically near the temple's protective wall, looking into the forest. He had replaced his armor with long black robes. Near him was a mound covered in bright green grass.

The grave of Slean, the green dragon they'd fought with Elidor. This place was the first place they'd really come together and helped each other. Fitting that it was the place where she'd reveal her decision.

Catriona opened her mouth to tell them, but her heart began to ache. Instead, she said, "Nearra, do you remember this business about a curse?"

"I do. My father was obsessed with it. He and Jirah left together to discover more, and then Mother fell ill, which is why I ended up working for Maddoc. I remember thinking maybe Maddoc could help me find out more about the curse, since it seemed so important to Father, but I never got the chance to ask. I didn't know I was the one foretold to break the curse."

Catriona turned from the window. "Are you going with Jirah, then? To try and break this curse?"

"I don't know," she said. "I'd like to see my parents, but Jirah says this is more important—" Breaking out into a fit of coughing, Nearra hacked into her closed fist, then slumped back into bed.

Catriona immediately leaped to her side. "Are you all right?"

"I'll be fine. It comes and goes. Nothing you can protect me from."

Catriona closed her eyes and leaned back. "I know. I . . . I have something to tell you all."

Davyn's eyes immediately narrowed into suspicion. "This doesn't sound good," he said.

"No, it's nothing bad," Catriona said quickly. "I don't think so anyway. It's just. . . ." With a sigh, she sat at the foot of the bed and leaned forward against her knees.

A small hand touched her shoulder. "What is it, Cat?" Sindri asked.

Looking into the kender's wide, inquisitive eyes, Catriona felt her heart jump. But she had to do this.

"I won't be coming with you on your journey, Nearra," she said, unable to turn and look her friends in the eye. "I realized over the past few months that there's some things about me I need to figure out, and I can't do it traveling with you. Not now."

"Are you going to go back to the knights?" Sindri asked.

"No," Catriona said. "I'm . . . I'm not even sure if I'm meant to be a knight anymore. I need to go home and do some thinking."

"Oh," Nearra said in a small voice. "I understand, Catriona. I know how you feel."

Catriona turned to meet the other girl's eyes. Nearra smiled a gentle, reassuring smile.

Davyn looked down, arms still crossed. "All right," he said, then looked up to meet her eyes. "But don't forget about us, all right?"

"It's not possible," Catriona said. Standing, she walked to the ranger's side and held out a hand. Grinning, he clasped it in his own.

"I suppose now is a good time to tell you all that I won't be going either," Sindri said from where he sat on the bed. "I'm discovering a whole lot about magic, and I just have to learn more. Maddoc said he'd take me in as his student."

"Are you sure that's a good idea?" Nearra asked. "He's Maddoc, after all."

"I'm positive," Sindri said.

Catriona swallowed, but did not voice her own doubts. Maddoc had proven himself in the battle, after all. And everyone knew there was no stopping kender when they've decided to do something.

"Perhaps I'll travel with you on my way home," Cat said. "For a little while at least."

Sindri tilted his head. "You don't trust I'll be fine?"

Cat shrugged. "Of course you will. I'd just like the company."

"I'll miss you both," Nearra said. Setting the mug on a table beside her, she reached out her arms and grabbed Sindri and Catriona's hands. "Just promise me we'll meet again."

"On my honor," Catriona vowed.

"Of course!" Sindri said with a wide grin. "I'm going to need to hear everything that happens to all of you while I'm away! And I know you'll be dying to hear my stories."

Nearra grinned. "Of course I will."

"So I suppose it's me, Nearra, and Jirah, then," Davyn said after a moment.

"You'll be fine," Catriona said. "I'm certain of it."

Davyn tilted his head. "You don't think you need to come along and protect us?"

She laughed. "I think all of us has proven that we can take care of ourselves when we need to. Besides, what could possibly be worse than Asvoria? If we can survive her, we can survive anything."

Sindri crawled through the sheets to plop on a pillow by Nearra's side. "Exactly. And since we're on the subject, Nearra, you have to tell me everything that happened! Being possessed has to be so interesting."

Davyn rolled his eyes, but Nearra only laughed. Sitting on the bed beside her, Catriona couldn't help but smile. Leave it to a kender to find being taken over by an evil sorceress an interesting experience.

For the last time before the companions went their separate ways, they sat together and enjoyed each other's company without fear of attack. With Asvoria gone, they could finally share their stories. Davyn told them about his journey into the cursed keep of the Dragon Knight. Sindri and Catriona told about their trials during the Dragon Day celebration in Palanthas. And Nearra finally got to share tales of who she was before this whole ordeal began.

Laughing as Sindri waved his arms in mimic of the discord demon, Catriona felt a little bit of peace return to her heart. Seeing her companions now, she knew that after all they'd been through together, she had three friends for life. She didn't know what lay in store in her future or theirs, but she knew that these people were some of the strongest she would ever know. No matter what, they'd be able to handle anything.

"Hello?"

Jirah peered into the trees before taking a timid step forward. Something small and furry skittered past her feet. She jumped.

"Just a rat," a boy's voice muttered. "It couldn't hurt you. Much."

Jirah took in a deep breath and clutched her shirt. "I'm fine," she stammered.

"Of course," a girl's voice said. "Thanks to us."

Two figures materialized out of the darkness and approached Jirah where she stood near the gates leading into the Temple of the Holy Orders of the Stars. Twin pairs of wide, almond-shaped eyes glinted like blue steel.

"Janeesa," Jirah said. "Tylari."

The Messengers smiled at her greeting. Tylari had been certain she wouldn't recognize them out of their disguises.

Janeesa stepped forward. Her blond hair hung long and golden down her back, parted behind her pointed ears. Blood red robes hung from her slender shoulders and flowed to her feet.

Tylari came to her side. Shoulders still stooped and eyes still dark and hidden behind his golden bangs, his face now bore the unmistakable elven features of his true form. He wore a long robe that at first appeared black. As he entered the light, the robe shimmered with metallic threads of red and silver.

"You're lucky that things ended so well," Janeesa said as Jirah bowed her head modestly. "I was almost certain for a while there that Davyn and his friends would fail to save Nearra. It was unfortunate that we had to step in to bring in reinforcements."

"But we did save Nearra," Jirah said. "And now the curse on the Trinistyr can be broken."

"That it can," Janeesa said, a sly smile playing at her lips.

"You almost failed," Tylari muttered. "If I hadn't told you how Davyn was to use his little sword . . ."

"And Rina could have ruined everything." Janeesa's smile fell into a sneer. "If she realized who we were, everything would have fallen apart. You were supposed to kill her."

"But it's all right now!" Jirah said, raising her hands in protest. "I did everything you asked for, didn't I? I . . . I failed at the chasm, but Rina's gone away and we won't have to worry about her."

Tylari's lips tightened. "We'd better not," he said. "You keep threatening to break our trust, Jirah. You wouldn't want me to do something drastic, would you?" Hands clenched tight, crackling energy appeared at his fingertips.

"N-no!" she said. "No, of course not. I won't fail, I promise you. I need this just as much as you do."

Tylari's lips widened into a crazed smile. The mystical energy on his fingers blazed into an electric ball.

"Tylari!" Janeesa snapped. She placed a stern hand on his shoulder and the look faded away. Dropping his hand, the ball of energy dissipated into the air.

"Here," Janeesa said, pulling a small pouch from within the folds of her cloak. "This is a stronger dose of the herbs. Give these to Nearra to keep her weak until we're ready. Tylari and I are going back to Caergoth to do more research on the curse. We were getting close before we had to come and help you finish this Asvoria mess."

Jirah grabbed the bag. She clutched it close to her chest and swallowed. "What should I do until then?"

"Just wait," Janeesa said. "We'll be in touch through the mirror, as usual. Until then, make sure Nearra stays here."

Lips trembling, Jirah backed away from the trees and toward the gate. "I will. I promise."

The human girl turned and fled through the iron gate, the two elves watching as she disappeared into the temple's courtyard.

"It would have to be someone like her that has the Trinistyr," Tylari grumbled.

"It will work out to our advantage in the end," Janeesa said. "She's young and fueled by jealousy. She won't get in our way."

Tylari snorted and crossed his arms. "I hope not. I don't trust her. She's out to destroy us. I'm sure of it."

"Oh, Tylari," Janeesa said. "Have a little faith. Shall we go home? There's still lots to do."

Tylari smiled darkly. "Let's."

With a knowing look in the direction where the fool human girl had run, the two Messengers disappeared into the shadows of the trees. Now wasn't the time, but events had been set in motion just as they had planned. Soon, it would be their time to strike.

At long last, their vengeance could begin.

Acknowledgments

Thanks to Linda Joy Singleton, who first alerted me to this project; Greg Fishbone and Kathryn Manchip, for their great comments during the final stretch; and everyone from Kidlit and Yellafantasy, for their unending support and advice.

A special thanks to Shivam Bhatt, the Dragonlance fan extraordinaire who was always there to answer every Krynn-related question I threw at him. Huge props to Donnie and M Flo for so graciously allowing me take over their computers during the wacky final draft deadline rush.

Finally, big thanks to Nina Hess, our amazing editor. This book wouldn't have been half what it is were it not for her, and I couldn't ask for a better experience than working under her guidance.

The battle may be over,
but the story has just begun.

Find out what happens next to Nearra and her friends in

WIZARD'S CURSE

TRINISTYR TRILOGY, VOLUME I
by Christina Woods

Once known throughout Ansalon as talented magic-users, Nearra's family has been barren of power for over three hundred years.

Until now . . .

Imbued with vestiges of Asvoria's power, Nearra is convinced she can restore her magical heritage. With family and friends by her side, she ventures south to Icereach, hoping to release the spirit of the wizard who cursed her family. But new enemies lurk where she least expects them. And the journey tests her every resolve. Will Nearra find the strength to break the wizard's curse?

THE NEW ADVENTURES

THE DRAGON QUARTET

The companions continue their quest to save Nearra.

DRAGON SWORD
Ree Soesbee

It's a race against time as the companions seek to prevent
Asvoria from reclaiming her most treacherous weapon.

DRAGON DAY
Stan Brown

As Dragon Day draws near, Catriona and Sindri stand as
enemies, on opposing sides of a feud between the most
powerful wizards and clerics in Solamnia.

DRAGON KNIGHT
Dan Willis

With old friends and new allies by his side, Davyn must
enlist the help of the dreaded Dragon Knight.

DRAGON SPELL
Jeff Sampson

The companions reunite in their final battle with
Asvoria to reclaim Nearra's soul.

**Ask for Dragonlance: the New Adventures
books at your favorite bookstore!**
For ages ten and up.
For more information visit www.mirrorstonebooks.com

THE NEW ADVENTURES

JOIN A GROUP OF FRIENDS AS THEY UNLOCK MYSTERIES OF THE DRAGONLANCE° WORLD!

TEMPLE OF THE DRAGONSLAYER
Tim Waggoner

Nearra has lost all memory of who she is. With newfound friends, she ventures to an ancient temple where she may uncover her past. Visions of magic haunt her thoughts. And someone is watching.

THE DYING KINGDOM
Stephen D. Sullivan

In a near-forgotten kingdom, an ancient evil lurks. As Nearra's dark visions grow stronger, her friends must fight for their lives.

THE DRAGON WELL
Dan Willis

Battling a group of bandits, the heroes unleash the mystic power of a dragon well. And none of them will ever be the same.

RETURN OF THE SORCERESS
Tim Waggoner

When Nearra and her friends confront the wizard who stole her memory, their faith in each other is put to the ultimate test.

For ages 10 and up

Want to know how it all began?

Want to know more about the DRAGONLANCE® world?

Find out in this new boxed set of the first DRAGONLANCE titles!

A Rumor of Dragons
Volume 1

Night of the Dragons
Volume 2

The Nightmare Lands
Volume 3

To the Gates of Palanthas
Volume 4

Hope's Flame
Volume 5

A Dawn of Dragons
Volume 6

Gift Set Available
By Margaret Weis & Tracy Hickman
For ages 10 and up

MORE ADVENTURES
FOR THE

FIGURE IN THE FROST

A cold snap hits Curston and a mysterious stranger holds the key to
the town's survival. But first he wants something…from Moyra. Will
Moyra sacrifice her secret to save the town?

DAGGER OF DOOM

When Kellach discovers a dagger of doom with his own name burned
in the blade, it seems certain someone wants him dead. But who?

THE HIDDEN DRAGON

The Knights must find the silver dragon who gave their order its name.
Can they make it to the dragon's lair alive?

**Ask for KNIGHTS OF THE SILVER DRAGON books
at your favorite bookstore!**

For ages eight to twelve

For more information visit www.mirrorstonebooks.com